NATIVE MOMENTS

a Novel

by

Nic Schuck

Merry Christmas, babydoll!
In 2019 you're going
to need more
Books!

#NOIR   *Love,*
                    y

WALDORF PUBLISHING

Published by Waldorf Publishing
2140 Hall Johnson Road
#102-345
Grapevine, Texas 76051
www.WaldorfPublishing.com

Native Moments
ISBN: 978-1-944781-18-7
Library of Congress Control Number: 2016930009
Copyright © 2016

From THE SONGLINES by Bruce Chatwin, Copyright © 1987 by
Bruce Chatwin. Used by permission of Viking Books, an imprint of
Penguin Publishing Group, a division of Penguin Random House
LLC.

Printed in Canada

Dedication
For my father

"Native moments—when you come upon me—ah you are here now, Give me now libidinous joys only,
Give me the drench of my passions, give me life coarse and rank, Today I go consort with Nature's darlings, to-night too, I am for those who believe in loose delights, I share the midnight orgies of young men, I dance with the dancers and drink with the drinkers, The echoes ring with our indecent calls, I pick out some low person for my dearest friend, He shall be lawless, rude, illiterate, he shall be one condemned by others for deeds done, I will play a part no longer, why should I exile myself from my companions? O you shunn'd persons, I, at least, do not shun you, I come forthwith in your midst, I will be your poet, I will be more to you than to any of the rest."

– Walt Whitman

"The anarchists, as always, are the 'gentlemen of the road.'"

– Bruce Chatwin, *The Songlines*

Chapter 1

The sound of the three-volley salute in his dream woke Sanch Murray. He shivered in the morning chill and looked up from where he lay on the bench seat of Buck's '78 El Camino through the condensation on the windshield at the sun that struggled to shine through the branches of the pecan tree under which the car rested in its shadow. He thought today would be the day that he confronted his father about his decision to not join the Navy. But now, lying across the car seat, he decided to wait a bit longer.

The last time he had seen his parents was about two months ago on the day of Buck's funeral. He was sitting on the couch of his parents' living room between two distant cousins that he hadn't seen since they were kids. He listened to the people in the living room talk about how good the cocktail wieners were or watched them as they picked out with toothpicks the sweet and sour meatballs from the crock pot. Every once in a while someone would say what a shame it was that Buck had died like that. The people making small talk on a day of mourning sickened him. He didn't want to sit there any longer. Not with these people. He stared at the wood paneling walls and wondered how long he had to stay before it wasn't rude to leave. His grandfather, at seventy-six years old, sitting across from him in a recliner opened his eyes after a five-minute blink and said, "What about you Brian? You decide what to do yet? What are you twenty now?" His family refused to call him Sanch.

"I am," Sanch said. He knew where this conversation was going and did not want to entertain it.

"I was in Anzio at your age," his grandfather said.

1

"Yes. I know."

"Well then? What the hell are you waiting on?"

"Can we not do this right now?"

"Now is a damn good time to do it. We just buried your brother and you don't have any intention to follow in his footsteps, do you?"

Sanch didn't mean to laugh. "Not anytime soon," he said.

"Goddamn it boy. You know exactly what I meant."

"I know. I'm going for a walk."

"Yep. Just walk away."

"I love you, Grandpa," Sanch said and patted his grandfather on the shoulder as he walked by. His grandfather waved a hand like he was trying to swat a fly.

Sanch walked a few houses down to see Jake Higdon, who lived in his parents' backyard in a rusted '68 Westfalia.

Jake sat out in front of his van in a lawn chair smoking a joint.

"Hey man," Jake said. "Was thinking of coming down there, but figured it was mostly family."

"It's cool. You have any beer?"

"No. Want to go get some?"

"Yes."

"I've been thinking of going to Costa Rica," Jake said. He passed Sanch the joint. "I heard they've got great surf almost every day."

"Yeah?"

"I heard you can camp there for like a buck fifty a night. And food is cheap. Heard for like a thousand dollars, you can stay for a month."

"I've got a thousand dollars," Sanch said.

"Bullshit."

2

"I do."

"From working at the car wash?"

"Not just from that."

Jake laughed. He knew Sanch sold pot, too. Not much, just enough to smoke for free and make a little extra cash.

"All we need is a birth certificate and an ID, and we can get in. Don't even need a passport."

"I've never flown in a plane."

"Me either."

That night they had tickets and in a week were on a plane.

Sanch stepped from the El Camino and through the window of the house saw his father drinking coffee and reading the paper at the same round Formica dining table they had since Sanch was a child. Sanch walked on.

He passed by Jake's house and saw the Westfalia sitting there and thought about Jake and about their recent trip to Costa Rica. He was sad that it had come to an end. He was afraid, as with all memories, it would fade, and he would only be left with a story he had to create, not how it had actually happened. He wanted to remember it how it had truly happened. He tried to remember specific details and knew that one day those details would be lost.

* * * *

Sanch and Jake stood in the customs line of the Juan Santamaría International Airport in San Jose, Costa Rica. Sanch was drunk from the free drinks on the plane.

The tall—maybe five-ten—California girl with sun bleached hair twisted in braids stood behind them. Sanch couldn't remember her name, although she had sat next to him on the plane. Sanch sat between her and Jake. Jake had washed down a valium with his first beer and fell asleep shortly after takeoff and slept the entire flight, his forehead leaving an oily smudge on the window. During the flight, Sanch tried to persuade California Girl to go to Tamarindo, where he was headed. She told him that a friend planned to meet her at the airport to take her to Dominical. Her friend recently bought a house there. Sanch didn't know where Dominical was. He didn't know where Tamarindo was either. He didn't bother to look at a map because Jake had sounded like he had a plan.

Waiting in the cramped, confined line of the sweltering warehouse of an airport, Sanch's head swirled.

"I might puke," he said.

Jake shook his head.

The drunken girl laughed. She laughed at a lot of things Sanch said on the plane.

"That's what you get," Jake said.

"I'm just hot. That's all," Sanch said. He laughed a bit as he wiped sweat from the back of his neck. "But seriously, I might puke."

"Yep," Jake said. "That's what it is. Not the drinks you were downing, huh? You were stoked they didn't card you."

The line moved a few steps.

After making it through customs, what little customs check there was, the three of them walked to the baggage claim area. Airport workers brought Sanch and Jake the board bags while they waited for their backpacks to come through on the conveyor belt.

"How many boards are in there?" the drunken girl asked.

"I brought four. My sponsor's messing with some different shapes and needed some feedback," Jake said. "Told me sell the ones I don't like. They say on them 'Custom for Boog.' Don't they, Sanch?" Jake said this

while running his fingers of his right hand through his hair.
Sanch bit his tongue but nodded.

"Who's Boog?"

"Me."

"Why does he call you Boog?"

"Yeah, Jake. Why Boog?" Sanch asked.

"Short for Boogaloo. He says it looks like I'm dancing
on the waves."

"Is that right?" Sanch said.

"Don't be a dick."

"So are you a professional or something?" she asked.

"Are you?" Sanch asked.

The girl looked confusingly at Sanch.

"You guys do know each other, right?"

"He's just being an asshole. I used to be a professional.
Now I do mostly photo shoots and whatnot."

"Really?" she said.

"So you're more like a model then?" Sanch said.

"Will you shut up?" Jake said.

Sanch laughed.

The next twenty minutes Jake talked about surfing and
listened very little when she said why she was visiting
Costa Rica. Sanch sat on the floor with his head in his
hands. Their bags circled around the conveyor a few times
before Jake flicked Sanch in the ear.

"Here they come," Jake said. "Grab them."

Sanch looked up through blurry eyes and held his ear.
He tried to punch Jake in the dick but missed and hit him
on the hip.

Jake laughed. "Almost got me," he said.

People rushed up to the new arrivals, yelling "taxi" and
grabbing luggage without waiting for a reply. New arrivals
followed their luggage like lost otherworldly simians.

Sanch pulled both his and Jake's bag off the belt, and the girl pointed her two bags out as well, and Sanch grabbed them and placed them on the floor in front of her.

Jake said to one of the taxi drivers, "Tamarindo, Tamarindo."

The taxi guy said, "Yes, yes. I take you."

"I," Jake pointed to himself, "need...to get...to...Tamarindo."

Sanch heard the drunken girl say, "Hey, baby. How are you?"

He turned to see her rush into the arms of a guy who looked dressed to go to supper at a yacht club.

Sanch left his things on the floor and strolled over to them. He stuck out his hand when the guy looked up at him and said, "I'm Sanch."

"Oh, honey. This is Sanch. I sat next to him on the plane. I told him all about you."

"Hey, I'm..." The guy told Sanch his name, but Sanch forgot it as soon as it was said.

"I was telling him..."

Sanch cut her off.

"Your friend from Dominical?" Sanch asked.

She ignored him.

"Your friend from Dominical?" Sanch said louder.

"Yes," she said, stopping what she was telling her friend.

"Well, I'm not from there, but my parents have a house there," the guy said. "Your first time in Costa Rica?"

Sanch nodded.

"Are you two drunk?"

"We might have had a few cocktails," she said.

"More than a few," Sanch said.

"We should get moving," her friend said. "My parents are expecting us for dinner."

"It was so nice meeting you Sanch," she said. "You are going to love Costa Rica."

Sanch reached in for a hug, but she stuck her hand out for a shake. He shook it and tried to pull her closer for a kiss on the cheek, but she pulled away from that, too.

He watched them walk off hand in hand and then he stumbled back to where he thought he left his things. Jake came running from outside and stopped at the threshold of the door. A sign that said "salida" hung overhead.

"Hurry up," Jake shouted. "They're out there with our boards."

A storm had just passed, and it looked as if another were on the way. Steam rose up from wet asphalt.

People rushed around the cars stacking up suitcases on roof racks and holding them down with bungee cords or rope. Tourists stood watching as the local men and boys worked. Kids stood off to the side in a circle waiting to be called for help and the possibility of a small tip.

Sanch looked across the lot and saw the girl from the airplane walking to an SUV, one that looked too new and too clean compared to the cars being used for taxis. Her boyfriend placed her luggage in the trunk and then ran around to open the passenger side door for her. He saw Sanch watching and waved. Sanch didn't wave back.

Jake helped the saggy-faced, dark-skinned man find a way to place the board bags in the small four-door hatchback that looked like it hadn't been washed in several years. They tried hanging the bags out the trunk. It looked dangerous, but the driver kept saying, "Okay, okay. No worry."

"Bullshit," Jake replied. He took the hard case out and tried shoving it in the back seat. That didn't work.

Jake and the taxi driver looked like a silent film comedy troupe, one person putting the bags in, the other taking them out.

On the outer pouch of his backpack, Sanch had shoved in a pair of soft-top, foam surf racks.

One of the young bronzed Costa Rican kids with no shirt and no shoes laughed when he saw Sanch hold up the racks. Sanch laughed with him. The kid said something in Spanish and laughed some more.

Jake heard them and looked at Sanch.

"Asshole," Jake said. He walked over and snatched the racks from Sanch. "We've got twenty minutes to get to the bus station, and you're standing around like a jackass."

Jake strapped the racks on the car.

"This is the last bus to Tamarindo tonight and I sure as hell don't want to waste today looking for a hotel," Jake continued.

"Asshole," the kid said and pointed at Sanch.

Sanch laughed harder. As he zipped the pouch on his bag, he felt a tap on the shoulder. Sanch looked up.

"La camisa," the kid said. He tugged on Sanch's shirt and pointed at his own bony, shirtless chest. "Camisa."

"You want a shirt?"

"Sí, sí. Chirt. La camisa."

Sanch grabbed a tee shirt, one with a national brand surf company logo on it. "You like this?"

"Sí, sí," the kid said. "I like."

Sanch handed it to him. The kid put it on. It hung over his blue frayed shorts. He smiled at Sanch and gave him two thumbs up and took off running towards a group of seven or eight kids. They saw the shirt and rushed over to Sanch.

"Shit," Sanch said and hurried over to the car.

Jake and the old man had finished strapping the hard case of boards on top of the car, but the soft case wouldn't fit.

"Where's your pack?" Sanch asked Jake.

"In the hatch. Put yours in the front seat. We're going to have to squeeze in the back with the boards."

Sanch put the pack in the front seat, shut the door, and turned around just as the band of skinny shirtless kids swarmed him.

"Tee shirt, tee shirt," they said in unison. "La camisa."

"No, no. No more," Sanch said.

"Sí, sí," the kid wearing Sanch's shirt said and reached for the bag through the window.

"You guys done yet?" Sanch asked, swatting the kid's hand away.

"What're you doing?" Jake said looking up at him from the back seat. "Get in."

Sanch did. The driver slid the rest of the boards through the back window obstructing their view. The kids shouted for more tee shirts. Hands reached in and grabbed some shirts from the bag. The driver scolded them in Spanish. The kids ran after the car as it drove out of the parking lot. Sanch managed to stick a hand out the window to wave. The kids waved back.

"What the hell those kids want?" Jake asked.

Sanch told him.

Jake shook his head. "You're seriously retarded, aren't you?"

Jake asked the driver how much longer it would be, but the old, snaggletooth man nodded his head and replied, "Sí, sí. Idiota."

Sanch lifted his head a little to see the rearview mirror. The driver's glassed-over eyes looked back at him in a squint from smiling, crow's feet stretching to his gray, thinned hairline.

Leaving the airport, they entered light traffic. What little could be seen over the boards didn't look like a Third World country. Mist-blanketed green hills surrounded a city set in the Valle Central, as it was known, but the two travelers looking out the window had not the slightest idea of the name.

San Jose and its surrounding suburbs contributed to about forty percent of the country's entire population. The bus ride they would soon be on would take them through poor and sparsely populated villages. The travel book that Jake had quickly perused at the Atlanta airport said a four-hour drive to Tamarindo. That was if they drove on the paved roads and took the route that would take them to Puntarenas, where they would take a ferry across the Gulf of Nicoya to the Peninsula de Nicoya, which had very few paved roads and took a good bit of navigational skill, eventually reaching Tamarindo and the Pacific Ocean. That was the quickest and most efficient way of getting there, if they had rented a car. But riding public transportation meant doubling or tripling the travel time. Jake hadn't read long enough to learn that little tidbit.

They made their way into downtown San Jose among the sounds of vehicles with no mufflers and the smell of exhaust inundating the two passengers. Sanch peeked over the bags and saw a metropolis.

"Not the way I expected Costa Rica to look," he said.

The cab screeched to a stop and then continued only to stop again. The cab driver shouted and waved his hands at kids whizzing by on mopeds within inches of the cars. Horns honked. The painted lanes on the street had worn off years ago.

"We won't make it," Jake said.

Chapter 2

The taxi pulled alongside a crumbling, gray building with a Coca-Cola logo painted on the entire left side of it.

"Whoa, Whoa. What're you doing?" Jake shouted out, but the driver ignored him, exited the car and pulled the boards from the back seat.

Sanch stepped out into the confusion of the city. The old man unstrapped the boards from the car's roof while Jake stood by shouting for an answer as to why they had stopped in the middle of the road.

About twenty people lined on the sidewalk filing through an opening in the wall that was big enough for a door, but there was no door or even a frame. It looked as if it had been hacked open with a chisel and hammer or blasted open with dynamite.

The line of people ended at a small window with a sign above it that read taquilla.

The old man guided the two errant wanderers to the back of the line. Jake fussed about leaving the luggage and followed the old man back to the taxi. Sanch stood in line staring at the back of a blond guy's head in front of him. His hair was unwashed, greasy and beginning to bald at the crown. He carried a book bag across his right shoulder and wore battered tennis shoes and a soiled, gray tank top. His skin looked like it was once of fair complexion, but now had that worn leathered look that comes from spending days in the sun without protection.

Jake came storming from around back of the Coca-Cola building and said, "That bus better not take off. They put our stuff on it already."

The blond traveler in front of them turned around.

"Where you going?" He was an American. Mid-forties, maybe.

"Tamarindo," Jake replied.

"Holy shit. And you haven't got tickets yet?"

"Is that bad?" Sanch asked.

"It was supposed to leave an hour ago. They're all packed up and ready to go. You won't make it to the window before it leaves."

Jake stormed off, leaving Sanch in the line.

"Where do you get tickets?" Sanch asked.

The blond American traveler looked at him and said, "At the front of this line."

"This isn't for tequila?"

"No. That sign says, taquilla."

"That's what I said."

"Tickets, man."

"Oh, well shit. I wanted a drink."

"You guys just arrive?"

"Maybe an hour ago."

The blond traveler pulled a flask from his backpack, took a swig and handed it to Sanch. "Been here before?"

Sanch took the flask and said "No. You?" He took a sip and scrunched up his face.

"You speak Spanish?"

"No."

The American traveler laughed. "You guys don't have a clue, do you?"

"About what?"

He stuck out his hand. "I'm Rick."

Sanch shook it. "Brian, but everyone calls me Sanch."

"As in Sancho? Like Sancho Panza?"

"No. Like in...I don't know. Just Sanch."

"And how'd you get that name, Sanch?"

"One of Jake's friends didn't know my name and called me Sancho. Everyone thought it was funny, and it stuck. But they just say Sanch now. Not Sancho."

"Never read *Don Quixote*?"

Sanch shook his head.

"Ever heard of it?"

"Wasn't he a cartoon character from the *Laff-A-Lympics*?"

Rick laughed. "A book by a guy named Cervantes."

"There's a street in Pensacola, where I'm from, called Cervantes. It's where all the whores and holy rollers hang out."

Rick nodded, took another sip from the flask and turned around. Then from over his shoulder he said, "This will be good for you."

"What will?" Sanch asked.

Rick didn't reply.

Jake came back with the tickets.

"What's the exchange rate?" he asked Rick.

"How many colones she give you?" Rick asked.

"Two seventy. She take me?"

"A little. Exchange rate's about three fifteen or so. Be careful, though."

"Now let's go," Jake said and sprinted to the bus.

"Thanks for the drink," Sanch said and followed Jake.

On the bus, Jake surveyed the seating options. The last two seats in the back of the bus were barely visible behind a large man. Jake stepped aside to let Sanch in first. Sanch sat down. His knees touched the seat in front of him. Jake stretched his legs in the aisle. They sat in silence for a few minutes, Jake with his head back and eyes closed and Sanch shifting his legs trying to find a somewhat comfortable position, finally settling with his knees pressed up on the back of the chair in front of him and he rested his head against the window.

After about ten minutes they were greeted by a familiar voice, "What's up, fellas?" It was Rick.

Rick shook the large man's hand and sat next to him.

"Good one," Sanch said.

Jake didn't open his eyes, but he lifted a hand and flipped Rick the bird.

"Just a little bus stop humor. This is Paco." He introduced Sanch and Jake to the large man in front of them.

Sanch laid his head back again.

"So you're going to Tamarindo, huh?" Jake said. Jake and Rick talked for a few minutes about what each other was doing in Costa Rica. Sanch listened although kept his eyes closed.

Rick was thirty-six with a wife and a daughter in Montana. He came to Costa Rica on a family vacation about four months ago and took a kiteboarding lesson.

"Why don't you just surf instead?" Jake went on to tell him that he had once come in third in the East Coast Surfing Championships.

Rick finally said, "You asked me a question. Are you going to let me answer it?"

"Damn dude. Go ahead," Jake said.

"Everybody surfs in Costa Rica and everyone who comes here wants to try it. Giving lessons to tourists is a quick dollar, but it's a competitive market. Kiteboarding though is still new. I paid fifty dollars for an hour. I've seen surfing lessons for as little as ten an hour. And the guy who taught me was the only one in the town doing it and had three other people in my group. That's two hundred dollars an hour."

"Where was this?"

"Limón. On the Caribbean side. If I can make five hundred a week, I'm moving my family back here. My wife gave me six months to make it work, or it's back to Montana for me."

"So what are you doing in San Jose?" Jake asked.

"I ordered a new kite."

"And you had to take a five-hour bus trip just for that?"

Rick laughed.

"Five hours? I wish it was that short," Rick said.

"The guide book said five hours."

"Yeah. I'm sure Frommer takes the bus when he travels. Anyway, internet service isn't so great in Tamarindo, you know. It's not the States. And Paco had to get some brake pads, too. So we took a little trip together."

"He had to come all the way here for brake pads?"

"Unless he wanted to wait an extra month and pay a hundred-dollar delivery charge. The conveniences of Third World living, my brother. Welcome."

That was the last bit of conversation Sanch heard before he drifted to sleep.

Chapter 3

Raindrops splashed through the open window. Jake laughed when he saw Sanch wake up and dry his face with the bottom of his tee shirt.

"I wondered when you'd feel that," Jake said.

Sanch looked around. Only a couple other windows were open. Fog had formed on the closed ones. Sanch put his up only halfway.

"Why we stopped?" Sanch asked.

"A couple cars in front got stuck in the mud," Jake told him.

Sanch looked out the window at the unpaved road.

"How far did we get?"

"Not far. We stopped every couple of minutes and spent half the time on dirt roads going five miles an hour."

Outside to the left, a hill raised fifty feet above them. To the right, on the other side of the bus, the cliff dropped off a couple hundred feet. Treetops to the horizon. A couple of shacks speckled through the timber. They weren't but thirty miles outside San Jose, but the city had disappeared quickly. It was now the majestic scenery that attracted so many hundreds of thousands of tourists each year.

The road narrowed, and if a car came in the opposite direction, it would have to pull over as far as it could into the overgrowth of vegetation to let the bus go by. Since the cars were stuck up front, the only thing the bus driver could do was wait. The soft murmur of voices and the pitter-patter of the rain drops hitting the bus lulled Sanch back to sleep.

About an hour later the clouds parted, and the sun shone through, creating a steam bath inside the bus. Sweat dripped from Sanch's armpit. He mistook the sweat for a bug and without breaking his sleep brushed it away. After doing that three times, he had enough and woke up. He wasn't drunk anymore. Now his tongue felt as if it had grown hair. And he had to piss. He looked over at Jake, who was staring straight ahead, eyes wide, sweat beaded on his forehead.

The bus moved at a steady pace and the passengers swayed with the motion of the bumps.

Rick turned around. He looked at Sanch and then at Jake. He looked like he wanted to say something, but hesitated. He scratched his head.

"Want another?" he asked Jake.

"Hell yeah. I've been waiting for you to ask."

Rick passed back a small baggie of cocaine and a small spoon. Jake grabbed hold of the spoon with his right hand and put a little bump onto the end. He set the baggie on his lap, lifted the spoon to his nose, shifted his eyes over to Sanch, gave a wink and with the thumb of his left hand closed off his left nostril and took a sniff through his right. He repeated the procedure, but this time with the opposite hand and opposite nostril. He offered the baggie to Sanch. Sanch dipped his pinky in and rubbed the powder on his teeth.

"That's all I want," Sanch said.

Jake tapped Rick's shoulder.

"Did he get any?" he asked, nodding to Sanch.

"A little," Jake said. "He's a pussy though."

Rick smiled and turned back around.

"That's the third time they've passed it back," Jake said to Sanch in a whisper out the side of his mouth. "But they been doing that shit every couple of minutes since you fell asleep. I think that's why they came to San Jose."

18

Sanch smiled. He rubbed his tongue over his already numb gums.

Night fell, and a chill passed through the windows. Rick and Paco continued passing the baggie back and forth, but they had stopped handing it back to Jake who sat with his head back, eyes closed and his foot tapping the floor. The crowd on the bus thinned the further they drove away from San Jose.

The bus stopped on an unpaved road. A line of houses, looking like tin sheds, some with blue tarp for a roof, sat between an abundance of trees. The muddy fenced-in front yards looked like pigpens. Some were pigpens. No light shone in the houses or along the road. The only illumination came from the bus's headlights and the waning gibbous moon. As the bus pulled away, a woman who had been on the bus shuffled her feet to one of the houses carrying two shopping bags of groceries in each hand.

They stopped for food at a lone cinder-blocked building that had been converted from a gas station to a restaurant. The rusted, non-working pump still stood in the center of the parking lot.

Sanch and Jake went inside. Rick and Paco stood off to the side of the building sharing a cigarette.

An older man with a cowboy hat and yellow glasses and a fat woman with a grease-splattered apron stood behind a countertop taking orders from the thirty or so bus riders. Behind them were two young boys, one tending to the chicken and pork on the grill while the other made the sandwiches. A young girl served the food and drinks. The only three tables in the restaurant were occupied. Most people took their food outside to eat or went back to eat on the bus.

"I gotta piss," Sanch said.

"Just wait till we order," Jake told him.

"I've been holding it."

"Pinch the head. You'll be all right."

Sanch did. "Not helping."

Jake laughed.

The menu hanging over the counter looked like it had been donated from the ballpark concession stand where Sanch used to play Little League ball. The only thing written in English was Coca-Cola.

Jake made a gesture with his right fist leaving only his thumb and pinky stuck out and acted as if he was drinking from his hand and said, "Two cokes."

Then he turned to Sanch, "How are we going to know what to eat?"

"I'm pretty sure pollo means chicken," Sanch said, still squirming.

"And what about bocadillo?"

"Hell if I know. Something to do with chicken."

"Two pollo bocadillos," Jake said to the lady. When he said bocadillos it rhymed with armadillos.

The lady nodded understanding and then turned to the boys behind her.

"This better be chicken," Jake said.

Sanch shifted his feet, squeezing his legs tighter. "It's about all I remember from high school Spanish."

"Did we order chicken sandwiches?" Jake asked the lady. He said it slow and loud.

"Why are you talking like that?" Sanch said.

"She doesn't know what I'm saying."

"Talking like an idiot ain't gonna help."

"Was it chicken?" He asked her again.

"Sí, sí," the woman replied. "Shicken."

"I told you."

Two people got up from one of the tables.

"Go grab that table while I pay," Jake said.

Sanch sat down and crossed his legs and rocked back and forth.

Jake joined Sanch at the table.

"You won't believe how much that was."

"Tell me when I get back."

The small bathroom looked like it was once an old storage closet and smelt like a French Quarter alleyway during Mardi Gras. There was no toilet, only a trough against the back wall and a hole in the floor. Sanch chose the trough. Mosquitoes swarmed out of the drain as the piss trickled down.

Returning to the table, Jake had already drank half of his soda.

"They serve cokes in the bottle like it's the nineteen-fifties," Jake said. "None of that plastic bullshit."

"How much was it?" Sanch asked.

"Guess."

"I don't know."

"Well, guess."

"Just tell me."

"Five bucks."

"Apiece?"

"No. All of it."

"Cokes too?"

"Cokes too."

"Cheap, huh?"

"We're going to be all right here."

The food came: grilled chicken with lettuce, tomato, and mayo between sliced bread. It was the first food they had eaten since a slice of pizza at the Atlanta airport.

When they finished, Sanch went back to the bus, and Jake went to the bathroom. Sanch sat in the aisle seat this time. Rick and Paco came in and sat down. Sanch asked Rick for the time.

"Eleven," Rick told him.

Sanch counted on his hands. It had been about seven hours or so.

"We even close?"

"Couple more hours," Rick said.

Jake got back on the bus. Sanch stood to let Jake into the window seat. Jake sat down in the aisle seat instead.

"What're you doing?" Sanch said to him.

Jake laughed his too-loud laugh.

"Come on. Get up," Sanch said.

Jake didn't. "You still gotta a couple more years to learn the ropes," he said. "I bet next time your ass won't get up."

"I didn't want you climbing over top of me," Sanch said.

"Well, thank you. I appreciate you giving up your seat to me."

"You're such an asshole sometimes."

Jake laughed, and as Sanch climbed over him, Jake poked a finger right on Sanch's butthole. Sanch jumped and hit his head on the ceiling. Jake laughed louder.

"What is wrong with you?" Sanch said.

Rick turned around. "You guys married?"

Jake laughed some more. Sanch didn't.

An hour or so later, back on the unpaved road, Paco stood up as the bus rolled to a stop. Rick let him out into the aisle.

"Is this Tamarindo?" Jake asked.

"No, Tamarindo is next," Rick said.

"I thought he was going to Tamarindo, too."

"You thought wrong," Paco said.

"You speak English?" Jake said.

"Of course. Why would you assume I don't?"

"I just…I thought…You didn't say anything the whole time. So, I thought you didn't speak English."

Paco patted Jake on the shoulder and smiled. "Don't stutter. It makes you seem nervous." He winked at Sanch and then said, "I guess he still has a few more years to learn the ropes too, huh?"

Sanch smiled. Jake didn't.

Paco shook all three of their hands. "Pura Vida," he said. Rick said it back.

When the bus moved again, Sanch asked, "What'd you guys say when he was leaving?"

"Pura Vida."

"What's that?"

"It's like the Tico's motto. Literally it translates to pure life. But it means more than that. It's a philosophy, a way of life here."

"Pura Vida," Sanch said. "Did I say it right?"

"Not bad for a gringo."

"What's that?"

"A gringo?"

"Yeah. That and Tico."

"Really? You never heard of either one?"

Sanch shook his head.

"Gringo means white person from the States. Tico means a Costa Rican native."

"Cool."

The bus's brakes squeaked at the final stop in Tamarindo at three in the morning. The remaining passengers retrieved their luggage from the belly of the bus.

A ponytailed man who had gotten on the bus about halfway through the ride stood with a board bag.

"You guys want to grab a beer before you go?" Rick asked.

"We're getting up early to surf. Maybe tomorrow," Jake said. "Where are you staying?"

"Place up the road. Hotel Abrigo. It's not really a hotel, just some small cabanas. What about you guys?"

"I heard there was a campground here. Chico's, maybe," Jake said.

"Yep. Go to the water and walk along the beach and when you think you are lost keep walking. You might see it. You're sticking around here for a while, right?"

"As long as we can," Jake said.

"Then I'll see you guys around."

"See ya," Jake said.

Sanch waved.

"You guys are looking for Chico's?" A non-American voice said.

Sanch and Jake turned around to face the ponytailed guy.

"You know where it's at?" Jake asked.

"I'm going now," he said.

Jake had a harder time keeping up. The board case he carried weighed twice as much and maybe even three times as much as Sanch's. Sanch walked a step behind the other guy. Jake fell further behind. Ponytail guy introduced himself as Antonio from Italy.

"Where in Italy you from?"

"Brindisi," he said.

"Never heard of it."

"No? Famous port city. Where the Appian Way ended."

"What is that?"

"The Appian Way?"

"Yeah."

"Really?"

"Really."

"The road that connected ancient Rome to Brindisi."

"No idea."

"Spartacus?"

"Sorry, man. Nothing."

"Pretty significant historical stories."

Sanch shrugged.

Antonio turned, looking back at Jake.

"Why did he bring so many boards?"

"Different boards for different waves, I guess."

"Is it really necessary?" Antonio held up his board bag. "Everything I need is in here."

"Clothes too?"

"Clothes, toothbrush, toothpaste, toilet paper. And only one surfboard."

"That's the way to do it," Sanch said.

"You take only what you need when you are on the road. Possessions weigh you down."

"You travel a lot?"

"I have been going for almost a year now."

"How do you do it?"

"What do you mean?"

"How can you afford it?"

"You work. How else do you afford anything?"

They passed a few restaurants and bars where the servers waited for the few late-nighters to leave so they could close up. They walked down a path between some palms and other bushes and trees that Sanch didn't know the names of and it opened up onto the beach. The tide lapped on shore, and distant laughter drifted out to sea.

They walked in soft sand and stopped after a few feet to make sure Jake saw them when he emerged from the path.

"Thanks for helping guys," he shouted.

"It's your stuff, no?" Antonio said. "You don't hear us asking you for help."

"Sanch," Jake yelled. "Come back here and help me carry some of this."

"It's not that much further," Antonio said.

Jake put the board case on the sand. He took off his backpack and sat on the ground.

Antonio turned and continued walking.

"What're you doing?" Sanch shouted back at Jake.

"Go take your stuff and then come back and help," Jake said.

Sanch turned and followed Antonio to the campground. Sanch couldn't see much except the outline of the Italian in front of him. They walked through another path that cut through some thick foliage and into a clearing known as Chico's Camping.

Chico greeted them. He was a short, fat, long-haired Tico who didn't speak English. Antonio and Chico spoke in Spanish.

A lone tent was pitched in the distance. A small stucco house sat in the middle of the complex. A lantern hung by the door shone light on the seating area. A tin roof hung over two small wooden tables made from tree trunks that had been lacquered, the age rings making a remarkable design. Chico sat on a wooden swing hung from the tin roof, and Antonio set down his board bag and sat next to him. Sanch, glad to take off his backpack and set down the board bag, took a seat at a table. Chico and Antonio spoke in Spanish. Sanch tried to pick up on a few words but gave up.

Sanch said, "Antonio, I'll be back. Going to check on Jake."

A barely moving shadow dragged a board case in the sand.

"What's taking you so long?" Sanch said as Jake got into earshot.

"Fuck you."

Sanch laughed. Jake dropped the board case.

"Where's this place?"

"Up ahead a ways. There's a little path that cuts through the bushes."

Sanch picked up the board case. He used both hands to lift it overhead.

"See you at camp," Jake said and ran off, laughing in the night.

Sanch trekked to the camp.

Jake had his tent sprawled on the ground ready to go up when Sanch arrived. Antonio sat under the lantern light. Chico had retired for the night. Sanch set Jake's boards down. Jake laughed and asked if he enjoyed the walk. Sanch ignored him and retrieved his boards and backpack from the seating area.

"Why'd you carry that for him?" Antonio asked.

Sanch shrugged and lugged his stuff to a clearing.

Jake finished putting his tent up and sat with Antonio.

After erecting the tent, Sanch crawled inside. He zipped shut the mesh door still allowing the breeze to enter. He had taken the two surfboards out and set them next to him on top of each other. He had his sleeping bag out on top of the board bag which now served as a mattress to add some comfort to the hard ground. His backpack was on the other side of the surfboards giving him plenty of room to sleep. He took off his shirt and pants and lying there naked, the cool air felt pleasant enough to close his eyes and think about the recent past before becoming suspended in that moment of consciousness just prior to falling asleep.

He hadn't camped in a long time and it reminded him of when he was a child and his father would take him and his older brother camping out at Fort Pickens on Santa Rosa Island. They would spend the weekends there, fishing for Pompano and Sheepshead and sometimes King Mackerel. That felt like a lifetime ago. Childhood, a vague memory. He knew one day those memories would disappear and in their place would be stories that he told himself, not quite sure which parts were true and which parts he had made up to fill in the gaps.

He said goodnight to what he hoped was God and to his brother who he hoped was there with God if there was one and then wished his parents a good night, hoping that by saying it aloud the words would float through the cosmos and somehow his parents would know that he was thinking of them. He couldn't remember when he had stopped praying, but on the day his brother died he began praying again. He didn't know why he started. He prayed to his brother though, more so than to God or Jesus. At least he knew his brother had existed at one time.

He knew his dad had favored his brother over him. Not only because they shared the same name, Barry, but because Buck, what they called him, followed in their father's steps. Buck was an all-star third baseman who played college ball on scholarship and later joined the Navy after a shoulder injury prevented him from a chance at the Majors. Sanch played right field in Little League, got cut from the high school team and flunked out of NJROTC his freshman year.

Since Buck's death, Sanch would lay at night trying to imagine what his brother went through that day on the Arabian Sea when a small boat loaded with explosives rammed into the destroyer while Buck was in the galley serving lunch. He thought of the sixteen sailors who died that day and wondered how their families coped with the tragedy. He wondered how he was supposed to cope with it. Sanch told himself, being as far away from everybody was a pretty good way for him to cope now.

Buck may not have died while on the ship, but he died as a direct result from it. He died from the guilt of having survived. He died from the pain of his back injury. He died of depression from losing his closest friends. He died from the embarrassment of not being able to serve his country anymore. He died from the drugs that he used to numb the hurt that kept him awake at night.

Sanch wondered what Buck thought before shooting up that last dose of heroin that ended his pain forever. He wondered if Buck had purposefully shot up enough to kill himself. He wondered if it was possible for a just God to punish suicide by eternal damnation as he was taught as a child. As if Buck hadn't suffered enough while alive. After the injury and the discharge, Buck had become a different person. It seemed as if everyone was different; as if that explosion had sent out ripples of misfortune that reached all the families associated with the sailors aboard that ship. He tried to keep thinking about Buck to keep himself from falling asleep because oftentimes in that moment just before sleep he felt himself dying. Or what he imagined dying to feel like, his soul or what he thought of as his soul, swiftly leaving his body and it frightened him to be aware that he was dying.

Eventually, beyond his control, Sanch fell asleep with those thoughts and to the sounds of tree branches rustling in the breeze and the sounds of crickets and other nocturnal noises and the salty air circulating in his tent.

Chapter 4

Sanch, possibly five or six years old, stood on the
beach with his father, brother and several other men under
a pavilion looking out over the water at the approaching
storm. Sanch couldn't place where he had seen the other
men before, but they were familiar. Except for Sanch, they
held rifles, yet there was a jovial spirit about them. Sanch
did not know why he was afraid, and the men watched as
the child's fear grew. It was a game to them, as if they had
experienced that type of fear before and now enjoyed
watching someone else go through it. Sanch grabbed onto
his dad's pant leg, burying his face in the jeans as kids who
are frightened often will. His dad laughed along with the
other men and pushed little Sanch away. Sanch clawed for
his father trying to avoid looking out at the water at a void
where the sun should have been. There was nothing visible,
but it was unbearable to look at. The more he looked at the
nothing the more frightened he became. He felt that there
was a secret he hadn't been let in on. His dad pushed him
away harder, and little Sanch fell to the ground and then
hurried to get underneath a nearby picnic table, but there
was no hiding from the encompassing fright. Wanting help,
he ran back to his dad for protection. His dad laughed
louder and said, "I can't help you, bud. But I can give you
this." He offered Sanch a gun. Sanch didn't want it. His dad
said, "Suit yourself" and turned his back to walk off with
the other men. Sanch's brother said, "It's not as bad as you
think." Sanch said to his brother, "I thought you were
dead." Buck smiled and turned, following the other men.
Sanch went back underneath the table and cried for

someone to help him. He watched as the men walked out to the water's edge toward the void.

Sanch's tent shook violently. A famished, beastly unknown awaited him to emerge. He now knew he was dreaming but couldn't force himself to awaken out of the hypnopompic state. The harder he tried to open his eyes, the harder he squeezed them shut. In his dream, he was in the tent, and he was shaking his head violently in an attempt to wake. He tried screaming, but no sounds exited his opened mouth. He could hear Jake say, "Get up. How long you gonna sleep?" His eyes dripped white globs of Elmer's glue. His breathing became labored. From his mouth, he pulled a never-ending wad of pink bubble gum. He kept pulling at the stringy, spongy substance. He was now looking at the inside of his tent at geometrical shapes swirling in front of him.

"You jerking off in there?" Jake said from outside the tent.

Sanch blinked a few times as he came to the realization of being awake.

Jake, Antonio, and the one lone camper from last night sat at the tables. Antonio and the other camper drank coffee. Although just breaking the horizon, the sun's heat already made a presence despite the campsite being well shaded. The heat made the slight breeze from the ocean more noticeable and welcoming.

Jake laughed as Sanch, shirtless and barefoot, lazily made his way over. He rubbed the sleep from his eyes, said good morning, and introduced himself to the new guy before sitting down next to Jake.

The new guy's name was Rob. He had a head full of frazzled gray hair and an equally gray beard. He wore thick yellow-tinted glasses, low on the bridge of his nose, and he had gray eyebrows that looked like a squirrel's tail, one long, bushy streak across his lower forehead. He was small in stature. He didn't say much after the introduction, just sat quietly cupping the coffee mug. The coffee's steam fogged his glasses when he took a sip.

Sanch looked at the three tents set up.

"Where'd you sleep?" Sanch asked Antonio.

The Italian laughed. "Here." He patted the tables. They were pushed together now. "Chico will give me a tent tonight."

"You ready to go?" Jake asked Sanch.

"What about breakfast?"

"Let's surf first. It's still early."

It was ten minutes past seven.

"Drink some coffee. It'll hold you over," Rob said in a raspy voice that sounded like it hurt him to talk.

"All right," Sanch said.

Rob went inside the cinder block structure.

"We can go in there?" Sanch asked.

"Just the kitchen part up front. The rest is Chico's house," Antonio answered. "Chico said he had to leave for the day, but would be back later, and you guys can discuss payments then."

Rob came out with a steaming cup of coffee for Sanch.

"Sure you don't want any?" he asked Jake.

"No, I wanna surf. I didn't come all the way here to sit around and drink coffee."

"But that's what this place is known for, the coffee," Rob said.

"No. It's known for Witches Rock. Hurry up. I'll wait in the tent."

"The surf isn't going anywhere," Rob said to him as he walked off.

33

Sanch, Antonio, and Rob drank their coffee in silence.

Sanch finished his coffee and went back to his tent to get his toothbrush and toothpaste.

"You ready?" Jake asked, sticking his head out of the tent.

"I'm going to brush my teeth first."

Jake stepped from his tent with his toothbrush.

"Where's the bathroom?" Sanch asked.

"Don't know. I pissed behind your tent."

"Why behind mine?"

"Cause I didn't wanna piss by mine."

Sanch shook his head but did the same.

Behind Chico's house, on top of the tallest tree on the property, was a black, plastic five-hundred gallon water tank that collected rain water. A hose ran down the tree with a shower head attached to the end of it. A hand-painted sign with red letters was nailed on the tree that read: CINCO MINUTOS DUCHAS, POR FAVOR. GRACIAS.

"Even if you're poor in the States, at least we have running, drinkable water," Sanch said. "Hell, we even flush our shit and piss in drinkable water."

"No curtains or anything. I can't wait to shower naked," Jake said. "Flop this big ol' dick out. Hopefully, some chicks'll camp here."

"You'll scare'em off with all those pimples on your ass," Sanch said.

Jake laughed.

While Sanch started brushing his teeth in the trickle of water that fell from the shower, Jake found a sink attached to the side wall of Chico's house.

"Holy shit," he shouted, "you've got to come smell this."

Before Sanch made it that far, he gagged. Jake laughed more and took an exaggerated deep breath as if he had just stepped out into the mountains and inhaled the purest air possible. Sanch dry-heaved a few times sounding like a cat with a hairball.

Next to the sink was a wooden structure about the size of a porta potty. They walked around looking for the source of the stench. Inside the stall with no door a pile of bottles of every size and shape covered the shattered toilet. Flies buzzed about and maggots crawled on the muddy floor. Sanch gagged again and Jake laughed harder.

The next stall had a door hanging crookedly on the hinges. Jake kicked it. It swung open and quickly closed again. The top hinge broke, and the door slouched on its side. The smell of shit hit them full force. Jake kicked the door again. They jumped back as it fell off the hinges and thumped on the ground. The toilet now showed in plain view. Both of them cupped a hand to their noses and peered in. A sign hung over the toilet painted like the one on the shower reading: NO RAS DE PAPEL.

Sanch braved closer but quickly jumped back.

"What?" Jake said.

"Look next to the toilet."

Next to the toilet was a wastebasket filled with shit-streaked toilet paper. Flies and mosquitoes buzzed about.

"We've got to find somewhere else to shit," Jake said.

At the tent, Sanch asked, "What about our money? We leaving it here?"

"Probably shouldn't."

Jake went back in his tent and came out with his money rolled into a film canister. He gave Sanch an empty canister. He shoved ten rolled-up hundred-dollar bills inside it.

"Why'd you bring film canisters?"

"In case we want to take pot seeds back home."

"You don't think we'll lose these surfing?"

"I ain't leaving it here. That's for sure."

They headed down the beach side by side, barefoot and shirtless and each carrying a surfboard.

As they crossed the threshold from the foliaged pathway to open beach, the view was not what they expected. The ocean was like a lake with no trace of waves.

"I don't get it. I thought this area gets waves every day. I could've stayed home for this," Jake said.

Sanch laughed. "What if we came all this way and there is a month-long flat spell?"

"This is bullshit. People said Costa Rica never goes flat. Even on small days, there is still something surfable."

Tamarindo Beach was U-shaped. Two points, miles apart, jutted out to make the tree-bordered beach into a little cove.

Standing in thigh-high water next to an anchored skiff, an old man balanced on black, exposed rock threw a cast net, beautifully. With one end in his mouth and the other end flung over his forearm, the old man tossed it with a delicate touch and the net spanned out like a web and floated down to the surface. Then the old man brought the net back to him hand over hand and tossed it into his skiff where he began pulling out the bait fish.

Beyond the fisherman, a line of sailboats and two larger fishing charter boats moored in the bay. Schools of bait fish jumped in the wake of the dinghies headed out to the larger boats.

"See those sailboats," Jake said. "That's where I wanna live."

Sanch and Jake approached the old man, slipping a few times on the algae-covered rocks.

"Surf. Where is the surf?" Jake asked, slowly.

"No, no. Fish," the old man said pointing to himself. He returned to pulling bait fish out of the net. He threw the baitfish into a styrofoam cooler, not caring if some missed and swam away to freedom. He had plenty.

"No. We want to surf," Jake said. He pointed to his surfboard and then pointed out to the water. "Where is surf?" he repeated.

"Punta," the old man said. He pointed up the beach and continued working.

They backtracked from the walk last night, noticing what they had missed previously in the dark. A trail next to an abandoned boat inclined slightly under a wooden archway with a hand-painted sign dangling at the peak saying "El Pescador." A few yards after that was another restaurant with a sign out front that read "American Food."

Passing the main beach, most of the waterfront property had been bought up. There were restaurants, cabanas, hotels. What wasn't already developed was for sale.

"Let's ask him," Jake said pointing to a Tico, who had a body built like an Olympic swimmer and a solid bronze tan, a tan that looked set in for good, not one that came and went with the seasons. His dark hair hung in his eyes. An old, banged-up single fin, red surfboard, a throwback from the seventies, rested at his feet.

"Hey, buddy," Jake said as he approached the Tico. The kid stayed seated on the rubble of concrete. He nodded acknowledgment and went back to studying the ocean.

"Where's the surf?" Jake asked.

The Tico pointed to the same spot as the old man.

"Where? All the way to the point?"

The Tico nodded, again. "Get some surf here, but smaller."

"That's the closest surf?"

The Tico nodded, still looking at the ocean.

"What's it called?"

"Grande."

"What?" Jake asked.

"Playa Grande."

"How long's it take to walk there?"

The Tico shrugged, "Depends how fast you walk."

They walked over crushed shells in the light brown sand, stepping over driftwood that had washed ashore. Two dogs raced behind them barking at the incoming tide.

They stopped at the estuary and looked out to the ocean.

"Over there," Jake said. Waves broke just on the other side of the river. "If that's surfable, I ain't walking all the way to Playa Grande or whatever the hell he called it. What do you figure this river is? Twenty yards?"

"About that."

Jake jumped in.

Sanch looked around. Behind him the dogs finished with the water and now chased after the gulls that pecked at the sand. He turned back and seeing Jake half across, entered the brackish water.

Jake, now on the other side, watched as Sanch slowly came across. Jake strained to see something.

"What is it?" Sanch shouted. He picked up the pace.

Jake laughed. Sanch looked behind him and continued in a rushed paddle.

"What are you laughing at?" he yelled.

"I think it's a gator."

Sanch dug deep into the muddy water.

"Where at?" Sanch said rushing out.

Jake turned and pointed, but kept his eyes on the surf.

"That's a log, asshole."

"Looked like a gator."

"Gators don't live in saltwater."

"How am I supposed to know that?"

When Sanch turned his attention to the surf, the log's eyes blinked.

"How big you think it is?"

"Can't really tell with no one else out. Maybe waist-high," Jake said.

"You gonna surf it?"

Jake nodded. "Damn right. First we gotta find somewhere to stash our cash." He looked around. "Up toward the trees."

Jake made sure they weren't being watched before digging a few inches below the surface and placing his and Sanch's film canister in the sand and then covering them up, setting a piece of driftwood on top as a landmark.

"I don't know if this is a good idea," Sanch told him.

"What else we gonna do?"

Sanch shrugged.

Paddling out was easy, unlike paddling through the wind chop of the Gulf of Mexico. The waves came in sets and were clean and smooth. If it had been Pensacola, there would be twenty people out trying to catch the same wave. But it wasn't Pensacola, and Sanch and Jake were the only ones out.

Waiting for a set to show on the horizon, they looked at each other, and Jake threw his hands up in disbelief, "Can you believe we are here?"

Sanch looked around for a minute, absorbing the scenery and then, as if unable to contain his joy any longer, let out a hoot and splashed the water like a child in a bath.

Jake took the first wave of good size. Although smaller than they expected, they had never surfed anything as clean or with as much power for such a small wave or had a ride ever last as long. Jake swung down with a large bottom turn and then back up, hitting the lip just as it curled over.

Sanch caught a wave as Jake paddled back out. Unfamiliar with such a quick wave, Sanch remained crouched, grabbing the rail of his board with his left hand and stuck his right hand in the face of the wave to slow down. The wave curled over him and for an instant, he thought he would ride in the barreling wave, something he had never experienced, but the board sucked up into the whirling water.

He came up through the white water of the passing wave.

"I thought you had that one," Jake said. "What happened?"

"I'll get the next one," Sanch said with a smile he hadn't known his face to make in a long time.

The next set of waves came, and they both paddled for the same one. Sanch was closest to the peak, but Jake didn't want to let him have it, and they both stood, riding the same wave, Sanch riding just behind Jake. Sanch leaned over to grab Jake's board to shake him off and instead fell. Jake rode the wave to the inside sandbar.

They spent the next two hours playing like that. The waves were easy and forgiving, and falling was of no concern.

The waves started to break less frequently and people, most with surfboards, walked by on the way to Playa Grande.

"Looks like everyone is going down there. We should check it out," Jake said.

The sky darkened over the rocky point of Playa Grande. The waves were twice as big there as the estuary break they had just surfed, and the crowd was large on the beach and in the water.

"Look at that one," Jake said pointing to someone paddling into a large wave. The surfer wiped out on take off and didn't bother paddling back out.

"Looks big," Sanch said.

"It is," Jake said.

"You nervous?"

"Hell no. This is what we came for." Jake looked at Sanch. He smiled. "You scared?"

Sanch shook his head no. "How big you think it is?"

"Overhead, easily."

With no hesitation, Jake paddled for the main peak where the surfers waited for the larger waves.

Sanch took his time entering the water and paddled to a smaller peak that was less crowded.

He sat in the lineup with four guys and one girl. None of them surfed much. Instead, they sat on their boards, facing the horizon with their heads cocked to the right watching the bigger waves and better surfers. After a few minutes, Sanch rode a slow, mushy wave. The water was too deep to give it any power.

Sanch once paddled out alone at Pensacola Beach during a two-foot overhead hurricane swell. It took him thirty minutes to make it out past the breaking waves and at times, he wanted to give up and go back in. He could hear

41

the thunderous roar as the waves pounded into the tide
rushing back out. He sat out there alone for twenty minutes
and didn't ride one wave. He had paddled for a few, but
when he peered over the edge just before it pitched he
would pull back. Finally, a smaller set rolled in, and he
rode in on his stomach, just wanting to get to shore as
quickly as possible. No one witnessed his inability to surf
large waves, but he was embarrassed about it nonetheless.
And oftentimes, that day would creep into his thoughts, and
he would be awash with shame. He remembered that
moment while sitting in the Playa Grande lineup.

He paddled over to another peak, not the largest where
Jake sat, but still a bit bigger than where he was just at.
About fifteen people shifted their eyes his way as he joined
the crowd. The bigger the waves, the more surfing became
a machismo testament, unlike the previous peak where it
was more for fun. He paddled for a few but didn't drop in
on any. The waves continued to build, and the rain moved
closer. Sanch knew the safest thing to do would be to
paddle in, but he couldn't make himself do it. He didn't
want to be scared anymore.

The waves had grown at least another foot, maybe two,
easily approaching six to eight feet, similar to the hurricane
swell of his past. As the surf grew larger, the crowd thinned
and he knew a stupid mistake by an amateur could have
grave consequences with waves that large. He spotted Jake
at the next peak. The waves were larger there, but he
paddled that way anyway.

"They're getting big, huh?" Jake asked. "You catch
any?"

"A few," Sanch said. "Not since they got this big
though."

A wave came up behind them.

"Watch this one," Jake said. He paddled for it, and so did another surfer. Jake was in position, but the Tico wasn't letting up. The wave lifted at its peak, and Jake was up. The Tico continued paddling. Jake hollered a warning. The Tico pulled out of the wave allowing Jake to ride it. Jake took this opportunity to make a statement and rode up close to the Tico and turned the board quickly just before hitting the local surfer and sprayed him with what looked like a bucket of water being dumped on him. Some people in the lineup laughed, but some shook their heads at such an arrogant move.

A wave came in Sanch's direction. He paddled for it. Another guy paddled for it as well. Sanch was in position, and the other surfer knew that and pulled away. Sanch's board lifted, and he looked out to his right. He panicked and pulled back.

The other surfer who let him have the wave shouted something to him in Spanish and splashed water his way. He felt resentful eyes look at him for letting such a thing of beauty go unsurfed.

Jake came up beside him, "See what I did to that dude?"

Sanch nodded.

"I said…" And Jake made a reenactment with his hands of what he did.

A couple of seconds went by. "How big was it?" Jake asked.

"It was big."

"Eight foot?"

Sanch nodded. "Could be." At that time, another wave raised behind them.

"Get this one," Jake said. "It's all you."

43

Sanch turned and paddled hard. He paddled before he had the chance to get intimidated. He glanced over his shoulder at Jake just as his board began to rise and Jake was looking toward the horizon, waiting on the next one. Sanch turned back and peered down the face of the menacing drop. The wave was closing out, and it was too late for him to stand and too late to pull out. He kicked free of his board and twirled his arms to stay upright on his fall and just before impact covered his head with both arms in case the board came down on top of him. He penetrated the rushing tide and was lifted back up by the cycling water and flung over the falls once more. His board shot through the back of the wave. After the wave had flattened out on the inside, Sanch broke through the surface into the disorienting eddy. He vomited a bit of water that had rushed up his nose. He turned to look at the horizon and saw another wave break in front of him. He pulled the board towards him by the leash and was able to crawl on the board and while staying on his stomach, he rode the pounding whitewater to shore.

He tried not to look at the people who he thought were looking at him as he walked from the ocean. His shoulders were burnt, and he was tired. He scooted underneath the shade of the trees at the end of the main beach away from the crowd to sit in the hot sand as the sky turned gray and rain fell in large, heavy drops.

Chapter 5

"How long you been up here?" Jake said.

Sanch looked up and shielded his eyes from the soft drizzle of rainfall.

"I can't believe how big it got in just a couple of hours. That one you tried to catch was huge. I didn't see you after that."

"I didn't make it," Sanch said.

"No shit. Nobody could've made that. Why didn't you come back out?"

Sanch looked at him with furrowed brows and flashed him the middle finger.

Jake laughed.

Walking back to camp, the rain continued.

"It was over here," Jake said dropping to his knees along the line of trees by the estuary.

"This was the marker," Sanch said, lifting a piece of driftwood a few feet from where Jake dug frantically.

After a minute Jake stood nearby watching Sanch dig with two hands, water filling the hole as fast as he could dig out sand.

"This was such a stupid idea," Sanch said.

"You probably already dug it up. It wasn't that deep," Jake said. "Check the pile you just made."

Sanch started sifting through the pile while Jake continued feeling around the soupy hole.

"Maybe it was deeper than this," Jake said.

"I'm not listening to you anymore this trip."

Jake laughed. "It's gotta be here. Just keep looking."

A second later, Jake held up a film canister.

"Told you it was in here," Jake said.

"It's probably yours, isn't it?"

"Yep," Jake said. He sat on the ground, opened up the canister and counted the soggy money.

Sanch looked at him. "Little help?"

"I'm sure it's there." Jake stood up and held his board up to the sky to rinse off the sand.

Sanch felt around until he ran his hands across it.

"Told you it was there," Jake said.

The rain continued as they arrived at the empty campsite. They placed their surfboards in the tents and went in search of a restaurant.

"Let's just eat here," Sanch said, pointing to the El Pescador.

"What makes you think that's a restaurant?" Jake said.

The next restaurant overlooking the beach had a white cloth on the table and glasses turned upside down next to neatly folded cloth napkins. They kept walking.

Through the path that led into the heart of Tamarindo, where they were dropped off the previous night, they stood on a dirt road that made a circle at the end of the town. Trees formed a canopy over a few benches next to pay phones on the inside of the circle.

They walked through the circle to the main road. To the south, the road ended at a ten-foot wooden fence painted bright yellow with words Mambo Bar painted bright orange. The door in the fence had a padlocked chain running through where the doorknob should have been.

A few people scurried out of the rain near a row of street vendor carts covered with plastic tarps. Only one brave or desperate man in a poncho sat on a stool waiting on customers, exposing his wares to the weather. Beyond the vendors, on both sides of the street, were single story, stucco buildings painted in different hues of orange, yellow, and green.

A restaurant called Fiesta del Mar looked well lit and empty except for a young local boy, maybe fifteen, sitting behind the bar watching a surf video. The chair cushions and tablecloths looked like they were ordered from a Magnum PI catalog. The plastic south wall could be rolled up to make al fresco dining. Sanch and Jake sat at the table closest to the street. A couple of minutes passed before the boy stood to serve them, not taking his eyes from the TV as he walked over to them.

He said nothing without a smile as he set forks and knives on the table. He wore an aloha shirt and khaki pants.

"Morning," Sanch said.

The young waiter handed them menus and went back to the video.

The menu was written in Spanish with English translations. The items were also numbered.

"You think they take American money?" Sanch said.

"You gotta get that changed. I can't keep buying everything. You already owe me twenty bucks."

"It's only ten, but whatever."

Jake waved the boy back over. The boy looked up and said, "Dime."

"What?" Jake said.

"Tell me," the boy said.

"You still serving breakfast?" Jake asked.

The boy nodded and pointed to a chalkboard sign by the entrance: Desayuno Americano. 24 horas.

"I don't know what that says," Jake said.

"American Breakfast. Twenty four hours," Sanch said. "It's written in English next to it."

"Didn't see that," Jake said. "Do we just tell you what we want?"

"Dime," the boy said again.

They both ordered the American breakfast: two eggs, bacon, toast, and coffee.

The young waiter disappeared and brought them their food a short time later. Then he sat back down at his chair behind the bar to continue watching the video.

"What is this?" Jake said. "Where is the bacon and toast?"

"No tienen."

Sanch scooped egg, beans, and rice on the fork in one bite. With his mouth full he said, "Taste yours."

"What's it taste like?"

"Just taste it and tell me what you think."

Jake took a bite and made a scrunched up face. "Tastes like soap."

"I thought that, too," Sanch said. He scooped another forkful into his mouth.

"Why're you still eating it?"

"I'm hungry."

"Why's it taste like soap?" Jake asked the kid.

"No soap. Cilantro."

"What?"

"No soap."

"Fuck it. At least we know the dishes are clean," Jake said.

The street vendors had come from somewhere and were pulling the tarps, preparing for the many tourists who paid ten dollars for a few shells on a string or a pirate-faced coconut—souvenirs to sit on a shelf or hidden in a closet as a reminder of that seven to ten day trip to paradise. A pack of mangy dogs scurried down the road. A symphony of birds rang out from the trees and lizards scattered into the bushes. Restaurants offered pizza, ice cream, and hamburgers. There were cabanas and hotels and signs for apartments that were for rent only ten minutes from town. A few newer hotels looked out of place. A Rottweiler came up behind the two clueless wanderers and snapped at Jake's hand before running off.

"What the fuck was that for?" Jake said.

Sanch laughed.

"Look at this," Jake said, showing his hand to Sanch, a small bit of blood dribbled down from his pinkie knuckle.

"He barely touched you," Sanch said laughing.

"Fuck you, you didn't get bit." He wiped the blood on his shorts.

They passed a hotel with a gated courtyard surrounded by lush greenery.

"How much you think these places are?" Sanch said.

"Let's find out." Jake pushed open the gate door and followed the red brick pavers through the manicured garden. A young woman opened up the tiki bar next to the pool.

An overweight lady wearing a tropical flowered dress watched TV in the office.

"Welcome," she said.

"An American," Jake said. "I can dig it. What are your prices like here?"

"Right now good. How long do you need?"

"Till our money runs out."

"Next week starts the dry season; prices go up. Starting the week of the fifteenth, I'm booked up for a few weeks."

"What do you mean the dry season?" Jake asked.

Sanch looked at brochures on her desk while the lady told Jake that Costa Rica didn't have a winter and summer, only a wet and dry season. The dry season, running from mid-November to April and being the most popular among travelers, was also the season of higher prices. At the moment, the hotel cost fifty dollars a night and in the next couple of weeks, the price would inflate to eighty a night.

"That's for the standard room with two twin beds. Of course, we have some suites with a king-size bed, satellite TV, A/C, and a kitchenette for a bit more."

"Too rich for us," Jake said.

"Do you need a band-aid?" she asked.

"What? No," Jake said looking at his hand. He wiped the bit of blood on his shorts. "Damn dog jumped up and bit me."

"Hope it wasn't a black dog," she said.

"It was. Why?"

She laughed. "I was just making a joke. You know? Bad omen and what not?"

"No," Jake said. "That's not a funny joke."

They continued on.

Walking by a bank, Jake said, "You better go in there and change some money."

The bank teller gave Sanch three hundred for the exchange rate.

They entered a surf shop called Aqua Blue next door to the bank.

"What's up?" Jake said to the ponytailed Tico sitting behind the counter watching a surf video.

"Hola," the Tico said.

"Does everyone in this town surf?" Jake asked.

"Yeah, bro. A lot of surfers here. More every day."

"Jake." Jake stuck out his hand.

"I'm Alex," the Tico said and shook his hand.

Sanch, looking around the store, lifted a hand. "I'm Sanch."

"So this is it, huh?" Jake said.

"What?"

"The surf shop of Tamarindo."

"Not the only one. But the best. There is Tamarindo Adventures and Lagarto Surf."

"Where are they?"

"You keep going that way," he pointed down the road in the direction they had just walked. "Take the road on the left. Halfway up the hill you will see Tamarindo Adventures. Keep going, staying to the right because it will fork to the left also and you'll see Lagarto Surf."

"Is it far?"

"Nothing far in Tamarindo."

"A mile?"

"Sure."

"Walking distance?"

"Everything's walking distance."

"You walk everywhere?"

"No. I have a motorbike."

"Where is really big surf?" Jake asked. "Got a little taste of it today and I want big. Reef breaks even."

"Only reef break in Costa Rica is on the Caribbean side. Puerto Viejo or Salsa Brava. Only breaks sometimes, but when it does, it's big. Everything on this side, small. Gets bigger in April or May."

"Small? Today was big. Wasn't it Sanch?"

Sanch nodded.

"He couldn't even surf it."

Sanch looked at Jake. "I surfed it."

"About killed yourself."

Sanch shook his head, "I was all right."

51

"I caught a wave that was, at least, eight foot. Wasn't it?"

"Look here," Sanch said. He pointed to a poster hanging next to the boards. The poster showed surfers with a large rock sticking out of the water with the words "Surf Witches Rock—famed wave from the *Endless Summer II*."

"Yeah, that's where I wanna surf. How do we get there?" Jake said.

"We have a boat that can take you." Alex showed him a photo album with pictures of charters that Aqua Blue ran.

"How much does that cost?"

"Two hundred a person."

"Any other way?"

"Some people drive it during the dry season. It's not easy. It's inside a national park. You have to let the river fully dry up. I never tried it. I always take a boat."

"So Grande's the best surf around here?"

"Grande's good. I like Langosta, too. And Negra is not too far. Negra's a rock bottom. Gets big. Need a car, though. It's one of the best waves on the Pacific side."

"We don't have a car."

"Langosta then. On the other side of the point." He pointed south.

"You're the man," Jake said, and they headed out.

They followed the road up to the other surf shops. Dirt roads ran throughout the town. The side roads were more primitive than the main road. There were no hotels or restaurants and only a few townhouse complexes, but mostly trees. Downtown Tamarindo was a half of a mile stretch of dirt road along the ocean front.

Sanch and Jake walked into Tamarindo Adventures and looked around. There weren't any workers around and didn't look like much of a surf shop. There were more motorcycles, ATVs, kayaks, and canoes than surfboards. A ten-foot-tall chain-link fence surrounded the store. The bottom floor had no walls. The vehicles were on the ground, covered by the second floor which was an enclosed wooden circle. A sign that said "surfboards" directed them up the stairs. Still no one was around. Mostly all they had were longboards or funboards. The few shortboards they had looked like boards from the eighties, single and double fin thrusters.

They left and continued up the road.

"We really could sell our boards for a lot. Both surf shops we looked at so far had crap. What were the prices at the other place?" Jake said.

"Some as much as three hundred," Sanch said.

"That's used boards, too."

Sanch nodded.

"I can get brand new ones shaped for two fifty. Sell them here for five hundred. Let's see if this last shop is the same. Then we could have three shops competing for our prices."

Lagarto Surf looked out of place. Maybe it was a sign of things to come. It was a huge wooden structure, well-made as if a Florida architect was hired to give it a rustic feel. An illuminated neon sign of a Disney-like lizard holding a surfboard invited consumers in. Entering, they followed a small wooden bridge that crossed a pond filled with Koi. There were racks of tee shirts for fifteen dollars apiece and racks of hemp necklaces, some with a shark tooth and some without, for as little as five dollars, but some were more expensive depending on how big of a shark's tooth was wanted. Hanging on the walls were beach chairs with and without cup holders, floats, snorkel-mask-fin sets, sunblock, flip flops, towels, umbrellas, shot glasses, sunglasses, postcards, coffee mugs, ground coffee and whole bean coffee, henna tattoos, beaded hair wraps and anything else needed for a beach vacation.

The girl working the counter was an American with shoulder-length, blonde, frizzy hair, pale skin, and a hook nose.

"Hello," she said, a little too loudly and bit too friendly.

"American? Right on," Jake said.

Her name was Beth. She moved to Costa Rica from Texas with her husband, Vince, after graduating college.

"Where is he now?" Jake asked.

"Giving a surf lesson."

"How much does he make giving surf lessons?" Jake asked.

"Ten bucks."

"A day?"

"A lesson. People pay forty dollars a lesson, and he gets ten for every lesson," she said.

"How many does he do a day?"

"It depends. Today he's got four, but sometimes he does seven or eight at a time."

"Wait. So he's making forty dollars right now? How long is a lesson?"

"Two hours."

"And what do you make?"

"Pretty personal, aren't you?"

"Just curious. My first day here. Trying to figure out how things run."

"I make two dollars."

"Two dollars what?"

"An hour. Minimum wage is only a buck an hour."

"Are you kidding me?"

"No."

"Anything else you guys need?"

"No. Just looking around," Jake said. Once out of earshot from Beth he said to Sanch, "I'm taking that dude's job."

A hundred yards or so past Lagarto Surf, the road continued straight, but smaller trails branched off, and they took one that went back in the direction of the town center. The trail was not big enough for a car, only foot traffic or maybe a bike. On the left two paltry homes, similar to Chico's, shared about a quarter acre of land. Chicken wire separated the two. The land had been cleared some, but there were still enough trees left to keep it shaded throughout the day. Chickens roamed freely.

Hopping over puddles along the trail and occasionally struggling to maintain balance on the slippery surface, they approached Fiesta del Mar from the rear. They had walked the town in its entirety in less than an hour, with stops included.

About thirty feet behind the restaurant another insignificant home sat at a slight angle like an earthquake had deformed its foundation. The roof was a blue plastic tarp. The wire fence around the property made a small yard on either side of the house. There were too many chickens to count, and the smell didn't invite anyone to leisurely stop and take inventory.

Unless tourists ventured off the main street, they would not be exposed to such a site. The restaurant did its job covering up the offensive living quarters and made Tamarindo the sleepy little surf town as described in travel guides.

An old woman, her frame more fragile-looking than the house's, stepped outside. She watched Sanch and Jake walk by. The chickens scattered with her every step. Some ran inside the house. Sanch waved to her, and she smiled and waved back.

At the campsite, Rob sat alone at the table, reading. Sanch and Jake joined him.

"What're you doing?" Jake asked.

Rob held up the book.

"Whatever, dude," Jake said. "Should've seen the waves. I was killing it. Sanch about drowned."

"I'm glad you didn't drown, Sanch," Rob said without looking up from his book.

"Want to go get a coke?" Jake asked Sanch.

"We just walked through town. I'm just going to chill for a little."

"And do what?"

"Take a nap, maybe."

"Just come with me to get a coke real quick."

"I'm good."

"Well, I'm going."

"I'll be here."

Jake left.

"Kid can't sit still, huh?" Rob said.

"He's always like that."

"Why do you hang out with him?"

"We're friends."

"Really?"

"We've known each other since I was about five."

"How old are you now?"

"Twenty."

"And him?"

"Twenty-six."

"Want to get high?"

"Yeah."

Rob pulled from the front pocket of his shirt an Altoids tin of cannabis and a small spiral shell. He dipped the bigger end of the shell into the cannabis, packing it full and handed it, along with a lighter, to Sanch.

"What kind of pipe is this?"

"A turritella shell. They're all over the beach." He pulled another one out of his pocket. "You just snap the end off like this." He pressed the small end of the shell against the table, snapping off a little from the end of it making it a perfectly good one-hitter.

Sanch lit it up and took a puff. He handed it back to Rob. Rob told him to finish it. Sanch took a few more puffs and handed it back to Rob.

Rob packed it again.

"It's nice here, huh?" Sanch said, looking around.

Rob took a puff. "I've been to some nice places. This is a bit better than nice."

Rob packed another bowl and handed it to Sanch.

"Been here before?"

Rob shook his head.

"How long have you been here?"

"Couple of weeks, I guess. I was traveling with a friend of mine over on the Caribbean side. We're going to meet up again here and then go to the volcano."

"What volcano?"

"Arenal. The lava flows constantly. At night, you can see the peak lit up. Plenty of hot springs and lakes."

"How long you been here, in Tamarindo?"

"Two days. Three. No. This is my fourth."

Sanch handed the shell back to Rob. Rob repacked it.

"How much longer you here for?" Sanch asked.

"Another week."

"Then back to reality, huh?"

"Something close to it. It'll be a different reality than when I left." Rob stopped talking to smoke.

"Why's that?"

"I quit my job before coming here." He blew out the smoke. "I might not go back."

"Where is back?"

"Minnesota."

Sanch nodded. He was high now. The thirty seconds of silence seemed much longer. Sanch looked at Rob and Rob nodded. Sanch nodded back.

"I was diagnosed with brain cancer a month ago. Told I only have maybe six months left."

"That sucks."

Rob looked at Sanch and laughed. Sanch smirked, not quite sure why Rob was laughing.

"Yeah. It sucks. It sucks bad," Rob said through laughter. Rob's rough laugh turned into a few harsh coughs.

"I didn't mean it like that," Sanch said.

"It was perfect. It is about the best way to sum up my situation. It sucks."

"Sorry, man."

"For what?"

"You know."

"You're sorry I'm dying?"

"I guess. I mean, yeah."

"It will happen to you too."

"Damn dude."

Rob laughed. Sanch did too, probably for a little too long.

"Where are you from?" Rob said.

"Pensacola."

"No shit?"

"You've heard of it?"

"Was stationed there in the seventies. Haven't thought of it much since then."

"Probably hasn't changed much since then," Sanch said.

"What are you running from?"

"What?"

"What brings you here?"

"I'm not running," Sanch said. "I just came to surf."

Rob looked at him for a bit. "Don't bullshit me, kid. Or yourself, for that matter."

They sat in silence for a moment.

"I don't know," Sanch said. "A lot of stuff, I guess."

Sanch sat quiet, waiting for Rob to say something. Rob didn't. Instead, he just sat nodding his head slowly.

"My dad wants me to join the Navy."

Sanch waited in an uncomfortable silence.

"Like him and my brother did, but it's not for me." Sanch stood up from the table and rubbed his eyes. "I'm pretty fucking high right now."

Rob looked at him with a crooked smile.

"I've gotta piss," Sanch said. He went around the corner by the shower, turned on the spigot and washed his face. Thinking about his brother still choked him up. But he hadn't really cried since he got the call from his dad saying Buck had been found in his car at Ft. Pickens with a needle still in his arm. He cried that day but hadn't been able to cry since. That bothered him. He couldn't cry at the funeral either, not even during the three-volley salute when he knew he should've. He looked over at his father who was crying, and he felt embarrassed. He had never seen his father cry before.

59

He walked back. Rob looked up from his book and said, "You okay."

"Yeah. I'm good."

"Want some acid."

"What?"

"LSD. Want some?"

"No. Definitely not."

"Have you done it before?"

"Yeah. Quite a few times. It's been awhile."

"I've got plenty."

"No. Seriously. I'm good."

"Bad experience?"

"You could say that. I thought I was dying."

"Eschatological experience. Happens to the best of us."

"I don't know what that means, but I'm in no hurry to experience it again."

"You broke free of this false reality and had a reunion with the divine."

"No clue. But it was pretty damn intense."

Rob looked at him until Sanch started talking again.

"It was as if all these thoughts hit me at once. No. It wasn't even thoughts. It was more than that. At first, I told myself it was nothing to be scared of. That it was the whole point of doing it. It was just the drugs. It would wear off. But it didn't. For hours, I felt I was stuck in a constant loop. It felt like it would never wear off."

Rob chuckled. "LSD can give you a taste of it. Not like DMT though. Ever try that?"

"What is it?"

"Oh, man. Want to visit the cosmos? Try DMT. That will take you there quickly."

"No thank you. I thought I had a heart attack. I might have even left myself for a while. I saw myself die. It sounds so stupid, but I was aware that I was dead. And then I wasn't. I was back in my body. I didn't want to tell anyone what I was experiencing because it sounded so stupid. So I just walked. I walked pretty much the rest of the night. It was the only thing I could do. I was convinced if I stopped walking I'd die. I never prayed so much in my life."

Rob laughed. "Maybe you experienced a fragment of hell. Who knows?"

"I figured, after that, I didn't want to know what was out there."

Rob laughed harder now. "But you do know. You can't unsee it. That's the thing. You saw it. You broke on through," Rob said. "You can't deny that you have experienced something greater than yourself. You just don't know what the hell it was."

Sanch laughed. "I guess. But I'm cool if I never experience it again."

"It happens, man. You wanted it, and you got it." Rob continued laughing. "But you know it doesn't have to be drugs. Some people can experience it through meditation. Kundalini."

"You've experienced it without drugs?"

"Shit no, man. Not because I haven't tried."

"Well, I'm cool never experiencing it again. Whatever it is?"

"You know what IT is. It might not have a name. Because, it's beyond words. If we gave it a name, we would humanize it and diminish it. It's the opening of our pineal gland."

"What's the pineal gland?"

"Really? You've never heard that word."

Sanch shook his head no.

"Our third eye. Our spiritual antenna. Hell, some will even say that's where our soul is located. Our whole existence."

"Sounds a bit new agey, Rob."

"Look, you are experiencing your astral body through a physical body. Doing psychedelics and meditating, that's as close to the real that we, as humans, can get in this physical world and what some would say, imaginary world."

"Imaginary world? Come the fuck on?"

"Well, maybe illusory is a better word. Or, let me see. Holographic, maybe. Some people say that all we see is just a symbol for what's real, that the physical stuff is all just a representation of the real."

"Has anyone ever said you are insane?"

"Maybe I'm the sane one. Look, the real scared you because it was too damn real. We aren't able to understand it in this physical world. But you've experienced it. I've experienced it. But that's all we can do with it. Experience it. Or experience something that resembles it even. Maybe we can't even actually experience it, but we think we are experiencing it, but we can never truly access that astral plane while stuck in human form. So we become frightened by getting as close to it as humans can. And it frightens us even more when we come back because we can't talk about it because people may think we are crazy. Or even if people don't think you are crazy, the words won't do it justice. Because words are just symbols too, you know?"

"Sure, man." Sanch smiled at Rob, but didn't look fully convinced.

"When you reached that moment of terror, of fear, you were there. You just didn't know what it was or what to do with it."

Sanch looked at him for a second and then turned his attention away. Rob didn't speak for a moment either then held up the book in his hand and said, "When I'm done with this, you should read it. It might fuck up your whole belief system."

"Not sure I have one."

"That's not always a bad thing. Means you are open to learning."

"What's it called?"

"Ever heard of Terence McKenna?"

Sanch shook his head. "Nope."

"You've done psychedelics and have never heard of Terence McKenna?"

"I haven't."

"Drugs are just recreation to you, huh?"

"Basically."

"No, they aren't and you know it. McKenna basically says human civilization spawned from Psilocybin mushrooms."

"Oh yeah?" Sanch said.

"Oh yeah."

"I'm listening."

"Shrooms were the original tree of knowledge. A certain breed of prehumans began incorporating psilocybin into their diet, and that led to a separation from primates. Ancient shamanistic societies were well-advanced for their times, more advanced than any civilization now, in relative comparison. And governments outlaw psychedelic drugs because of the influence it could have on male-dominated, capitalistic views. Basically, they don't want us to access our pineal gland. So they do things to calcify it. Fluoride in our drinking water and things like that. Without access to our pineal gland, we create a spiritually empty society. So people search for that spirituality from false substitutes: Religion, caffeine, tobacco, alcohol and TV. But mushrooms are different. They can lead us to a greater consciousness, and further evolve us."

"Hmm."

"Some like to call it the Stoned Ape Theory."

"Sounds like that guy was a bit stoned."

"He was."

Rob stood up, stretched and said, "But just because someone is stoned doesn't mean you discount what they are saying."

"I guess so."

"Want to hear a joke?"

"Of course."

"A lizard walked down a path smoking a joint and didn't see the koala bear sitting in the tree. Koala bear shouts down, 'Hey buddy. Climb up here and let me get a hit.' Koala is always mooching off everybody, but the lizard is too nice to say no, so he climbs up there and says, 'Look Koala. This is some strong shit so take it easy.' Koala says, 'Motherfucker, I've been smoking longer than you've been alive' and takes a large drag and starts coughing up a lung. Lizard says, 'Told you,' gets his joint back and says, 'I'm going to the river to get a drink.' Koala says, 'Bring me back a glass, will ya?' So lizard goes down to the river and sees an alligator coming out and heading back towards the path. Lizard says, 'Hey man, can you take this glass of water over to Koala for me?' Alligator agrees. Koala is sitting in the tree stoned out of his mind when he sees Alligator approaching with the glass of water, and he shouts down to him, 'Goddamn Lizard. How much water did you drink?'"

Sanch chuckled and then that chuckle became a laugh and then that laugh continued until tears streamed down his cheeks.

"Good one, huh?" Rob said.

"Great," Sanch said through the hybrid laughter-cry.

"Want to join me for a swim?" Rob asked.

"I'm going to wait for Jake. Thanks for the joke. I needed that."

"No problem. Somehow, while traveling the road, you get exactly what we need."

Shortly after Rob left, Jake walked up.

"I just had a snickers and a coke and that shit was good," Jake said. "And I found out where to score some pot."

"Sounds good," Sanch said. He then started laughing again.

"You're stoned now, aren't you?"

"I am," Sanch said. "But I was thinking of a joke Rob just told me."

"I knew that old fucker smoked. How is it?"

"Listen to this joke."

Sanch told it.

"Pretty funny."

"Pretty funny? It's fucking hilarious." Sanch laughed again.

He then told Jake that Rob was dying and some of the things Rob had said.

"Damn. This is his last hurrah, huh?"

Chapter 6

"Did you try the phones?" Sanch said.

"They don't work. You want to call what's-her-face, don't you?"

"Whatever."

Jake laughed. "Let's call Frank then," he said. "That pussy should be here with us."

"I'm sure he doesn't want to talk to me. He's probably still pissed I left him with the rent."

"Fuck that. He makes enough money."

The weather was now less hot after the rain.

"I found the weed hookup right across from the ice cream and pizza shop," Jake said. "It was closed when we walked by before, but this time, there were two guys setting out chairs. I walked by and a dude called me over. Asked if I was looking for anything. Whatever I want, he said."

The place Jake mentioned didn't have a name, just a chalkboard A-frame sign that said: Hamburgers and French Fries - $5. The smell of reefer drifted with the breeze. Two guys stood near the bar, and another six or so huddled around two café tables. Two girls sat alone behind the group of guys. No one there looked over thirty. A few of the guys didn't wear shirts and the ones who did wore ragged and ripped surf tees. A chessboard sat on one of the empty tables. A small television on the counter displayed a surf video. The girls didn't seem as interested in the video as were the guys. However, all eyes turned to the two unfamiliar guests as they strode through the crowd.

"What's up?" Jake said to the guy behind the counter. He had dark, curly hair to his shoulders, no shirt on and a well-toned, tanned upper body that seemed to be the look of most of the men who lived there. Muscles formed long and lean from the hours upon hours out in the water. It wasn't the short and bulky look of steroids and protein shakes and dumbbells. "Where's that other guy?" Jake asked. "The one who was here earlier with you?"

Some of the guys went back to watching the video.

"Johnny?" The man behind the counter said with a French accent.

"I guess. The guy from earlier who asked if I needed anything."

"I don't know. Do you want anything from the menu?" The man said and pointed to the chalkboard.

"Not really. What about phones?"

"We don't have phones. We serve food." He pointed to the town center. "Check down at the circle." He turned his attention back to the TV.

As they left, one of the girls grabbed Sanch by the wrist. With a French accent, she said, "Up the road is a small grocery store. They have phones. It's painted bright orange. If you see the Alamo Rental Car place, you missed it."

"Thanks," Sanch said.

She smiled and winked.

Sanch smiled back.

Walking away, but not quite out of earshot yet, Jake said, "Why didn't you ask her name?"

Sanch looked behind him, and she waved. Sanch waved back.

They walked by rusted vans lined up in front of hotels. Men leaned on the hoods of the vans or sat in rusted lawn chairs next to the vans, smoking cigarettes. They yelled out to Sanch and Jake, "Taxi, taxi. You need taxi?"

Built behind the bright orange store, several cabanas were painted the same bright orange. Vespas chained together out front had a sign next to them that said RENT ME.

Inside the store were rows of chips, sodas, and candy. There was a stand-up cooler for beer and another for ice cream.

A man and woman stood behind a counter in the back underneath signs for laundry service and check-in. The woman folded towels, and the man watched a soccer match on a small television set on top of a milk crate.

"Can I help you?" the large man said in a German accent. The woman, a small, wrinkled Tica with black hair braided in a ponytail hanging over her right shoulder, smiled at the visitors.

"We heard you had phones," Jake said.

"Yes." He pointed to the phone on the counter. "It is forty cents a minute international. What is the number?"

"What's Natalie's number?" Jake said.

"I only know her dad's number."

Jake laughed. "I still can't believe she already moved in with that other dude," he said.

Sanch nodded. "Me either."

"And she wouldn't move in with you? You guys have only been broken up, what? Two months?"

"Less than that."

"She had to have been fucking him while you guys were still together."

The German store owner looked at Jake and said, "Don't talk like that in my store."

"I apologize," Jake said.

"What is the number?" the German said.

"What's Frank's number?" Jake said.

Sanch told him. The owner dialed, said something in Spanish and then handed Sanch the phone.

"I don't wanna talk to him. What am I gonna say?"

"He's your friend," Jake said.

"Probably not anymore. You wanted to call him."

Frank answered the phone.

"What's up?" Sanch said. "I don't know. Jake wanted to call somebody...Yeah, it's cool as hell here."

Sanch paused as Frank said something.

"Believe it or not, it's not so bad not knowing how to speak Spanish," Sanch said into the phone. "Everyone pretty much speaks English. Hey, let me ask you something: you're not still sore at me for leaving you with rent, are you?"

"Tell him about the surf," Jake interrupted. "Tell him how I smacked the lip right in front of a local boy. Tell him about that wave I dropped in on. Is he coming down? Tell him what he's missing because he's too big of a pussy to get over here."

"Hold on," Sanch said. He handed the phone to Jake. "You tell him."

Jake grabbed the phone. "What's up, faggot? Why ain't you over here? We got barreled like crazy on our first day."

"Where are you guys from?" the store owner asked.

"Florida," Sanch told him. "You?"

"Germany."

"How'd you end up here?"

The German told him that he had visited Costa Rica some fifteen years ago on a vacation, decided to buy a little property and sold everything he owned in Germany. Back then, he said, he never imagined Tamarindo would turn out how it did. When he started the store there were no cabanas in the back, but after he saw the tourists continue to come, people began to pay him to camp on his land, and it wasn't long before he expanded. He met his wife, the lady that was sitting with him behind the counter. At the time they met, she didn't speak any German, and he didn't speak any Spanish. He had studied English in school; he said, thinking that if he ever left Germany, it would have been to go to America. Who would've guessed Central America, he said. He laughed at his own joke. She still didn't speak any English or German, but his Spanish had gotten better.

"The phone went dead," Jake said cutting the store owner off from reliving his past.

"You're lucky you got to speak as long as you did," the store owner said. He looked at the clock. "Seven minutes."

A girl walked in the store wearing denim overall shorts with a bikini visible underneath. She was an exotic beauty with some Tica features but taller and with blonde hair. Sanch and Jake flashed each other a sly smile as they watched her grab ice creams out of the cooler. She bent over a few extra seconds looking for the right ones. She flashed a flirtatious smile at them and said something in Spanish to the owner and then leaned over the counter to kiss him on the cheek. She said something to the wife, kissed her on the cheek and then turning to Sanch and Jake said "Hola" and smiled again before skipping out of the store. Sanch and Jake watched her until the door shut.

"Goddamn," Jake said. "I'm in love."

"She's only sixteen," the German said.

"I'm cool with that," Jake said.

"She's my daughter."

Sanch laughed. The dad, not so much.

"Can you introduce me?" Jake said.

"How about you give me the four dollars for the phone, and I don't kick your ass."

"You said forty cents a minute. Seven minutes," Jake paused to calculate the numbers, "that's only two-eighty."

"That was before, when I didn't know you."

"I'll give you six if you give me her name."

"Two if you leave and don't speak to her on your way out."

"Deal. Give 'em two bucks," Jake said and went out the door.

Sanch paid for the phone call. "Let me get a six-pack, too." There were two kinds of beer to choose from. He chose the one with an imperial eagle design.

Outside Jake talked to the girl.

"Are you two dating?" Jake asked, pointing to the boy sitting next to her.

"No way," the girl said.

"What did I tell you," the German shouted from the door.

"Dad!" the girl yelled back.

"Was just leaving," Jake said.

They walked down the road drinking a beer and Sanch held the remaining four beers by the plastic rings that kill fish.

"I'd marry that girl. You didn't think she was hot?"

"She was hot, but only sixteen."

"I could wait. I wonder if that's the law here."

They sat on the beach.

"I could do this the rest of my life," Jake said.

"Sit on the beach and drink beer? Me too."

"Not just this. I mean the whole thing. Live in a tent, surf all day and drink beer."

"It wouldn't be a bad gig," Sanch said.

"Let's do it."

"We are doing it."

"You're damn right we are," Jake said. They toasted their beers to that.

After the six-pack, they went back to the store and grabbed another one. Jake sat outside while Sanch went in to get it. The German owner was alone now.

"Pura Vida," the store owner said as Sanch left.

"Pura Vida," Sanch said back.

Sanch and Jake took the beers to the beach behind the cabanas.

"I wonder if I could catch her at her dad's house?" Sanch said.

"Natalie? That's what you are thinking about right now?"

"I don't know. It just sucks."

"Don't be that guy."

"I'm gonna call her."

"Bullshit."

"I just don't understand what happened. It drives me crazy not knowing why she broke it off after two years. Just out of the blue."

"It wasn't out of the blue. She was fucking someone else."

"You're an ass."

"All you have to do is get laid, and you'll start to forget about her. You had it bad for her, didn't you?"

Sanch laughed. "I did. Now I feel like an idiot."

"Chicks are good at that."

They finished the beers and walked back to the campsite.

Chapter 7

Sanch woke up the next day and joined Rob and Antonio at the tables for coffee. Rob had prepared Sanch a cup when he saw him step from the tent.

"How'd you know?" Sanch asked.

"I heard you guys come in last night. I figured it'd be a rough morning."

"Jake still sleeping?" Sanch asked.

"I reckon. Unless, he's dead in there. I heard him hurl a few times outside his tent last night."

Sanch finished two cups of coffee before Jake woke up. Antonio left to meet a friend for breakfast.

"Not too thrilled about surfing this morning?" Rob said as Jake stood there with his hands down his shorts, scratching. He then smelled his fingers.

"I'm still surfing today, but I need some food first."

"I don't see how ya'll drink that shit."

"Keeps you regular," Rob said.

"Tastes like sweaty socks."

Every time Sanch moved he could feel the sting on his shoulders. "I need to get some sunblock."

"I've got some you can use," Rob said. He grabbed it from his tent.

"Rub some on my back," Sanch said to Jake.

"Just wear your shirt."

"I don't like surfing with a shirt on. It irritates my nipples."

Jake laughed. "You don't hear me bitching about it, and I surfed longer than you."

"Well, my shoulders are burning."

"Then you've got to suffer."

73

"Don't be a dick. It's not gonna mean you're gay if you rub it on me," Sanch said.

Jake laughed. "Turn around," he said and smeared a white streak across Sanch's upper back.

After breakfast, they crossed the river mouth and the surf, no different than the day before, was mid-sized and slow rolling on the outside, but then fast on the inside. They learned their lesson with the money and didn't bring it with them.

It was later than when they entered the water yesterday, and the glassy surf didn't last as long. After the tide shifted, they made the long walk to Playa Grande.

The lineup was half as crowded because of the smaller waves.

After a few waves Jake paddled next to Sanch and said, "Maybe you should try my funboard. You don't surf bad if you just ride down the line. But when you try to hit the lip or do a cutback you lose all momentum, and it looks weak. The bigger board'll help your turns. Just try it."

"I'll try it tomorrow."

Sanch surfed for a little while longer but as the day progressed and the waves lost form he had a harder time dropping in while Jake still caught every wave he paddled for. On shore, Sanch crawled underneath the shade of a palm and watched Jake surf for another hour.

"Why'd you get out so early?" Jake asked.

"My back's burnt and now my balls are hurting, too."

"Burnballs? You didn't bring any spandex?" Jake asked. He pulled his shorts down a bit revealing black spandex underneath.

"I forgot that, too?"

Jake laughed because Sanch had to walk the rest of the way back to camp holding out the crotch of his shorts so the inseam wouldn't rub against his testicles.

There were only two people at the Frenchman's café, one behind the bar and one sitting at the bar with him. Sanch and Jake sat down at the table with the chessboard set up and the two guys looked at them.

"Who are they?" the guy at the bar said, an American. The one behind the bar didn't respond or if he did he said it in such a low voice that neither Sanch nor Jake heard anything.

"You want anything?" the man behind the bar asked them in a French accent.

"A couple burgers and beers," Jake said.

Another guy came up. They recognized him also as one of the guys from the day before. He had long, curly light brown hair and wore a tee shirt with sleeves ripped off. He was short for a grown man and walked with his shoulders pulled back and his chest puffed out in an arrogant strut.

"You guys surf today?" Jake asked the two guys, the one having gone in the kitchen to grill the burgers.

They didn't answer.

Jake had his back to them, so he turned in his chair to face them.

"Did you guys surf today?" Jake said louder.

The two guys laughed.

"Something funny?" Jake asked.

"Nah, man. Just wasn't any waves. Thought you were making a joke," the American said.

"Yeah, we like when it gets big," the short one added in a French accent.

"How about yesterday?" Jake asked.

"Yesterday wasn't big, either," the American said.

"Well, where we're from it was pretty big. I've surfed bigger but it was pretty good and today wasn't half bad. Shit, I got barreled both days, didn't I Sanch?"

Sanch nodded and moved a pawn.

"I didn't see any barrels," the American said.

The two guys laughed again. The first Frenchman came out with the burgers.

"What about the beer?" Sanch asked. The Frenchman pointed to the cooler next to the bar. "Just grab it?" Sanch asked.

"Yeah, you grab it," the American said. "Tourists expect to be served everywhere they go."

"I don't expect to be served anything," Sanch said. "But where we're from, it's polite not to help yourself when you're a guest unless you get the okay first. I guess I got the okay." Sanch grabbed the beers.

"Where is this place of polite people and where head-high surf is considered big?" the American said.

"LA," Sanch said.

"LA? That's where I'm from. What parts?"

"Pensacola," Jake said. He took a bite of his burger. Sanch took a long pull from his beer.

"Where the hell is Pensacola?"

The two Frenchmen lost interest and went back to watching the surf video.

"You know. Blue Angels. Roy Jones Junior," Sanch said. Jake continued eating.

"I've lived in LA my entire life, and I've never heard of Pensacola."

"He was making a joke. LA as in Lower Alabama," Jake said.

"You guys are from goddamn Alabama?"

"It's in Florida," Jake said.

"Don't you mean Flori-duh?" The American said and laughed to himself. "Are you guys here for a week and then back to your knee-high surf?"

Jake stopped chewing and said, "We ain't going home."

"That's what everyone says, but this kind of living isn't for everyone. People like it for a few weeks. Maybe a month. But then people get homesick. They miss fast food. They miss their family, their old way of life."

"Well, I ain't going back. And we may get knee-high waves most of the time, but I'll guarantee I can surf as good or better than anyone you know," Jake said.

"I know twelve-year-olds that will surf circles around you." The two Frenchmen regained a slight interest in the debate. "I'll tell you what," the American continued, "You surf Langosta yet?"

Jake shook his head. "Heard about it."

"Let's surf Langosta tomorrow. Four o'clock."

"Why not in the morning?"

The American closed his eyes and shook his head and took a deep breath before saying, "Because that's when the kooks are out. They surf all day and are too tired in the afternoon. And low tide's in the afternoon tomorrow. That's when Langosta gets good. Just be careful of the exposed rocks."

Sanch stopped chewing. Jake shook his head and said, "He's full of shit. It's all sand over this way."

"What was that?" the American said.

"I said you're full of shit. There ain't exposed rock over this way."

"Okay," the American said. "You'll see for yourself tomorrow."

Jake and Sanch ate their food, ignoring what they thought were snide comments being said too low for them to hear. They then continued playing chess. The loser bought the beers. Sanch won three in a row. During that time more people had shown up, most were the same from the day before. Sanch looked for the girl who had told him about the phones, but she didn't show. In the middle of the fourth game, Sanch had Jake on the defensive when a local with a shaved head arrived. He said hello to the crowd with high-fives and hugs then pulled up a chair to watch the chess match.

He shook Jake's hand and nodded to Sanch.

"This is Johnny. The guy I was telling you about yesterday," Jake said to Sanch. "The one with the hookup."

Johnny nodded. "Anything you need, come see me."

"We came here looking for you yesterday. They acted like they didn't know you. Who are those guys?" Jake pointed to the two Frenchmen and the American.

"The guy behind the bar owns the place, and everyone calls him Boss. His sidekick, the other Frenchman, he's Gerard. The gringo's name is Drew."

Johnny wore a white tank top undershirt and had a cross tattooed on the side of his neck. He had a scar above his left ear that showed through what little hair he had on his closely shaved scalp. He didn't look much older than Sanch.

"What were you looking for anyway? Cocaine, heroin, women?" Johnny asked.

"Just pot," Jake said.

"You don't want women? Forty dollars gets you three hours. Nice girls, too. Clean. Virgins are a bit more."

"Just pot for now," Jake said. "Maybe women later."

"I can play the winner?" he asked.

78

"You any good?" Jake asked.

"I'm okay."

"Let him play, Sanch," Jake said.

"I've won enough," Sanch said getting up.

"Finish," Johnny said.

"I'm all right. Play."

The game didn't last but two minutes. Johnny knew a four-move checkmate.

"Damn, he whooped your ass worse than I did," Sanch said.

He beat Sanch just as quick with the same strategy.

"I thought you were just okay," Jake said.

"I am. That was pretty basic stuff. Let's take a walk."

They left the café and headed up the street that led to the surf shops. They stopped at the top of the road, behind Lagarto Surf, in front of a house that was much nicer than others they have seen. A sign posted out front said "Police."

"How much you want?"

"In front of the police station?" Sanch said.

"Isn't there somewhere else we could go?" Jake asked.

Johnny shook his head. "No. I need to go this way after." He pointed further up the road. "Nobody's here. They are out of town. And if they were, they don't care."

"Pot's legal here?" Sanch asked.

Johnny shook his head. "No. It's not really the police. It is just the guy you go to who may be able to contact the police. We don't have police in Tamarindo."

The ten dollars worth they purchased was twice as much as they expected.

The rest of the day drifted by rather quickly. Jake surfed again. He didn't walk down to Grande but stayed right out front in Tamarindo's cove. About twenty people were learning to surf on thigh- to waist-high rollers. Jake weaved between the beginners and their boards that washed ashore after each wipeout. Sanch didn't want to expose his shoulders to the sun again and stayed on the beach taking puffs from a shell and watching dogs chase birds. A lady selling hemp necklaces asked if he wanted to buy any. He said no. Later, a man asked if Sanch wanted to buy seashells that he had collected. Sanch said he didn't. Sanch watched the surfing, and the world seemed right for a suspended moment.

They then played poker with Rob and Antonio at the campsite. They played with colones and Sanch was up the equivalent of twenty dollars as night fell. He had learned how to play poker from Jake, and this was the first time he had ever ended ahead in the same game with him. Sanch relished the moment by offering to buy Jake dinner.

"I never turn down a free meal."

Rob and Antonio went along for dinner, too. Rob had been eating nightly at a small stand called Pedro's so they went there.

"I thought this place was closed up," Sanch said. It had been boarded up earlier in the day.

"Nope. It opens at night. Closes when they run out of fish. Pedro goes fishing in the morning, and his wife cooks up whatever he catches," Rob said.

They sat down at a fold-up table that looked like it should be used at a garage sale instead of a restaurant.

A local girl wearing a tight floral sundress placed forks and knives on the table. She asked, "Full dinner?" It was about the only English she knew.

Rob and Antonio said yes.

"Menu?" Jake asked.

"No. No menu," she said.

"What do you mean, no menu?" Jake said.

"It's either full dinner or half dinner," Rob said. "Full dinner is with fish. Half dinner is just rice and beans."

"How much is the full dinner?" Jake asked.

"Get the full dinner," Rob told him.

"I ain't paying," Jake said.

"Dos más," Rob told her. "Cuatro cervezas."

Sanch and Jake watched her walk back to the stand.

"She's too young for you guys. I bet she's no older than fifteen," Rob said.

"She's a little thick," Jake said.

"You're an idiot. She's cute," Sanch said.

"You guys are going to mess around and fall in love with a local girl," Rob said.

"When she comes back, ask her how old she is," Jake said to Antonio.

Antonio shook his head no. "She's young," he said.

"Find out," Jake said.

"I want no part of this."

"Don't be a pussy. Just ask her how old."

When the girl came back out, Antonio asked her. She didn't reply, only giggled. A big lady, hair pulled tight in a bun, looked out the door and when she saw the girl hanging around too long, she marched over. The girl hurried back. The big lady came to the table and said something in a stern voice.

Antonio said something to the lady.

"What did she say?" Jake asked.

"I told her my friend here," pointing to Sanch, "liked the girl."

"And?" Jake asked.

"She's seventeen. Mom said to stay away. She isn't allowed to hang out with tourists."

The girl peeked out. Jake waved and she giggled and went back inside.

"That's the way to live," Jake said. "This Pedro dude has got it figured out, huh?"

"Simplicity," Antonio added.

"It's the competitive spirit of the American culture that makes us think we need a bunch of bullshit to be happy," Rob said. "People go to work every day to a job they hate to buy shit they don't need. If they didn't buy so much worthless bullshit, they wouldn't have to work so much. I did it my whole fucking life. Every day someone is trying to sell you shit. Trying to convince you that you need shit and that their shit is better than other people's shit. But it's all shit. I learned that late. But it's not too late for you guys."

"To Rob," Jake said, and they all took a long drink from their beers.

The lady brought out a whole Red Snapper with slits in the side, head and tail still attached and fried until the skin was crispy and the flesh flaky. Rice and beans and a tortilla were served on the side.

"We get some kick-ass seafood in Pensacola, but this is the best goddamn fish I've ever eaten in my life," Jake said.

They paid and went their separate ways. Rob went to an American bar called Expatriado. Antonio met Italian friends at a restaurant they owned. Sanch and Jake smoked from a shell and walked about, stopping at the beach by the estuary.

"What's up?" Jake said. "You seem a bit off since dinner."

"Nothing."

"You thinking about Natalie again?"

"I wasn't," Sanch said.

"Bullshit. Look at you all sad and shit."

"Was thinking about Buck."

"Yeah man. That's a bummer," Jake said. Jake and Buck were the same age but were never friends. Buck would tell Sanch that Jake was a bum, and it was strange of him to hang with someone that much older than him. Sanch liked hanging out with him for obvious reasons, booze and women, but also, it seemed as Jake had become more of a big brother to him than Buck had ever been. Sanch sometimes felt guilty about that.

"Doesn't even feel like he's dead sometimes. For a brief moment, I can even forget he is dead. I can convince myself that he's on duty or whatever. He'll just come back in a few months and start giving me shit about not doing anything with my life. But he won't. He'll never come back."

"It's pretty heavy."

"I think it fucked my parents up even worse though. They are completely different people now. My parents talk all kinds of bullshit like 'He's in a better place. We'll see him again one day. He's up there with Nana.' But I can tell they don't believe it. They still go to mass. But they are just going through the motions. Just doing it because they don't know what else to believe anymore."

"Do you still believe in God?" Jake said.

"I don't know. You?"

"I'm too afraid not to," Jake said.

"Only thing I know for certain anymore is that I'm getting drunk tonight."

When they stood, Jake put his arm around Sanch in an awkward attempt at comforting him.

They bought a six-pack at the German's and sat outside the store.

Jake held up the can for a toast. "To living the dream."

They both took a long pull from their beers.

"What about Brianna?" Sanch said. Brianna was Jake's three-year-old daughter.

"She would love it over here. Are you kidding? She'd surf all day, get home-schooled. It'd be great."

"Her mom would let her move over here?"

"Fuck her mom. You know that bitch is crazy. She would have to let her visit me, right?"

"I don't know how any of that works."

"It would probably be best for her to finish school in the States and move over when she's eighteen. Until then, we have to leave the country every three months anyway. I'd visit her then."

"I guess that could work."

"You act like you don't want to live here?"

"I do."

"We're living out every surfer's dream. What more do you want?"

"I don't know."

"German dude did it. French guys are doing it. American dude, what's his name? Drew. He's doing it. Rick the kiteboarder. What are you going to do? Wait until you are like Rob and about to die before you start living?"

Sanch shook his head no.

A young guy and two girls walked up.

"What's up?" the guy said. He had shaggy hair, blue eyes, and a thick neck. The girls both said hi.

"How's it going?" Jake said.

Sanch nodded as the three passed by, going into the store.

"Look," Sanch said. But Jake waved him off.

"I thought we were going to get drunk. I mean for fuck sake, look where we are at. Let's just enjoy it."

The young guy and two girls came back out with a six-pack. They introduced themselves. Oliver, April and Mary. Oliver and April were from Canada. Mary was from California. Oliver rented an apartment near Lagarto Surf for three months. Had two more months to go.

"An apartment?" Jake asked.

"The room isn't much. Kitchen and bedroom are in the same room. But there is an outdoor pool, and we can flush the toilet paper. There are five rooms like that in the complex, and two two-bedroom units."

"How do you have enough money to just move over here for three months?" Jake asked. "You don't look any older than nineteen."

"I'm twenty-three," Oliver said. "Was supposed to be for med school. I got my degree in Philosophy. All I had to do was get a degree and I got access to my trust fund."

"You staying three months, too?" Jake asked April, Oliver's girlfriend with the pixie cut.

"No. I'm leaving soon. Just came down for two weeks."

"What about you?" Jake asked Mary, the dark-haired girl.

"I have a room next door to Oliver."

"Wait," Jake said. "You are his girlfriend and are leaving, but you two will be living next door to each other? You're cool with that?"

"Whatever," April said. "I'm not going to waste my energy on being jealous. If he says he's faithful, why shouldn't I believe him?"

"Marry her," Jake said. "You can have a new flavor any day of the week, and you'd just have to say, baby, don't waste your energy."

"You're kind of an asshole, aren't you?" Mary said.

"I've been told that before," Jake said.

"Well, we are heading to Expatriado. I'm sure we will run into you guys again," Oliver said.

"Later," Jake said.

Sanch waved.

They finished their beers outside the German's store.

"What do you want to do now?" Jake said.

"Apparently Expatriado is the spot to be."

It was a dark walk to Expatriado, more like a nature hike than a stroll through town. Insects buzzed about and the bushes rustled with shadowed creatures.

Expatriado's stucco bungalows each had a window unit air conditioner. People lounged around the lit-up kidney-shaped pool listening to Jimmy Buffett tunes coming from outdoor speakers disguised as rocks.

Inside the bar, Rick the kitesurfer played the acoustic guitar and belted out a song about howling at the moon. Two women, both middle-aged, danced drunkenly. A big screen television showed NFL highlights.

An American flag covered the wall behind the bar where Rob leaned with his elbows on the bar rail molding and his legs crossed at the ankles. He nodded at Sanch.

Trophy-sized fish and pictures of the proud fisherman who had caught them decorated the rest of the interior. Jake set his sights on the pool table. Sanch moved towards Rob, who drank a Budweiser, seemingly the drink of choice for the men at the bar.

"Budweiser?" Sanch said.

"It's an import. High-class stuff."

Sanch ordered one. The stunning bartender opened a bottle and told him it was four dollars.

"How much is Imperial?"

"A dollar," she said.

"Why the hell'd I order this then?"

"Reminds you of home," she said.

"I'm still trying to forget it."

She laughed and grabbed beers from the cooler for two overweight, red-faced men with visor hats and fishing shirts.

"She's cute," Sanch said.

"Beverly," Rob told him. "She's lived here a while."

Before Sanch finished his beer, the two fishermen marched over to him.

"Rob, who's your buddy here?" The one with the red goatee asked, too loudly and with too much spit.

"Sanch from Pensacola," Rob said.

"No shit? Pensacola, Florida?"

Sanch nodded yes.

"Well goddamn. We are practically neighbors," Red said, grabbing Sanch in a headlock and giving him a noogie, his knuckles rubbing hard on Sanch's scalp.

"We're from goddamn Ocean Springs," Red said. He set Sanch free, and Sanch could see Beverly looking at him. She smiled and turned away.

"So you come for the fishing?" Red asked him, beer foam on his whiskers.

"Surfing. Fishing is good here, though?"

Red looked over his shoulders, making sure the wrong person wasn't listening and then leaned in to whisper, "That's what we tell the women." He motioned to the two women dancing.

"Right on," Sanch said.

Red leaned in closer, practically touching his lips to Sanch's ear. Sanch tried to back up, but Red had a good hold of him around the shoulders. "The fishing is great. Don't get me wrong. But the girls here sweeten the deal. You know what I mean?" He squeezed Sanch harder. "I gotta little sixteen-year-old for thirty bucks the other day. She wasn't a virgin, but damn, sweeter than pecan pie. You want me to set you up with her?"

"I'm good," Sanch said.

"Why is that? You a fag?"

Sanch squirmed away. "I'm not," he said.

"Suit yourself. When you get my age, you'll be singing a different tune," Red said.

"I'm going to play some pool," Sanch said and backed away.

"Playing partners," Jake told him and tossed him a stick. He then quietly told Sanch the plan, "I let him win the first one. Scratched on the eight. Now you're about to see a hustler at work." He winked.

A kid came back with an older man and said, "My dad wants to play."

"You're hustling a kid?" Sanch asked.

"Kid has to learn sometime, right?"

Jake purposefully lost the first game.

"Play for money?" Jake asked.

"Not trying to hustle us, are you?" the dad asked.

"That is exactly what I'm trying to do," Jake said. "Five a game?"

"Been known to win some money in my younger days."

"Really?" the son said.

"A lot you don't know about your old man."

"Where you guys from?" Jake asked.

"Indiana," the dad said lining up the cue ball for the break.

"Family vacation, huh?"

"We come here every year," the dad said and broke. No balls went in.

Sanch knocked in two. The son hit in two. Jake ran out the rest, like a movie montage.

"Get lucky sometimes," Jake said. "Double or nothing?"

"I, at least, want a chance," the dad said.

The next game, Jake ran all the balls out on the break. Jake gave Sanch money to buy some beer. The father cursed under his breath.

"Trying to embarrass me in front of my boy?"

"Just trying to win some money," Jake said.

Sanch brought back four beers.

"He's not old enough to drink," the dad said when Sanch handed the kid a beer.

"He's old enough to gamble, he's old enough to drink," Jake said.

The father glared at Jake. Jake smiled.

"Hurry up before your mom sees," the dad said.

The kid downed half in two quick swallows, let out a loud belch and then finished the rest.

"I don't think that was his first beer," Jake said.

Sanch and the kid laughed. The dad not so much.

"One more game. Double or nothing," Jake said.

"Dad. It's fine. I don't want to play anymore, anyway. It was just for fun."

"No. One more," the dad said.

They played one more. Jake was now up thirty dollars.

"You weren't lying," the dad said to Jake. "You really did hustle me."

"I don't lie," Jake said. "One more?"

"No," the dad said. "Let's go, son. Don't tell your mom."

"That was fucked up," Sanch said. "Embarrass that dude in front of his son like that."

"Fuck 'em. They both learned a valuable lesson thanks to me." Jake gave Sanch more money for drinks. He came back with two beers and two shots of tequila.

Sanch and Jake shot some balls around waiting for the next challenger. Jake, a left-hander, played right-handed. Sanch still lost.

Red and his brother slogged over while Sanch racked.

"You guys playing for money?" Red said.

"Only way I play," Jake told him.

"Twenty bucks a game too rich for you young'uns?"

"We got it covered. But you look like you've had a bit to drink," Jake said.

"Just getting started, buddy."

"How about I play you left-handed?"

"Grew up in pool halls, boy. Been shooting pool since before you could walk. Don't go around offering handicaps like that to me, motherfucker."

"I hear ya," Jake said.

Jake walked up to Sanch, leaned in and whispered, "I might've just fucked that one up. You've gotta break now."

Sanch did. No balls went in. Rob took a seat closer to the pool table to watch. Sanch made the ones he needed while Jake played defense. They were down to the eight ball and Red still had two balls left. Sanch missed.

"Goddamn it," Jake yelled across the table. "You gotta make those shots."

"You're the one that said we'll play for twenty bucks," Sanch said.

"I thought you could make an eight ball when it counts."

Red's brother hit in their two balls but missed the eight ball. The cue ball rested close to the rail leaving a straight shot for Jake.

"Care to raise the wager before I knock this sumbitch in?" Jake asked.

"That's not a hard shot," Red said.

"I'll do it left-handed then," Jake said.

"Still ain't hard."

"Left-handed and one-handed."

"Now you got yourself a bet."

"Another ten bucks?"

"Hell, I'll make it another twenty."

Jake made it. Not only was it left-handed and one-handed, but also he did it while looking at Red and not the ball.

Red's face got redder. Rob smiled and shook his head. "Now I know better than to play poker with you two," he said.

"Sumbitch," Red said and threw two twenty dollar bills on the table. "Gimme another twenty," Red said to his brother. "This asshole thinks he can hustle us."

"I don't think anything," Jake said.

"One more game and you play left-handed the whole goddamned time," Red told him.

"That doesn't seem too fair. Give me ten on your twenty."

"Fuck that," Red said. "You are a goddamn cheat."

"Okay. Left-handed," Jake said. "Tell ya what, though. I'm going to give you a chance to win your forty back."

"How's that?"

"For forty bucks. Not only will I play left-handed." He paused. Timing was part of the reason some people kept betting. "I'll beat your ass with a broomstick."

This was a classic Jake trick in Pensacola that locals knew to stay away from, but the tourists continued to fall for it over and over. Jake had learned about hustling from stories he had heard from his dad about a man named Amarillo Slim. One of the stories told was of Amarillo practicing ping-pong with an iron skillet for a month. When he got good at using it, he challenged the world ping-pong champ at that time to a wagered game. Amarillo had one condition; he wanted to choose the paddles. The champ accepted as long as the paddles were identical. Amarillo said they would be and would even allow the champ to choose which of the two paddles he wanted. Amarillo showed up the day of the game carrying two iron skillets. The champ couldn't back out because he never specified what the paddles had to be made of. The amount of the bet was never disclosed, but it was speculated to be around ten grand. Jake didn't win that much.

Chapter 8

Sanch awoke with Jake's saliva-covered finger in his ear. He lay on the porch swing, never having made it to the tent the night before.

"You didn't see or hear shit last night, huh?" Jake asked. Rob sat nearby. Antonio and Chico stood inches from each other in a heated argument. Sanch rubbed his eyes.

"I don't remember coming back here," Sanch said. "What's going on?"

"Antonio's board was stolen."

Sanch focused his eyes, cleared the fog from his brain and swallowed the bile that bubbled up his throat.

"When'd this happen?"

"Last night. I just said that. I was the last to get here, besides you, and Rob was still awake when I showed up."

"You remember seeing it when you came back?" Rob asked.

Jake laughed. "He doesn't remember shit. Look at him."

"I really don't," Sanch said. "I don't remember walking back here."

Jake pushed Sanch's leg around so he could sit next to him. Sanch sat up. They listened for a moment as Antonio and Chico continued back and forth in Spanish.

"Where'd you go last night?" Jake asked. "After we won the money from Red and took a couple more shots you said you were going to the bathroom and never came back."

93

"I remember that," Sanch said with a smirk. "I walked outside by the pool. I think you were talking to the bartender."

"Yeah, she was hot," Jake said. "She's lived here since she was nineteen. Ran away from home. Didn't say why. I tried asking her questions, but she wouldn't answer nothing."

"I wanted to go swimming in the ocean," Sanch said.

"Why didn't you come back to get me?"

"I was drunk."

"We were wasted, huh? I know I was," Jake said.

"This asshole fell asleep at the bar," Rob said, pointing to Jake. "Beverly asked if he was with me. I told her, no way in hell."

"Thanks, dick. Way to look out for each other," Jake said.

Rob shrugged. "I don't babysit."

"I looked all over for you," Jake said to Sanch.

"First he threw up in the bushes," Rob added.

"I damn sure did," Jake said.

"I ran into those Canadians we met at the store, the dude and two chicks. I remember that," Sanch said. "We walked together to the beach. They had a bottle of some liquor, some local stuff. Started with a G. I don't remember the name of it."

"Probably guaro," Rob said. "A Costa Rican liquor. Packs a punch."

"Was it good?" Jake asked.

"Hell if I know. I took a few swigs, but it could've been anything at that point." Sanch paused, trying to recall the night. "I think I went swimming."

Jake laughed.

94

"Now that I think about it, I'm pretty sure we got naked and went swimming. I kind of remember being naked at some point."

Jake and Rob laughed.

"But I'm not really sure."

Chico stormed off. Antonio came back to the tables.

"Can you believe this bullshit," Antonio said. "Everything I owned was in that bag. I've got nothing."

"Your money too?" Jake asked.

"No. But everything else."

"What did Chico say?" Rob asked.

"Said he will see if he can find anything out. I think he knows something."

"Well, that sucks. I'm going surfing though. You ready Sanch?"

Sanch looked up with red eyes.

Playa Grande was clean, but not so big, the smallest they had seen it yet. The crowd bunched in tight on two peaks.

Jake went to the main peak. Sanch hung out in the outskirts waiting for the rare wave, away from the majority of the people.

Sanch caught three half-assed hung over waves and told himself only two more and then he would paddle in to sleep on the beach.

On his next one, just before the sandbar, another surfer paddling back out threw his board away from him as the wave broke in front of him. There are no steadfast rules to surfing, but a few unspoken ones are, don't drop-in and always hold on to your board. Instead of keeping straight and duck-diving under the wave, letting the one riding the wave maneuver around you, the surfer in front of Sanch jumped off his board, launching it in Sanch's path. Sanch already turned to go around the inside of the guy and didn't have time to adjust. Sanch felt the bump as he sped across the abandoned board. He immediately jumped off his board.

"Are you okay?" Sanch shouted. "Did I hit you or just the board?"

The surfer held his board out of the water, looking it over, inspecting it for dings.

"Did I hit it?" Sanch asked. He knew he did.

The other guy said something in Spanish, threw his arms up in frustration and paddled in.

Sanch paddled back to the lineup instead of going in.

A large Tico, looking more like a bear than a human, paddled next to Sanch. "You should go in, too," he said.

"For what? He jumped off his board. There was nothing I could do."

"To make sure there are no hard feelings," he told him. "Pura Vida."

Sanch looked at the shore and saw the other guy looking out at the water, motioning for Sanch to come ashore. Sanch did.

A group of five guys passed the board back and forth, each inspecting the damage. They accosted Sanch as he exited the water, creating a semicircle around him.

"You ruined my board," he told Sanch.

"You jumped…" Sanch tried to defend himself but was cut off.

"Give him your board, kook," the tall one to his right said.

"I'm not doing that," Sanch said. He had a suspicion that this was not the first time this scenario had happened. It all seemed well orchestrated.

"You owe me a board."

Sanch looked around. The Bear Tico had followed Sanch in.

"I said give me your board, kook."

The tall one inched closer.

"Let me see your board," Sanch said. "Where did I hit it? I can get it fixed for you."

The Tico held his board up for Sanch to grab and Sanch set his on the ground.

Jake walked up and said, "What's going on?"

Sanch turned around. "Nothing. Minor misunderstanding."

"Then why are they walking away with your board?"

Sanch jogged after them. They stopped just at the edge of the lot.

"It wasn't a trade," Sanch said. "I can fix this one."

"You fix it then. It's your board now," the Tico said and continued walking. He strapped his board on the top of the other boards on the roof of a ragged out Ford Escort.

"You jumped off your board. There was nothing I could do."

"Deal's done, kook."

His buddies laughed. The tall one said, "Go back home, gringo."

"Deal is not done," The Bear Tico said from behind Sanch. "I saw you jump off your board. He said he will fix it for you. So give him his board back. Find out where he is staying and take him your board to get fixed. And then you go home. Because you don't live here either."

The other Tico hesitated a moment. He looked at his buddies, but they started getting into the car. He unstrapped the board and handed it to Sanch.

"You sticking up for the gringos now?" he said to the Bear Tico.

"I'm sticking up for what is right," Bear Tico said.

The young Tico strapped his dinged board to the car and sped off, kicking up dust on the way out.

Bear Tico explained to Sanch that those guys are what the locals called "weekend warriors." They lived in San Jose or one of the other cities and drove to the coast once or twice a month. They didn't live the Pura Vida lifestyle; they just liked to cause trouble. "We would rather surf with tourists any day than with those young punks."

Sanch thanked him. They shook hands.

Jake had a great time retelling the story back at camp. "Sanch was getting pushed around and was about to trade boards to keep from getting his ass kicked. I walked up just in time," Jake said to Rob.

"Not quite how it happened," Sanch said.

At the Frenchman's café, Drew the American and Gerard, the long-haired, peacock-strutting Frenchman watched TV.

"Boss isn't around," Gerard said, "but I can cook you some food if you would like."

"Don't forget about Langosta today at four," Drew said.

"I'll be there," Jake said. Then quietly he said to Sanch, "I forgot all about that."

Gerard served them shredded chicken wrapped in tortillas and french fries, and they watched a western movie while they ate.

"Sanch. Jake," Johnny said as he walked up, shook the other two guys' hands and then began setting up the chessboard. "Who's got first game?"

"I'll play," Jake said with a mouth full of fries.

"You were pretty drunk last night," Johnny said to Sanch. Then to Jake, "I found this guy sleeping naked on the beach."

"Was I really?"

Jake laughed.

"Said he was swimming with some girls. You believe that?" Johnny said.

"I was," Sanch said. "I told you," he said to Jake.

"Wait," Jake said. "So you may be able to piece some things together."

"Yeah. Like how'd I get home?" Sanch said.

"I walked with you. You wouldn't have made it."

"You walked me back to Chico's?"

Johnny nodded.

"Anybody else there?" Jake asked. "One of the people staying there got their surfboard stolen last night."

"I'll ask around," Johnny said.

He then beat Jake and Sanch two games apiece at chess. Before they left, Drew reminded them one more time about the meeting at Langosta. Jake asked how to get there.

"Around the bend on the south side of the cove. Just keep following the beach," Drew said.

"Shut up, Drew," Johnny said. Drew and Gerard laughed. "The walk on the beach is nearly impossible. They are fucking with you. Take the road by Lagarto Surf and keep walking. You'll see it. If a car drives by, hitch a ride."

"Really?" Jake asked.

"Yes. People pick up hitchhikers here."

After eating, they returned to the campsite to nap off the hangover that still lingered.

Beth from Texas saw them walking by on the way to Langosta. She stood outside with a guy.

"This is my husband, Vince," she said.

"Are you from Texas too?" Jake asked.

"El Paso."

"What beach is by there?"

"Beach?"

"Where'd you learn to surf?"

"When I moved here."

"And you give surf lessons?" Jake said.

"I do."

"Are you serious? Come surfing with us at Langosta," Jake said.

"I've been out all day," Vince told him.

"Right."

"You know how to get there though?"

"Was told to just keep on this road."

"When you get to the big construction site, where they are building a resort, you'll see where to go."

Jake turned to Sanch as they continued down the road and said, "If that goofy motherfucker can move over here and get a job teaching people how to surf, we've got this made. I'm gonna take his job. Maybe that hooked nose chick of his, too."

"That's his wife."

"She'd fuck me."

"Something is really wrong with you," Sanch said.

Jake laughed.

The road turned from packed clay to pebbles and rocks. Sanch and Jake walked barefoot, thinking they didn't want to leave anything on the beach while in the water. Now they wished they hadn't. They stepped on rocks more than once. When Sanch stepped on a rock and shouted a profanity, Jake stopped to laugh, only to have the same thing happen to him a couple minutes later. Sanch would laugh then, but only until he stepped on another. Eventually, they stopped laughing.

A truck rumbled down the road going in their direction.

"Stick out your thumb," Jake said.

Sanch did. The truck slowed. The driver waved them in to the bed while the truck still inched forward. He wore a cowboy hat and Willie Nelson sang through the tape deck about *Pancho and Lefty*. The driver shouted out the window, "Where to, amigos?"

"Langosta," Jake shouted back.

The man nodded and punched the gas. Sanch nearly fell out backward into the black cloud of smoke that billowed from the exhaust.

"If you fall out, make sure you hold the board up," Jake said. "Or you'll owe me five hundred bucks. I could easily get five hundred for that board."

The truck slowed when they neared the construction area. He pointed them in the direction even though you could see the ocean from the elevated road. They stepped from the truck, and the old man lifted a hand and drove off. Tractors and other earthmoving equipment rested in a fenced off parking lot next to the hollowed concrete shell of a soon-to-be mega resort. They crouched through a rolled back portion of the fence and trampled through the grassed lot, making sure to avoid bits of broken glass, to a well-worn trail that sloped down to the beach which was more shells than sand and down to the exposed black rock on the water's edge. About twenty more yards to the south was a river mouth larger than the river mouth on the way to Grande. Two bikini-clad girls dangled their black soled feet from a lookout tower built on the point overlooking the break.

One guy paddled out, hugging the jetty on the north side of the river and then paddled over to the break, his hair still dry. The waves rolled in much bigger than either Tamarindo or Playa Grande. One surfer rode the hollow wave, standing fully erect as the wave barreled over the top of him. He disappeared from view and a few seconds later emerged still standing, hands behind his back.

"You see that?" Jake said watching the guy kick out of the wave just before crashing into the jetty's jagged rocks.

"Let's do it," Jake said and entered the water, following the route the previous surfer took along the rocks. Sanch followed, a little less enthused.

Sanch picked a spot among the crowd that allowed him to be out of the way. Jake paddled directly between Drew and Gerard. Drew caught a smaller wave, not waiting for the larger sets to come in. As one of the large sets loomed on the horizon, Jake, Gerard, and another guy paddled for position of the first wave. Gerard caught it. It wasn't his to catch. The other guy had better position, closer to the peak. Jake had backed off, but not Gerard. He took the wave from the other surfer, laughing as he did so. The hefty wave barreled, but Gerard didn't get down the line quick enough to get inside it and rode it straight into the river mouth. A wasted wave. He shouted and pumped a fist in the air as if he had just scored the best wave of the day.

Jake caught the next one. It didn't barrel either but had a considerable crumbling face and from behind the wave, Sanch could see all the fins leave the water as Jake hit the lip and fanned a beautiful spray of seawater. Drew took notice and nodded his head in approval. He looked over at Sanch and said, "That asshole really is pretty good, isn't he?"

"Best I know," Sanch said.

That settled the debate. Jake proved himself in the water, and Drew and Gerard witnessed it.

Drew caught the next wave and as he paddled back out he stopped next to Sanch and said, "You're not going to catch anything here. You have to take off at the peak. Come with me."

Sanch did.

For fifteen minutes, wave after wave the surfers had an organized yet unspoken priority on who surfed the next wave. Sanch, Jake and Drew waited patiently watching as others took off. Gerard didn't. He paddled for everything but rode very few.

Sanch paddled for a wave. He paddled hard and should have caught it, but pulled back as he saw the steepness of the face. Jake paddled next to him and saved the wave from being unridden. Sanch resumed his position next to Drew.

"You've got to go for those," Drew said. "Only way you'll learn. Just go for it."

"I thought it would close out."

"They won't. Just go for it. Worst that will happen is that you bust your ass. We'll come save you." He winked and took the next wave.

Sanch paddled for a couple more, but couldn't drop-in. Jake, Drew, and only a couple others were the only ones actually catching everything they went for and surfing them well. The rest of the crowd sat out there and paddled around or went to the smaller inside break.

"This is way better than Grande," Jake said.

"The best I'd ever seen," Sanch said.

"You aren't still scared because of what happened at Grande, are you?"

"No. I'll catch one."

Jake paddled for another one. Gerard started in beside him. Jake hollered him off. But just as he had been doing all day with everyone else, Gerard dropped-in on Jake. Jake kicked out of the wave so as not to collide with him.

"I've had it with this fucker," Jake said.

Gerard rejoined the lineup.

"That was a good one, yeah?" he said to Jake.

"Get over here you little shit," Jake said to him.

"Hey bro," Gerard responded. "Pura Vida, man. We are just here to have fun."

"I've watched you drop-in on people all day," Jake said to him. "You did it to me the first time and I let it slide, but twice is too many. I'm about to take you up on shore and whoop your ass if you don't stop."

No one said anything for a few seconds, and then the people within earshot started clapping.

"You don't like it? Go home," Gerard responded. Then he shouted it to everyone in the water. "I live here. This is my wave."

"Your wave?" Jake said. "You don't belong here any more than we do. Why don't you go back to wherever the fuck you're from?"

"I was here first. I've lived here for seven years. Before any of you heard of Playa Langosta."

"You might've been surfing this wave longer than us, but I'm only gonna tell you one more time: Keep dropping in on us and I'm gonna fuck you up. You hear me? If you drop-in on anyone else, that's it. We will go to shore, and I'll beat the shit out of you. We clear?"

"Whatever, bro."

"It's not whatever, bro. If you're too big a pussy to leave the water and get your ass beat, I'll whoop your ass right here in the water in front of everyone."

People clapped again. A few shouted out at Gerard, threatening to join in and kick his ass, too.

"Whatever," Gerard said again, but on the next wave, he didn't bother paddling back out. When people saw him get out of the water, people cheered once more.

"If we watch closely enough," Sanch said to Drew, "we might literally be able to see Jake's head swell a few inches."

For the next hour, Sanch rode the small inside shore break having given up on the larger sets. The crowd thinned and the large full moon hung opposite the setting sun. The sky to the west shone different hues of red and purple and orange. Drew stopped to chat with Sanch before heading in.

"Now's your chance," he said. "Crowd is gone. Get back out there and go for it."

Only two other guys still surfed the shore break. Jake was alone on the outside in the twilight hours. Sanch joined him.

"I was just going in," Jake said. "It'll be dark in another minute." He caught one last wave, leaving Sanch out alone.

The waves continued coming in at sizable strength, crashing onto the inside sandbar with thundering power.

Sanch let a set pass. The last sliver of sun drifted below the horizon creating a magnificent green flash.

Sanch had no choice but to catch the next wave. He paddled, and the board lifted. The reflection of the moon glared off the curl of the wave. He had to go, either on his feet or in a head over heel wipeout reminiscent of the one he experienced at Playa Grande, maybe worse with the exposed rock being so close. He didn't stand but remained crouched with his right hand holding tight to the outer rail, fighting the urge to shut his eyes and give in to his fear, to take the wipeout and paddle to shore, a broken spirit. Before he could make a conscious decision, the roaring wave connected with the fast moving surface below him, placing him deep into a twilight translucent dream tube. Sanch slowly loosened his grip on the board. The cave opened wide, and he eased himself from the crouch and stood half erect. The fear lifted, and he experienced a stillness unknown to him as he sped through the oceanic vortex. But it ended as quickly as it started, fleeting and momentary, but at the same time infinite. He was now bonded to the ancient tradition of surfing that was first recorded by Joseph Banks who sailed under Captain Cook on the first European visits to the Polynesian Islands in 1769. The past and present collided. All one. As had always been. One. All there ever was and ever could be.

Sanch emerged from the barrel still standing. His back arched, face to the heavens. He pumped both fists twice, the only outlet for the excitement within. Two hundred and thirty years of tradition pumped through his veins in just a matter of seconds.

Jake stood watch with his board under his arm. He had a half-smile on his face.

"Whatcha think?" Jake asked.

Sanch smiled. He did his best to contain himself. He nodded, unable to speak.

"You did it."

Sanch nodded again, his smile growing.

"You still looked like the one-nut, wiggle-butt wonder, but you did it. You got a full stand up barrel."

Sanch nodded. "I damn sure did." He wanted to shout, to twirl, to run, to do something but smiled and nodded his head. "It was unreal."

"Didn't think you were gonna make it."

"Me neither," Sanch said.

"Could barely see you under the lip. Good job. Didn't think you had the balls to go for it."

Sanch smiled and turned back to the surf to look at the biggest waves he had ever seen in person.

Jake began walking and said, "Now you gotta learn to hit the lip like I do. Should only take you another ten years."

Sanch caught up with him. "I'll be surfing better than you soon."

"One barrel and you get cocky, huh? Until you get another one, you can just chalk that up to a Mother Nature pity fuck."

No cars came by on the walk back to camp. It was dark, and they stepped on rocks from time to time. None of that mattered. They didn't stop to yelp or complain. Jake talked for about ten minutes about being the one who finally shut down Gerard when Sanch broke in and said, "I just got barreled."

Jake stopped walking for a second and said, "All right. I'm gonna let you have this one. I remember the stoke of my first barrel, too. But you did see me shut him down. I did what nobody else had the balls to do."

And then their ego trip was brought to an abrupt halt as a loud, obnoxious, guttural scream like a lion roar echoed through the trees and bushes that surrounded the dark, barbarous road they walked. Without hesitation, Jake ran. Sanch held out his board like a bayonet. He yelled for Jake to stop.

"What the fuck was that?" he shouted.

"Come on," Jake shouted back, slowing down.

"Stop for a minute," Sanch said.

107

"For what? A panther to jump out?"

Sanch stood planted, holding his board out for protection. "I'm serious. What was that?" Sanch said.

"I don't know, and I don't wanna wait to find out either."

The trees rustled above and in the bushes, on both sides of the road. The roar came again. Two. Then two more. From both directions and from above. Sanch turned toward Jake. Jake laughed but just as quickly turned to run. For a good minute, they laughed at each other's fear and yelled profanities because of their own fear and laughed some more before slowing to a jog and then slowing to a walk. Nothing followed them and the bushes no longer rustled.

Realizing they had won, the six howler monkeys went back to their young, leaving Sanch and Jake unsure of what lurked in the trees.

Chapter 9

Sanch stepped from his tent. Jake's tent was already folded and his backpack leaned against a tree. The boards were inside the case next to the pack. Rob and Antonio had their tents down as well. Rob and Jake shared a smoke from a shell.

"What's going on?" Sanch asked. Rob handed him a shell and went to the kitchen.

"We're getting outta here. I don't trust Chico," Jake said.

"What happened?"

"You didn't hear anything last night?"

Sanch shook his head, took a puff from the shell and gave it to Jake. Rob came out and handed Sanch a mug of steaming coffee.

"You didn't hear Antonio and Chico going at it?" Jake asked.

"No. I just said I didn't hear anything."

"Me and Rob came out at the same time. They were yelling at each other. Antonio accused him of stealing from him." Jake smoked and passed the shell to Rob.

"They fight?"

"Just about," Jake said. Rob nodded in agreement.

"No shit?"

"No shit. Johnny showed up and said he knew where Antonio's stuff was and that for a hundred and fifty bucks could get it for him. Antonio tried to talk him down in price, and Johnny told him he was already doing him a favor just by telling him how to get it back."

"He paid him?"

"Had to."

"That sucks."

"That ain't all. Antonio said he wasn't gonna pay for the nights he stayed and was gonna leave in the morning. Me and Rob sat out here smoking, watching the whole thing. Antonio went to his tent. About three minutes later, Johnny came with some other guy. They went to Antonio's tent and told him it was better he left now. Wasn't allowed to use the tent anymore."

"No shit?"

"Yeah. He left. Just like that."

"He paid?"

"Of course. So this morning, me and Rob said we're getting the hell out too. So you owe me like ten bucks. I went ahead and paid Chico. But we gotta go before they try that shit with us."

Sanch and Jake stood in the middle of the town circle with backpacks on and boards in hand.

"Where was that guy from the bus staying at?" Jake said. "Whatever the hell that kitesurfer's name is?"

"Rick. Somewhere down there." Sanch pointed down the road. "Said it was cheap, didn't he?"

They walked and after a few minutes spotted him bellied up to a bar in one of the restaurants overlooking Tamarindo Bay.

"That's him there, isn't it?" Jake said.

"Damn sure is," Sanch said.

Being such a small town, running into someone you knew or were looking for wasn't too coincidental.

The menu out front said lobster and steak dinners for twelve dollars American.

"Hey guys," Rick shouted when he saw them. "I was wondering how things were going with you two." He was red-faced and happy. Ten in the morning and already drunk. "These are my buddies," he said to the waitress at the bar. He stood up, hugging them both at the same time.

The waitress placed a plate of eggs and rice and beans next to his half-full Bloody Mary.

"Who's this for?" he asked her.

"That's for you Mr. Rick. I was told you needed to eat something."

"I will eat something," he said and took a bite of his celery.

"Either of you want this?" He pushed the plate of food towards Sanch and Jake.

"I'm good," Jake said.

"I'll eat it," Sanch said and pulled up a chair, splashed hot sauce over the eggs and beans and filled a fork full of both.

"This fucker will eat anything if it's free," Jake said.

Sanch gave him the finger and continued eating. He started to like the soap taste of the cilantro.

"What's that hotel you were staying at?" Jake asked.

"Abrigo? Fuck that fleabag, shithole," Rick said. "I got a new place at only twenty-two dollars a night. Warm showers. Air-conditioning. Satellite TV."

"How much was the Abrigo?"

"Seven dollars or some bullshit like that."

"Where is it?"

Rick pointed up the road. "Just keep walking. You'll see it." He drained his drink. He motioned to the waitress for another. "You guys want one?"

"No. We gotta find a place quick," Jake said.

Sanch scooped in one last mouthful and then followed behind Jake.

"You two be good," Rick said. "I like you guys."

A mile from the town circle, which felt like a much longer walk with the packs and boards, they arrived at the Hotel Abrigo. Slime green painted ramshackled cabanas with aluminum roofs, doors no thicker than cardboard, slits cut through the wall above the doors to circulate a little air and no windows. A slab of covered concrete in the center of the courtyard served as the community kitchen consisting of a faucet, a sink, and a rusted two-burner camping stove. An aged lady sat on a cot in the office watching a TV that cut in and out between white noise static and a Bob Marley concert. She gummed a strange looking fruit shaped like a star and hummed along to the songs. She held up half of an index finger, a small sharp claw stuck from the nub, to indicate, "Wait a minute." A few seconds later a skinny, middle-aged, dark brown man glistening with sweat led them to the rooms. He didn't speak English. He grinned and laughed a lot, his only way of communicating with foreigners. He waved over a barefoot girl wearing an unwashed dress. Her face riddled with acne. She translated what the brown man said in an English accent. Her name was Taylah.

"Only two rooms," she said. "For five dollars you can stay in the ones without bathrooms."

"Where do we go then?" Jake said.

She pointed to the community toilets.

"Can we see them?" Jake asked.

Spiders hung in the corners of the showers, and a shit-colored circle lined the toilets. Again toilet paper wasn't to be flushed. The smell was fecally offensive.

They took the room with a private bathroom. Toilet and shower. No door separated it from the beds, but for seven dollars a night each, Sanch and Jake didn't need privacy between them.

"It's a bit out of our budget," Jake said to Sanch, "but technically we are still using money we won shooting pool the other night. Let's just get this for now and we'll look around."

The middle-aged man opened the door for them. He and Jake took in the backpacks and boards. Sanch followed Taylah to pay the lady in the office.

"You work here?" Sanch asked Taylah.

"You could say that."

"From England?"

"God no. Australia."

"No shit? What're doing over here?"

She stopped walking and looked at him like he was the strangest looking person she had ever seen.

"Probably the same as you. Visiting Costa Rica. What kind of question is that?"

"Just making small talk. Australia is pretty far away from here, no?"

"That's the point." She continued walking.

"How long have you lived here?"

"A long time."

Taylah said in exchange for room and board she helped the lady in the office by taking money to the bank, going grocery shopping, cooking, and helping take care of the old lady's grandkids, aged two and five. She played with them, read to them, and when they get older she would home school them. The kids' mother visited on the weekends from San Jose. Nobody spoke about what the mother did for work in San Jose. Nobody spoke about what a lot of women did for work in San Jose.

Jake lay on the bed he had chosen as his.

"Cool," Sanch said. "I'm sure they are both equally uncomfortable."

"Bullshit. Mine is way more comfortable."

They unpacked their bags, putting their clothes in the lone dresser. Jake took all the boards out, stacking them one after the other against the back wall.

They smoked from a shell and went for a surf.

Staying at the Hotel Abrigo made for a quick walk to the river mouth through an abandoned lot of rundown cabanas, down a well-worn path through trees.

They surfed the river mouth alone for a good hour before a group of five guys paddled out. They had some girls with them who stayed on the beach. One of the guys was Oliver.

"We were going down to Grande, but saw you guys surfing some pretty good waves," Oliver said. He then turned to Sanch, "How'd you feel the other night after Expatriado?"

"Horrible," Sanch said.

"You were pretty drunk," Oliver said. "I take it you made it home okay."

"You could say that," Sanch said.

Jake told the Canadians about what happened at Langosta with Gerard.

"We heard," Oliver said. "Everybody has heard. He's notorious for dropping in on people."

"Well, he won't do that anymore as long as I'm in the water," Jake said.

The sun stayed out as a light drizzle fell, and the waves cleaned up even more. The waves were smooth, rippleless peaks of perfection in the soft sun shower. The rain pitter-pattered on the ocean surface, and the sun rays that beamed down between the clouds created a double rainbow in the distance over Playa Grande.

"Meet us tonight on the beach for some beers and bonfire," Oliver said as they finished up and exited the water. Jake and Sanch surfed a little longer.

The bonfire blazed bright as did the cone-shaped joints. Oliver stood with his girlfriend, April, and his dark-haired neighbor, Mary. April was leaving in the morning and told everyone this was her going away party. It would have happened if she was leaving or coming or if she had never existed at all. Jake retold the story of Gerard and Langosta once again. Mary pulled a joint from a cigarette pack and offered to share it with Sanch.

"You're Canadian, right?" Sanch asked.

"California. But pretty much everyone here tonight is Canadian."

"How long have you been here?"

"Five months."

"Have we had this conversation already?" The cannabis exacerbated Sanch's drunkenness, and his speech slurred.

"Probably, but it's cool."

"How've you been able to live here for five months? Is it easy to find work here? I don't want to go home."

"I'm blowing my inheritance," she said. "My grandparents died last year. But I work here, too. I waitress."

"But you don't get tips here, do you?"

"No. And I make a whole dollar an hour," she said. "It gives me something to do. After a while, you have to find things to do, you know."

Sanch swayed as she spoke.

"Are you okay?" she said.

"A little drunk," Sanch said.

The crowd had grown by about a dozen or more. The bonfire flamed five feet or higher and spewed fire-fly ash that twirled and painted the night sky, a spectacle that could be seen from a distance and attracted other revelers to join. Two of the revelers joined Sanch and Mary. Mary passed them the joint as they made their introductions. Both were from Massachusetts, just graduated college and were spending a semester traveling before starting graduate school. Both were literature majors. One, a beautiful Asian American with two strands of braids tied back around her head like a headband. The other was a pretty strawberry blonde with faint freckles across her upturned nose. Sherry and Cindy.

"What are you studying in grad school?" Mary asked.

Sherry said fourteenth- and fifteenth-century writing like the *Divine Comedy*, *Sir Gawain and the Green Knight*, and Chaucer's *Troilus and Criseyde* and *The Canterbury Tales*. Cindy said the Romantics: William Blake, Mary Wollstonecraft, William Wordsworth and Samuel Coleridge.

"I've never heard of any of that," Sanch said.

They found that funny. "None of it?" Cindy, the blonde, asked.

"Nope."

"What's your favorite book then?" Cindy asked.

"Fuck if I know."

"Well, what's the last book you read?" she asked.

"Does a surfing magazine count?"

"Wow, an intellectual," she said.

"I'm joking. Give me a second." He tried to remember the name of the book Rob was reading.

"It's okay," she said. "But you should probably start reading. It's good for you."

116

"Maybe, I'll do that," Sanch said.

Mary left and blended back into the crowd.

"Women like smart guys."

"So I would have to have a college education to have a chance with you?" Sanch asked. He did his best to keep his eyes affixed to her green eyes, but he kept feeling them shift down to her cleavage.

Cindy pulled her dress a bit to cover them better.

"It's not necessary, but it would be a good start."

"Be nice," Sherry said.

"It's just we wouldn't have much to talk about, you know. I'm afraid you would bore me."

"That's a bit rude," Sanch said.

"I think you're a bit drunk. We are going to walk over by the fire. Sorry."

"Fuck you," Sanch said under his breath. He knew he shouldn't have said it, but her attitude reminded him of Natalie, and he felt his face flush with anger.

"Excuse you?"

"You heard that?" Sanch said, forcing a smile out of embarrassment. "It wasn't directed at you."

"That is definitely not a way to talk to a lady. I'm not sure a college education could even help you."

"Is she always this mean?" Sanch asked Sherry.

"I'm not mean. Maybe you just feel threatened?"

"I wasn't talking to you. But what would I be threatened of?"

"A smart, beautiful woman."

"You are hot. I'll give you that. And maybe smart, too. But shit…"

"It's a bit sad, really."

"Goddamn. Sherry, you want to go for a walk? Leave this bitch on her own for bit?"

Sherry laughed, "No thank you. And that's a little offensive. Don't talk about my friend that way."

"You're the one acting like a little bitch," Cindy said to Sanch. "Look, take this as a learning moment. Where is your passion? Your drive? What do you want from life?"

Sanch shrugged.

"Aren't you excited about life? What the future holds?"

"Not really."

"See. You're just drifting through life with no goals, nothing. That's not me."

The more Sanch stood there without saying anything, the more enraged she became.

"What do you love? What is it that you like most out of life? If you had to do the same thing every day, what would it be?"

He looked around. "This?"

"What?"

"Surfing. Drinking. Getting high. Shooting pool, sometimes. Hanging out."

"That's pretty pathetic," Cindy said. "I kind of feel sorry for you."

"I like fucking, too." Sanch didn't like talking to her like that, but he felt attacked.

"You're a Neanderthal. And a misogynist."

"I'm pretty sure Neanderthals don't exist anymore, but I'm not quite sure what the other word means. So I'm going with no. I'm neither."

"You sound like you're proud of your ignorance."

"Look. I'm just trying to have a good time. Sorry for calling you a bitch. I mean, what else is there besides having a good time? Before you know it we'll be dead, and life was wasted doing shit we were supposed to do instead of what we wanted to do, you know? It'n that why we're all here right now? It'n it why we all came to Costa Rica? Because we were looking for something more?"

"Are you saying, 'It'n it?' You mean to say *isn't it,* right? *Isn't* that why we're all here?"

"You're fucking with me, aren't you?"

"It's just hard to take you serious with that country accent."

"What is your problem?" Sanch said. He never knew he had a country accent. "I'm just trying to have a conversation with you."

"By staring at my tits?" she shouted.

"Sorry. I didn't realize I was doing that again."

"Sanch," Mary said walking back towards him. "Come over here for a second."

"Hold on. I'm trying to find out what this bitch's problem is."

Mary put her arms up in frustration and turned back around.

"Such strong words from such a weak man," Cindy said.

Jake made his way over now and put his arm around Sanch.

Sanch flung Jake's arm off of him.

"Are you his brother?" she said.

"Basically," Jake said.

"You guys proud about being rednecks."

"Nothing we can do about it. That's where we're from," Jake said.

"Where?"

"LA," Sanch said. Jake laughed.

"We're from Pensacola," Jake told her. "Florida."

"Why did he say LA?"

"He still thinks that's funny," Jake said. "Don't listen to him. He's drunk and just being stupid."

"I ain't drunk. She's just a bitch," Sanch said.

"You're drunk," Jake said.

"I'm a little drunk," Sanch said.

Jake laughed and then said to the girls, "Why don't we let him chill a bit? You girls come by the fire?"

"Thanks, but I think we'll be going now. I think I'm actually losing IQ points the more I hear this guy speak," she said.

"Don't leave," Sanch said. "I apologize. I'll go for a walk. You two stay here." He stuck out his hand for a handshake. "I was out of line."

She shook his hand and said, "It's good you are getting out of your little southern bubble. You might learn something."

Sanch let go of her hand. She turned away.

And he should've too. But he said, "Least there ain't no pretentious cunts like you there." She turned around and Sanch smirked when he saw the disgusted look on her face. "What's the matter? Didn't think I knew such big words?"

"You're a pig."

Jake jumped in the middle and turned Cindy away. Sanch overheard him say one more time that he was drunk.

"Fuck her," Sanch yelled. The girls were walking towards the bonfire, and Jake turned back to him.

"What's your problem? I'm trying to get laid here. And you're trying to argue with some females?"

"You wanna fuck her?"

"At this point, I might fuck you." Jake laughed. Sanch didn't find that funny. "Just have a seat and chill for a bit." Jake went running after the girls, squeezed between them and led them into the darkness away from the fire.

Sanch walked back to the crowd by the bonfire and squatted next to Mary, who sat cross-legged in the sand finishing another joint. She handed Sanch the roach. He took a few tokes before sucking in the ash and coughing for a few minutes. People stood around watching him, and Mary handed him a beer. He took a swig.

"You okay?" Mary asked.

"I just don't like people who think they're so damn smart cause they been to college or read a few books. How smart are you if you make fun of people's accents? Fuck them."

"I think that's Jake's plan," Mary said.

Sanch smiled.

Oliver walked by Sanch and rubbed his head. "It'll be okay, dude," he said and continued on.

One of the other Canadians walked up to him and said, "Florida, eh?"

Sanch didn't say anything for a moment. He was caught unprepared for the "eh." He thought that was just a stereotype. He struggled to his feet.

"Yeah, Pensacola," he said, holding back from commenting on the "eh."

"I didn't think Florida gets many waves, let alone Pensacola."

"You know where Pensacola is?"

"Why wouldn't I?"

"I don't know. But yeah, we get waves. Not too big but during a hurricane it gets pretty good. You guys get waves in Canada? That's something I wouldn't think either."

"BC gets waves as good as California."

"What's BC?"

"You don't know where BC is? I know where Pensacola is and that's some tiny podunk town. BC's an entire province. That would be like me saying I've never heard of Florida. "

"Never heard of it."

"You've never heard of British Columbia?"

"I don't know anything about Canada."

"What are they teaching you in school?"

"Not about Canada, I guess. Not like I really went to school much anyway."

"You ever been to a library? They have these books there called an atlas."

"Yeah, I've been to a goddamn library before." Sanch had not been to a library since he was in the 7th grade.

Oliver shouted over to them, "You guys cool it over there. Just leave him alone. He's drunk."

"No," his buddy said. "Kid has to learn some things. I know the names of all fifty states and their capitals and this guy has never even heard of BC."

Sanch didn't know what to say. He couldn't name all fifty states, let alone the capitals, too.

"Say something. Call me a cunt," the Canadian said to Sanch.

"You can name all fifty states? And their capitals?"

"Seriously? Can you guys quit already?" Mary said. She stood, and others had crowded around now.

"I knew you didn't have the balls to call me a cunt. But you'll disrespect a female, huh?"

"I called her a cunt because I couldn't kick the shit outta her," Sanch said. "I don't need to call you a cunt."

"Pretty American of you. Can't think of a response so you go straight to ass-kicking. Kick my ass then."

Mary stepped in, seeing as no one else would. "Come on. We are in Costa Rica. There's no fighting here. Pura Vida, remember that? Pura Vida."

Sanch looked at her. She may have been the most sincere person he had ever met.

"She's right," Sanch said. He stuck his hand out for a shake. "Pura Vida." After they shook hands, Sanch said, "Let's just have a good time and try to forget you're a cunt."

"I thought you guys were finished," Mary said.

"Sorry," Sanch said. "Bad joke."

"This assclown won't shut up. Always has to get the last word," the Canadian said.

Sanch put his hands up, a beer still in his left hand. "I'm done. Mary, you're right," he said. "This is stupid. Pura Vida. I'm just going to go back to the room and go to sleep." He gave her a hug. "I'm sure I'll see ya around."

"You want me to go with you?" she whispered.

"Nah, I'm good."

"I'll see you tomorrow." She kissed him on the cheek.

"You guys have a good night," Sanch said to the others. "Didn't mean to cause a scene at your going away party."

He turned to go.

The Canadian said, "That's right. Walk it off, champ."

Sanch stopped for a second, took a deep breath, started walking again and then stopped. He pursed his lips and then threw his beer to the ground. He turned around and saw the Canadian staring him down. Sanch rushed him. He played one season of freshman football, but he remembered the tackling technique he learned, and he put a shoulder into the Canadian's gut, bringing him to the sand inches from the orange glow of the fire. His coach would've been proud. Sanch jumped to his knees, straddling near the Canadian's chest, pinning one arm under his knee and with his left hand pinned the other hand to the ground. With his

free hand, Sanch could have pummeled him, but he held his
fist above and never brought it down. He held it there long
enough for the others to rush over and throw Sanch to the
sand. They were not as forgiving, and a few landed some
pretty solid punches. Oliver pulled the others off of Sanch
and helped him to his feet. There Sanch stood and looked at
the crowd. He could taste the metallic tinge of blood as he
rolled his tongue across his bottom lip. He walked off
alone.

The German's store was closed. Sanch went to the first
bar he found. A few patrons watched a subtitled American
movie. Sanch had seen it, but couldn't remember the name.
The locals loved it, laughing about every couple minutes as
if someone were recording a laugh track. He sat down and
ordered a beer and a shot of tequila. He downed the shot
and ordered another, then drank that one just as quick. The
other drinkers watched him. He paid, taking the beer with
him.

The rain started again. A solid downpour and lightning
flashed across the sky. Everyone had run for cover and
Sanch sloshed through the forming puddles on the deserted
road. His hair dripped in his eyes, and he threw his hands
above him in despair, the beer can raised high as if he
extended an offering to the gods. He poured the beer from
the elevated position into his mouth, but most of it fell
down his shirt. He took the wet shirt off and slung it across
his shoulder, kicked off his flip-flops and walked. A drunk
savage. This was not a vacation. It never was. To go on
vacation, you must have a home to return to. As much as he
called Pensacola home, he had no home. His family saw
him as a disgrace for turning his back on tradition, and
according to his dad, also family and God. Killing terrorists
wouldn't bring Buck back. Nothing would. Buck was gone.

Nothing he could do and no one he could pray to would bring him back. There was no reversing what had happened. He couldn't face his father anymore. Not because he was afraid to join the Navy, but because he was afraid he wouldn't have the courage not to join the Navy. He was more afraid of not being able to say no, of being forced to live a life he didn't want to live. He thought in Natalie he had found someone that would take on this destinationless adventure with him. He thought she was as lost as he was. But she abandoned him, too. He thought there was something wrong with her, and that was why she couldn't be with him. But he was the problem. People liked having a destination, a cause to believe in or some sort of organized plan. Chaos and uncertainty was not the way people wanted to see the world, even if that was the way the world was. But he didn't believe in certainty. In fact, he wasn't even certain about that. He believed in nothing and everything. He believed nothing and everything were the same thing. He believed no one knew what to believe, and even those who were in control, those who were supposed to know—the presidents of countries, teachers, parents, police officers, scientists, priests—none of them had a clue what they were doing or how to do it. It was all just a charade of people walking through a dream pretending they knew where they were going.

He walked past the Abrigo and continued walking. He stopped outside of the Best Western and watched the neon lights pulsing "No Vacancy."

The rain slowed, and he stood like an effigy in the muddy road, swaying, staring at a corporate run hotel in a town that was largely unpopulated until the nineteen seventies when Robert Vesco bought one thousand acres near Playa Grande. Prior to Vesco investing in the area, the coastlines were considered useless, and only a few farmers moved out that way to raise cattle. In the eighties, with war going on in Nicaragua and twenty percent of the cocaine entering the United States from Costa Rica, Tamarindo attracted two types of people: ones wanted for crimes and the ones unwanted anywhere else. He knew none of the history of the area, but yet there he stood, one of the two types that had decided to settle the area and turn it into a tourist mecca.

"You going in?" a voice asked from behind.

He turned and belched, then drank from the can that was now a mixture of beer and rain water.

"You look fucked up." Drew said something else but to Sanch, it all jumbled together.

Sanch left. He headed back to the Abrigo. Seeing the boarded-up farmer's market stand he said, "Just wait till they build a Walmart."

He eyed a phone booth next to the stand and then spent twenty minutes trying to get an English-speaking operator on the other end. When he finally got one, he dialed Natalie's dad's house collect. Her stepmother answered.

"Is she around?" he said.

"Sanch? Is that you? Are you okay?"

"Yeah, I'm fucking wonderful." He tried taking another drink, but the can was empty.

"Are you still in Costa Rica?"

"Yes."

"Are you sure everything is okay? You don't sound okay."

"I'm having a...Is Natalie around?"

"You know she doesn't live here anymore."

"Yeah, I know that. Is she around though?"

"Are you drunk?"

126

"Yes. Very. Can I have her new number?"

"Look, I know it's hard. You loved her. And when a relationship ends it's always harder for one than it is for the other."

"I loved her," he said. "We were going to get married. She said that. I never brought that up. She did. She's the one who said all that bullshit."

"Try to get some sleep."

"Just give me her number. Please."

"I can't do that."

"Give me her goddamn number." He swallowed the vomit that rose up into his mouth. The world spun. He couldn't hold the vomit down any longer, not all of it. He spit some out on the phone.

"Hello. Hello." He shouted a few more hellos and then yanked the phone cord from its base and commenced to pound the receiver into the phone box until some of it splintered into his hand. He stopped when he noticed blood dripping from the fatty part of his closed fist. He wrapped his hand in his wet shirt.

At the Abrigo, Rob and his traveling buddy were sitting on the bench outside their room. They had gotten the room next to Sanch and Jake. Rob said something as Sanch stumbled towards them. Sanch stood, swaying, trying to remember where he was, who he was. Rob passed him a joint.

"The sky cleared," Rob said. He and his buddy had both their eyes towards the cosmos. A meteor made a bright line among the millions of stars and faded into the ether.

Sanch took a hit of the joint and blew out a veil of the medicinal smoke. He took another hit and tried to say thanks, but he felt the rush of bile coming up his gullet and swallowed it back. He hurried behind the community kitchen as he put his hand to his mouth to catch the vomit but instead it spewed in different directions between his fingers. He dropped to his knees and heaved again into the weeds. A steady stream of liquid continued before transitioning to dry heaves, his stomach still trying to evacuate the poison. Sanch wiped his mouth with the back of his good hand and then rubbed his hand in the grass. He slowly and cautiously and what he thought was steadily, walked back to the room; Rob watched him struggle with every step.

Sanch patted his shorts. "I don't have the key."

"Mercury in retrograde," Rob said.

"What?"

"The liminal stage, my friend."

"What?" Sanch asked again.

"Trickster, brother."

"I have no idea what you're talking about," Sanch managed.

"Yeah ya do," Rob's friend said. "Even if you don't, you do. You are there, man. We are all there, man. And this may not be our first time here. Might not be our last, either." And he laughed. And Rob laughed. And to Sanch it sounded like the same laugh as the dark void in his dreams. And all the laughs merged into one laugh and swam in his clouded brain. It was his brother's laugh. His father's laugh. His grandfather's laugh but Sanch did not laugh. Instead, his thoughts sunk in a horrid sludge.

"You can sleep in my bed," Rob said. "I won't be using it tonight. Don't think I'll be sleeping for a while."

"I'm fine," Sanch slurred and slumped up against the door and closed his eyes, the world whisked away in a helix of foul warmth that bubbled just below his Adam's apple.

For a brief moment, he thought he would die, but even that faded, and he disappeared into nothingness.

Jake kicked him awake.

"You all right?" he asked. Rob and his friend still sat on the bench out front like simulacra of ancient priests.

"He's been like that for nearly two hours," Rob said with a chuckle. "Kid was in a bad way tonight. I don't wish to go where he went." His buddy chuckled alongside him.

Sanch opened his eyes and belched, the warm rancor burning his throat and nose. "Where you been?" Sanch said, the words barely audible.

Jake laughed at his drunken friend. "I had a blast. That bar down on the end, the Mambo Bar, opened up. The owner just came back in town from a surf trip to California. Played the hell out of foosball. You ought've seen how much cocaine people were doing. Then went down to the Best Western. Heard you were around there and were all fucked up. Drew said you couldn't even speak. You oughta see it. Everyone wants to be my friend now. Drew was cool with me, the French guys were there, and they were cool. I'm about to own this place. People know my name, and if they don't they just say, 'you're that dude that shut up Gerard.' It's awesome."

"Didja fuck that girl?"

Rob handed Jake two bottles of water. Jake handed one to Sanch. Sanch downed half; some dribbled down his chin and onto his chest. He used that water to wipe away some of the caked on vomit that was entangled in his chest hair.

"Hell no, I didn't fuck her. Guess what she said to me."

Sanch looked at Jake, trying to find something to focus on and said, "Are you going to open the door?"

"She said, 'I didn't come here to fuck American boys.' Can you believe that?"

Sanch scooted out of the way, and Jake opened the door.

"Did you see what some idiot did to the pay phone down the road? Beat it all to hell."

"Fucking idiot," Sanch said.

Jake took a piss, climbed in bed and propped himself up against the wall.

"What happened to you tonight?" Jake said.

"Got into a fight," Sanch mumbled. He hid his head under the pillow.

Jake laughed. "You got fucked up, is what happened."

"Hmm, hmm," Sanch said and then drifted into drunken oblivion.

"I tried calling home again," Jake said. "Down at the pay phones in town. Nothing. Then saw this one and it was all banged up."

Jake looked over at Sanch.

"I'm going home in the morning. I'm catching the first bus out," Jake said. "I'm going to be a better father. My daughter needs me. I don't want to be the kind of dad my dad was," Jake said.

Jake's dad, who everyone called "Fat Boy," was partners in a hunting club. When Jake was young, up until he was 16 and able to drive himself, nearly every weekend was spent out there drinking and smoking and shooting guns. Fat Boy's brother, Jake's Uncle Dayday, was also a partner with eight other guys and their wives and kids.

The more the men drank, the looser they got with the tongue and sometimes those words turned into fights. Once the fight was over, whether from an ass beating or from exhaustion, everyone was friends again.

"Light that joint up," someone would shout. Getting stoned together was their way of showing no hard feelings.

"What about the kids?" One of the wives would ask on occasion even though she didn't really give a shit. Sometimes she wouldn't even get to the "kids" part of the sentence, and it would trail off into something incomprehensible.

"They don't fucking know," one of the men would say. And the grownups would get stoned, and the kids knew it.

Once the adults were stoned, some of the teenagers would be offered a couple of tokes or maybe a beer or two.

"I'd rather them do it with me than behind my back," was the most common rationalization from the parents of these teenage stoners.

When Uncle Dayday got a buzz, he would start making fun of one of the kids. He thought he was being the fun uncle, the comedian of the group, but the kids always wished he wouldn't choose them for the entertainment. For some reason, young Jake was his favorite to pick on.

"Your boy still a sissy?" he would say to his brother. Everyone at the camp thought that about nine-year-old Jake and no one tried to hide it from him either. In fact, for a while he was even called Sissy, like that was an appropriate nickname for a nine-year-old boy. He earned that name after his first hunting trip. He complained about getting up early. He complained about the cold. He complained about being bored. Jake never did shoot his first deer. He even refused to help field-dress any game that was shot. "Something must be wrong with the boy," DayDay would say, "maybe he's queer." After Jake watched *The Endless Summer* for the first time, he started to ask his mom to buy him surfing magazines, and his mom finally convinced Fat Boy to buy him a surfboard too. Uncle DayDay arrived one morning with a single fin that he picked up at a pawn shop. But the jokes never stopped.

"Boy's only nine. He'll grow out of it," Skeet said in an attempt to defend young Jake. Skeet was the fattest of the bunch and had the longest beard and no one ever challenged Skeet. All the men kind of looked alike though: uncombed hair, beards, and large bellies. A couple of the men had 1% badges sewed on the leather jackets. Skeet had one.

The men often talked about hunting, and every once in a while when they had really been drinking, stories from their renegade past would enter the conversation. Only Skeet had been in war, and that was not by choice. Fat Boy enlisted but didn't last long. He had been injured before ever being sent off to war. No one really knew what happened, but he had been on disability for most of his adult life. Uncle DayDay and a few others dodged the draft. From what Jake could gather Skeet had killed people during wartime, but also once he was out. At least one. He was arrested for killing a guy once but beat the charges on grounds of self-defense. Uncle DayDay had been to jail a few times as well. His crimes were a little less violent: drunken disorderly for pissing on a police cruiser, DUI, possession of controlled substance and criminal mischief/vandalism when he turned donuts in his neighbor's yard destroying freshly laid sod because he wasn't invited to their Fourth of July party.

"The kid may be nine, but he also might be queer," Uncle Dayday said.

"You ain't queer, are ya boy?" Jake's dad said. Jake looked up at him and said, "No sir," and then went back to poking the fire with a stick.

Jake's dad would smack Jake in the back of the head

132

and say, "Go on with your momma." And in his memory, older Jake would see little Jake run to the women who were always sitting in a group talking shit about their husbands or discussing what new drug they were prescribed and drinking homemade wine out of mason jars, waiting to do the dishes. Wasn't much else for them to do until after supper when they did the dishes. They didn't even cook. The men said women didn't know how to grill properly, but they could clean the hell out of some dishes.

As Jake got older he went to the hunting camp less and less. He took Sanch there one time, and Uncle DayDay asked if Sanch was his boyfriend. After they all got to drinking, Skeet laid out lines of cocaine and Uncle DayDay kept on about Jake being gay until Jake pushed his uncle and said he was going to kick his ass in front of everyone. And Jake was kicking his ass when Fat Boy tried to get between them. Jake started kicking his dad's ass, too. That was when Skeet pulled a gun on Jake. He pressed the barrel so deep into Jake's mouth it forced him to gag. Skeet told Jake if he ever tried any shit like that again he'd feed him to the wild hogs. That was four years ago, the last time Jake visited the hunting club.

Chapter 10

Jake, outside on the bench with a lit joint dangling from his lips, repaired a small ding on the side of a board. Sanch took the joint from Jake's lips and took a long drag, holding the smoke deep in his lungs. He closed his eyes, trying to recall the previous night. His head throbbed. His guts bubbled. He let out a fart that would have rattled the bench if he had been sitting on it. Jake stopped sanding.

"You feel better now?" he asked.

Sanch shook his head. "I ain't drinking tonight."

"What happened to your hand?"

Sanch looked at it. The river of blood that had once flowed from his hand to his elbow was now dried and crusty. He handed the joint back to Jake. "You saw the phone booth last night?"

Jake let out a loud laugh. "I knew that was you. You called her didn't you?"

Sanch nodded.

Jake laughed more and continued sanding the board. "I think I might have pissed off her stepmom."

Jake laughed again, even louder this time.

"Should I call back and apologize?"

"Told you all this repair shit I brought would come in handy."

"What happened?"

"It got knocked over last night. Either you or me. But it was one I planned on selling anyway."

Jake handed him the joint back. Sanch studied it. "Where'd you get papers?"

"Rob gave me a pack before he left."

"They left already?"

"Said something about a volcano."

"Rob was an alright dude."

"Them two were tripping balls last night. I don't think they ever went to sleep. But he gave me these." Jake held up a baggie of chocolate-covered mushrooms.

"Might have to wait a couple of days before I eat some shrooms," Sanch said.

Jake laughed.

Sanch took a couple more hits from the joint before giving it to Jake. He sat on the ground and looked at Jake sanding the board.

"How long have we been here now?" Sanch asked.

"A week, maybe."

"Why did it take us so long to do this?"

"What was that?" Jake said.

"Nothing. Just talking."

"You still fucked up?"

"Think about it: My parents think I don't know the value of hard work. I know the value of hard work and know we are being used. What has hard work got them?"

"I don't give a fuck about anything right now, but getting this board looking good enough to sell," Jake said.

Sanch looked at Jake and believed him.

Sanch went and lay back down in the room. He stared at a spider spinning a web in the corner above his bed and wondered if spiders ever spun webs for artistic purposes. Not much time passed when Jake shouted, "Let's go" from the bench.

Jake stepped into the doorway and stood with his hands holding on to the door frame above him.

Sanch looked over at him and said, "You think there is any work out there that you would be stoked about getting up every morning and doing every day?"

"Jesus. Can't we just go sell this board?"

"So no? No job you want to do every day for the rest of your life?"

"Look," Jake said. "We're just regular people. We don't matter in the big scheme of things. Look at our dads. My dad. He sits on his ass all day collecting disability. Hadn't left Pensacola since I was born. I said fuck it. I ain't doing that. I wanna do what makes me happy. If we don't get out and do it right now, all we are going to be is nothing but pawns in another person's chess game."

"My grandfather fought in fucking WWII. My dad Vietnam. My brother followed them right into battle. He gave his life for us to be able to do whatever the hell we want."

"Then honor him by not being another pawn. Might sound harsh, man. No disrespect to him either. But he was a pawn."

"You're kind of an asshole."

Jake laughed. "Sorry, I said no disrespect."

"It used to be you were already a man at twenty years old. But look at us. You are going be thirty soon and still act like a fucking child. When do we grow up?"

"Who says we have to? Look, all I'm saying is that I'm refusing to play the game. I don't even want to be on the board. And if you think joining the military is the answer, you've lost your goddamned mind. Just because I don't want to go to war or to college or do some bullshit job that I hate, I'm supposed to feel bad about that? Fuck that. I've never heard a bigger crock of shit."

"I'm not saying joining the military is the answer."

"I know it's not. Killing people or getting killed isn't solving anything. I just want to chill and get high and go surfing and right now sell this motherfucker."

"Let's go sell that motherfucker then," Sanch said.

"As long as what I do don't hurt anybody, why can't I do whatever the hell I want? We are told our whole life to be a hard worker because our parents were told that same shit and they believed it. But all it does is make someone else richer. You realize how short our life is? In the history of the world, this shit is like a millisecond or a fraction of a millisecond. And you think I'm going to sit around and do something I don't want to do. For what?"

"So the purpose of life according to Jake is to do whatever you want and be happy as long as it doesn't hurt anyone else?"

"I don't know what the purpose of life is. And to be honest, I try not to think about it too much. Maybe there is no purpose."

Sanch laughed.

"Work nowadays is just a more humane way of keeping people in slavery. All the middle class is good for is getting rich people richer. We will never be part of the elite. We will never be in the ruling class. They tell people you can be anything you want to keep us working hard because the harder we work the more money they make. We, the middle class, the working class, whatever the fuck you want to call it, we are what makes the world run, and we don't get shit for it in return. We get to buy a house we can't afford, drive a car we can't afford and work our asses off just to be able to pay off our debt when we die. I refuse to be a part of that. I don't want to be the reason some asshole that runs a corporation gets to sit on his ass while I'm working all day trying to survive. What you've got to face is that there are movers and there are shakers. And we aren't either. We won't change the world. It doesn't matter if we ever existed. So that's why I'm gonna have as much fun as I can. Might as well just enjoy the ride. That's all life is. One long motherfucker of a wave. And we just gotta figure out how to ride it. And shit, maybe everyone is riding a different wave, right? So only you know how to do it best for the wave you're riding. Goddamn, I'm fucking figuring this shit out, ain't I? You will never be elite. But y can you always be original."

"If you say so." Sanch laughed.

"I'll teach ya before it's over, grasshopper."

Sanch laughed again. "I didn't know you thought that hard about anything."

"You can laugh, but you know I'm right."

"I won't argue with you."

"Goddamn right, you won't. Let's go sell this motherfucker already."

On the way to Aqua Blue, Sanch spotted his flip-flops that he lost the previous night, but having spent the night in a downpour getting caked in mud and then drying in the blistering sun, the flip-flops were too stiff to walk in.

"Who needs shoes?" Sanch said.

"I'm glad I got mine. Them rocks hurt."

Jake had the board he had been working on, and Sanch carried one that hadn't been getting used. At Aqua Blue, Alex said, "I've got more than enough boards. You'd be better off selling it to someone on the street."

A middle-aged American man walked through the door and looked over Alex's boards. He wore a tank top. His shoulders bright red and his legs stuck out from his Bermuda shorts like a five-year-old's stick figure drawing.

"Excuse me," he said. "I've never surfed before and thought I might just give it a try. I don't want to spend too much, though. Do you rent surfboards?"

"Sorry," Alex said. "Just sell."

"I'm only here for a week."

"You're in luck," Jake said. "I'm selling this one for real cheap."

"What are doing?" Alex said. "You can't sell a board in here."

"I'll be outside if you want to talk price," Jake said to the man and winked at Alex.

Outside, the guy looked the board over. "You think it's a good board to learn on?"

"It's perfect for that. That's what this board is. It's a beginner board."

"I don't know anything about surfing. You're not trying to swindle me, are you?"

"I promise. All those boards were three, four hundred dollars, right?"

"Yeah. It was too much I thought."

"It was, but that's what boards go for here. But I'll make a deal with you because we just got too many with us."

"How many?"

"What is it twelve?" he asked Sanch.

"Something like that," Sanch said.

"Why do you have so many?"

"I'm a pro. My sponsors just give them to me. They want me always riding on the newest design, ya know?"

"How cool is that? What's your name?"

"Jake Higdon. Look. I'll sell this one to you for two hundred. When you go to leave, you can sell it for three hundred. Make you a profit. Maybe even more if you find someone that knows about surfing. Tell him it was Jake Higdon's board."

"Two hundred? Are you sure? You don't know of anyone that rents boards do you? It's still a bit more than I wanted to spend."

"Nah. This is the only surf shop that I know of in town. This board is a hundred times better than any of those in there."

"Two hundred is still a lot of money."

"One seventy-five then. But that's it."

"All right. One seventy-five."

The guy handed over one hundred eighty in twenty dollar bills.

"I don't have change," Jake said. "But I'll tell you what." Jake pointed to the camera around the guy's neck. "I'll take a picture with you so you can prove to people you got a board from Jake Higdon."

"Really?"

"Of course." Jake then said to Sanch, "Get his camera and take a picture for my newest fan."

Sanch smiled and took the camera.

"Much appreciated," the man said.

"Hang loose, brother," Jake said. Jake watched the man walk off.

"That was easy. Let's see if we can sell this other one at Tamarindo Adventures. That just gave us another two weeks here."

"You don't feel bad about bullshitting people?"

"That dude has plenty of money. If I didn't get it, someone else would."

Tamarindo Adventures wanted to buy Jake's board for one hundred twenty-five dollars.

"And then you turn around and sell it for four hundred? Kiss my ass," Jake said.

Lagarto Surf offered only seventy-five dollars. Jake laughed. As they were leaving, Vince walked up, having just finished giving another lesson. He told them about a guy up the hill named Chip, who would probably buy it. Told them to look for a sign outside of the house that said "Chip's Ding Repair."

"People are living here by just fixing dings?" Jake said.

"He's the only one," Vince said.

"So one more won't hurt him," Jake said. "Competition is good for business, right?"

"You fix boards?" Vince asked.

"Hell, I can shape boards. Fixing them is easy."

"We need someone to do ding repair here. There's a ton of boards in the back, like two hundred that need repairs, and we can't find anyone to do it. Chip said he makes more on his own than what we can pay him."

"What's the pay?"

"Don't know. The boss is gone today. You've got to ask him. Come back tomorrow."

"Let him know you found a ding repairman."

"I will," Vince said.

Walking away, Jake said to Sanch, "This is it. We'll live at the Abrigo, eat at Pedro's, fix a couple boards when it's too hot to surf. We've figured it out. Told you I would. Just stick with me, you'll be all right."

To get to Chip's Ding Repair they walked down a rutted, muddy driveway through dense foliage. The house had a hand built quality about it, similar to the clubhouse Sanch had built in his back yard when he was eight. And not much bigger either. Jake knocked. The door opened. A long-haired shadowed figure peeked out.

"Chip?" Jake said.

141

"Yes," The wiry man said. He had gray, nappy dreads down to the middle of his back.

"Heard you might like to buy a board."

Chip stepped out and took the board. He ran his hand over the rails, then held the board from the tail, put it about nose high and looked down the board lengthwise, checking the curves or what surfers called the rocker. All typical things people did before buying a board. But then he held it to his ear and closed his eyes. Sanch and Jake looked at each other.

"What's it say?" Jake asked.

Chip opened his eyes and looked at Jake. "Says, it'd like to get in the water. I'll give you two hundred."

"Sold."

They walked back to the Abrigo three hundred and seventy-five dollars richer and the prospect of a new job.

"You sure you could handle living like this?" Jake said.

"Why not?"

"What about what's-her-face? You're still not over her."

Sanch shrugged.

Jake laughed.

"What about your daughter?"

"What about her?"

"You just gonna forget her, too?"

"Fuck you."

"Just saying."

"Listen. I'm talking about you and that puppy love bullshit. It was your first real relationship, and you got caught up in it. That's what happens when you're young. She outgrew you, and you got hurt. It's completely understandable."

"I'm cool. Just had a bit of freak-out last night is all."

"Listen to me. How many girls have I slept with?"

"A lot, according to you."

"Fuck you. You know I have. Don't you think I learned something from them? Besides how to…" He did a few pelvic thrusts as he walked.

"What've you learned?"

"Ready? About to drop some more knowledge on you. Maybe you should be taking notes."

"I am. It's all up here." Sanch tapped his temple.

"So look, most people mistake infatuation for love. That sense of the word is bullshit. Romeo and Juliet, bullshit. Women and men only need each other for two things. You know what they are?"

"Let me take a guess. Fucking and making babies?"

"I'll be damned. You are listening. That's right, fucking and making babies."

"You don't really believe that, do you?"

"Let me explain. Women have been programmed to think if they're just with a man to fuck, then they're a whore. So they want them for companionship. And men, like you, believe them because you like getting laid. Sometimes you find a woman who understands that, and then you're set. Some women start off that way. They act cool at first, let you get some anytime you want. She'll blow you in the morning. But they can't keep that up. Sooner or later they change. Men change, too. Most men play the little game: take them out to dinner, pretend they're interested in whatever they ramble on about for hours, buy them flowers and shit like that. But guys can't keep that up either. Most men are too chickenshit to be honest with a woman, too. So when one fucks you, you don't ever want her to leave. That's how guys get trapped.

They think they won't ever be able to find someone who will fuck them. They sacrifice getting head once a year on their birthday because at least they get head once a year, right?"

"You're a genius," Sanch said. "No wonder you have women crawling all over you."

"Just shut up and listen. This is the way I see it: ninety-eight percent of women are bitches or whores and out of those, ninety-eight percent are both. Only a chump will settle for a whore, but most men will settle for a bitch because at least she ain't a whore. You follow me?"

"That's a bit harsh, no? Ninety-eight percent is a pretty high number."

"Just go with it for the sake of argument. I'm not gonna settle. If I ever find one that belongs to that two percent that isn't a bitch or a whore then I might get married. But if not, then a loner I was meant to be."

"Sounds like you got it figured out then," Sanch said.

"Motherfucker, that's what I'm telling you."

Sanch laughed.

"Just give me a few grand and I'll give you a diploma from the school of Boogaloo."

"Can I get a student loan?" Sanch said.

"Hell no. Cash, upfront."

Sanch spotted his flip-flops again. He picked them up and carried them with him. The sun was still high. The Abrigo was silent. Sanch waved to the old lady gumming a banana.

"What now?" Sanch said.

"I'm taking a nap. Might rub my balls on all this money we just got."

Sanch tried to nap as well, but the heat was unbearable. The only circulation in the room came from the door being left open. He closed his eyes for awhile but couldn't tell if he had slept. He stepped out and sat on the bench by the door. Two guys walked out from the room Rob had stayed in. They both had shoulder-length hair and wore nothing but board shorts. One was noticeably bow-legged.

Sanch nodded a hello.

The bow-legged one sat next to him. "Get high?" he asked. His English was not so good.

"What?" Sanch asked.

"Uhh. You." He pointed at Sanch. "Get high?"

"Like smoke pot?"

"Yes. Pot."

The one standing up holding a book laughed.

"Yeah, I get high," Sanch said.

The bow-legged one pinched the contents from a small baggie on his lap into a rolling paper.

"What're you reading?" Sanch asked, looking at the book's cover. It was of a man's face and the background behind the picture was red.

"I've seen that face on tee shirts and whatnot," Sanch said.

"Yes, yes. Che Guevara."

He handed the book to Sanch. Sanch thumbed through it but it was written in Spanish.

"Who is he?" Sanch asked.

"Revolución," the boy said, throwing a fist into the air.

"Revolutionary?"

"Sí. Revolucionario," the boy shouted. The one sitting next to Sanch smiled at his animated friend.

"From here?" They didn't understand. "Costa Rican revolucionario?"

"No. No. Argentina and Cuba."

145

"You Argentina-ian?" Sanch didn't know how to pronounce that.

"No. Venezuela."

"Don't get mad, but where is Venezuela?"

"I show you. One second." He left.

The bow-legged one lit up the joint. The other came out with a map.

"Look. I show you." He spread the map on the ground. He not only showed Sanch where Venezuela was, but also where their hometown of Puerto Cabello was, one of Venezuela's two most important harbors.

"Wish everyone was this cool when I didn't know where they are from," Sanch said.

"¿Cómo?" the boy asked.

"Nothing."

The joint was passed around and they communicated the best they could, mostly through hand gestures when Sanch didn't understand something.

They traveled by bus all the way from Venezuela and were continuing to go north until Mexico. Then they would fly home. The bow-legged one was the younger of the two, seventeen. He was just going to see the world, as he said. The other was eighteen and his purpose was to capture the spirit of Che. He was a writer and was keeping extensive notes on his journey. He stepped inside and then back out with two notebooks he had filled already. He was on his third. Bow-leg asked Sanch what he did.

"What do you mean, what do I do?"

"Back in America? A student? Work?"

"I don't do anything," Sanch said. "This is it, I guess. I used to work at a carwash. I put money aside and here I am. See how long it'll last."

Revolucionario asked what he planned on doing when he went back home.

"I'm not going back," Sanch said.

They laughed. Sanch smiled, but he wondered why they thought that was funny.

A few minutes passed with all three just scanning the Abrigo grounds. They watched an iguana about three feet long scurry by, his tail leaving a trail in the dust. The cannabis settled on them and conversation seemed unnecessary at the moment.

"I go inside for a little," Revolucionario said and went in with his notebooks.

Bow-leg looked at Sanch. Sanch nodded to him. Bow-leg smiled. "Good. Yes?" he said.

"Feeling all right," Sanch said.

"¿Tranquilo?"

"Tranquilo." Sanch assumed that meant tranquil which he assumed was a way of saying stoned.

A few seconds later, he felt a nudge.

"Look," the Venezuelan said. He pointed at two birds in a tree across the way.

"What?" Sanch asked, straining his eyes.

"Pájaros."

"I don't know."

"Pájaros." He then whistled like a bird and flapped his arms.

"Birds?"

"Sí. Birds."

"What about them?"

"Fuck. They fuck." He made a motion to help get his thought across.

Sanch started laughing because the Venezuelan said fuck but when he saw the birds, he thought he would never stop laughing. The more he laughed, the more the Venezuelan laughed until they both clutched their abdomens as they doubled over and tears filled their eyes. It was laughter with such force that it was just as cathartic as crying.

"What the hell's going on?" Jake said, storming out. "What the hell's wrong with you?"

Sanch could only manage to point.

"What are you pointing at?"

"The birds are fucking." This caused Sanch and the Venezuelan to laugh harder.

"What?" Jake said.

"Look," Sanch said. Revolucionario came out. He laughed without knowing what was funny.

"Are you stoned?" Jake asked.

Sanch nodded. The birds flew away. "The birds were fucking," he managed through more laughter. Bow-leg went inside to try and gather himself. Revolucionario was now laughing harder.

The laughter settled to the last remaining chuckles when Sanch made eye contact with Bow-leg as he came back out of the room and they started up again.

"You guys are retarded," Jake said. "I'm going inside to roll a joint." They followed him in, still trying to hold in their laughter.

They then surfed the river mouth and it was a good surf. Nice slow rollers, no bigger than waist-high. They stayed out until dark and the last bits of sunlight hung in the sky. As they walked back very few words were spoken. It was as if a passerby could sense the self-forgetfulness or inner silence that the long surf session created. Anxiety faded and although the euphoric feeling did not last long, a stillness lingered for the rest of the day.

The Venezuelans went out to eat that night. They were only in town until they head out on the morning bus and wanted to see a bit more of Tamarindo. Jake and Sanch were to use the community kitchen for the first time in order to cut back on food expense since they were spending more on lodging.

They shopped the little market down by the bank and bought a bag of rice, a couple cans of tuna fish, an onion, half a dozen eggs, a loaf of bread and some peanut butter. They were a bit taken back by the eggs sitting on a shelf as opposed to being refrigerated, but were assured that was the way to store them. They were told that America was the only country that stored eggs in the refrigerator.

The electric camping stove was rusted and dented sitting on a wooden bench with the cord plugged into an exposed outlet underneath the sink where a slow drip splashed on the concrete below. The drawer under the stove held the utensils and few plates. An iron skillet and a large pot for boiling water hung over the stove.

Sanch sat at the picnic table and diced the onion. Jake put the full pot of water on the burner and touched the igniter button for the stove to start and jumped back just as quickly.

"What happened?" Sanch asked.

"Piece of shit stove shocked me."

Jake tried it three more times and it shocked him every time.

"I can't turn the damn thing on," he said. "You try it."

Sanch shook his head.

"Try it. See if it's just me."

"I just watched you get shocked three times."

"It doesn't hurt."

"Then try it again."

The maintenance worker came in at that time. He laughed and said something in Spanish.

"This fucker thinks it's funny," Jake said.

The maintenance worker pointed at Jake's bare feet and then pointed at his own feet. The maintenance man then took off a flip-flop and pointed at the sole. He pointed again at Jake's bare feet.

"No. No have." He put his flip-flop back on and walked up to the stove and pushed in the igniter. The stove lit.

"What the hell?" Jake said and then tried it again and was immediately shocked. "Motherfucker," he said.

The maintenance man found that amusing. "No," he said. He pointed to Sanch and then at the stove.

"He wants you to try," Jake said. "He wants to see you get shocked so he can laugh at the stupid gringos. Go ahead, be his clown. Make him laugh."

The man insisted that Sanch try it. Sanch finally gave in and was shocked. He jumped back holding his hand. The man and Jake laughed.

"Told you," Jake said.

"What the hell?" Sanch said.

The man slapped his knee in laughter and pointed at Jake's bare feet again, then at Sanch's bare feet and then at his feet with flip-flops.

"It's because we're barefoot," Sanch said.

The man laughed, nodded his head yes.

"Get outta here. Let me see your shoes," Jake said. The old man gave him his shoes. Nothing happened. "Now you touch it."

"Hell no," Sanch said.

"Come on. It doesn't hurt. Just to see if that's it."

Sanch did and jumped back, shaking his hand.

"Dumbass," Jake said.

Sanch laughed even though his hand tingled.

The little old Tico loved it. He joined them for dinner. Jake boiled all six eggs and a cup of rice. Then he cut up three of the eggs and mixed it in with the rice and two cans of tuna and half of the onion. They each ate one of the extra boiled eggs. All they managed to understand from their dinner guest was his name. He wrote Jesus in the sand. He didn't pronounce it like that though. They wouldn't call him Hayseus. They called him Jesus.

"Not bad," Sanch said shoveling a spoonful in his mouth.

"We need salt," Jake said.

They looked at Jesus. He wasn't using any spoon or fork but was pinching the rice between his fingers and scooping it into his mouth.

"Acting like we just cooked him Filet Mignon," Jake said.

Jesus insisted on doing the dishes. When he came to the rice bowl, before washing it, he picked out the last few grains and ate those.

After dinner they visited The Mambo Bar. Behind the big fence, a thatched roof covered the bar to the left. Two pool tables and a foosball table were in the center of the property and were covered by another smaller thatched roof. Couches, recliners and a few chairs were spread about the dirt floor among wooden picnic tables. An outhouse was set away in the corner. Large trees and bushes lined the fence creating an intimate, secluded, secret atmosphere. The moon and stars served as lighting along with a disco ball. Bob Marley songs blared through the speakers. A few girls danced together. The men hovered around the pool tables.

Gerard was playing pool and rushed up to greet Jake as they entered, like they were lifelong friends. Jake gave the bartender money for tokens to shoot pool. He set some down to mark that he was next. In the meantime, he and Sanch played foosball. Sanch won two games and then two players challenged them, a man in his early forties, looking as if he hadn't showered or shaved in a couple of days, and his partner, who was just a kid that was maybe ten years old.

"What are you doing in a bar?" Jake said. The kid didn't speak English. His partner answered for him.

"It doesn't matter the age here."

"How old is he?"

"Eleven."

"He drink?"

The man shook his head and didn't respond to Jake. The man played defense, as did Sanch. Jake and the kid battled up front. The kid knocked in the first three balls within two minutes.

"Trade me," Jake said. "You suck." Sanch switched positions with him, but it didn't help. The game was over, seven-zero.

They played another game. The man sat out. Two against one and they only managed one score and even that was an own goal by the kid when Sanch mishit the ball, ricocheting it off the side with a strange backspin and the kid's goalie tapped it in his own goal. The kid didn't smile after his victory, just patiently awaited his next victims.

A six-foot Tico picked up Jake's tokens and put them in and began racking the balls as if he were next. Sanch sat down next to Mary who had just arrived. She had two beers in front of her and offered one to Sanch. He drank half on the first pull.

"Whatta you think you're doing?" Jake said.

Sanch looked over and saw Jake struggling with the Tico to rack the balls. They both stood and were nose to nose.

"Those are my tokens," Jake said. "You can't just walk up and use anyone's tokens you want."

Gerard and another guy stepped between the two. Sanch sat sipping his beer.

"Think Jake can take that dude?" Sanch said to Mary.

"You last night, him tonight. Pura Vida. You guys haven't learned that yet? There's no fighting in Costa Rica. You guys got to learn to handle things differently. This isn't Alabama," she said.

"We're from Florida."

"Well, people are calling you 'those Alabama boys.'"

Jake sat down next to Sanch, picked up the beer and took a drink, leaving about two sips at the bottom of the bottle.

"Might as well finish it," Sanch said.

"Not like I spit in it."

"No, but I saw a string of drool connected from your lips to the bottle when you were setting it down." Jake looked at him. He put the neck of the bottle in his mouth and simulated oral sex.

"You're disgusting," Mary said. Jake laughed.

"You try it," he said to her. "You're probably better at it."

"I'm sure of it. But you'll never find out," she said.

"She's funny," Jake said. "Did you see that asshole over there?"

"That asshole is hot," Mary said.

"Well, he thinks he runs the place. He knows he's good-looking and all the girls want him and all the guys are

153

too big of pussies to stand up to him. So he's used to getting away with shit like that."

"Or because it's just a game of pool, not really worth fighting over," Mary said.

"Well, this cowboy ain't gonna let that kind of shit slide. Those were my quarters."

"They're tokens," Sanch said.

"Tokens. Quarters. Who gives a shit? They were mine and it was my turn to play. He has to wait his turn like everyone else. He was like Gerard, dropping in on everyone. And you saw who put a stop to that. I don't care if this is Costa Rica and Pura Vida and all that hippie dippy shit."

"So why aren't you playing?" Mary asked.

"He apologized and gave me my money back. That's all I ask for. A little respect."

After the next game, the Tico who had the tokens came to tell Jake it was his turn. He shook Jake's hand. Jake accepted.

While Jake and the Tico played partners, Sanch and Mary downed a few tequilas and more beer and had a conversation about how they arrived at a stage in their lives where they were sitting in a bar drinking tequila and beers thousands of miles from home. Mary had come to Costa Rica after her fiancé broke off their engagement two weeks before the wedding. She was embarrassed and wanted to get away and fell in love, this time with a country and lifestyle instead of a person.

"It's easy to get stuck here," Mary said. "Every day you stay, it'll get harder and harder to leave. Your past will get further and further away until eventually you have no past life except the night before. That is until you run into someone like you, who is still new to the whole idea of expatriatism and asks questions about why I don't ever go back home."

"Sorry," Sanch said and then downed Mary's shot.

"You may," she said.

"Didn't look like you were drinking it."

"I was, just not at the moment."

A friend of Mary's joined them. She was a caramel-skinned Tica. Mary told him that she made money by doing piercings.

Two beers later, Sanch was getting his ears pierced in the light by the outhouse. She put ice behind each earlobe, had a needle that she said was in a sealed plastic bag, never been used, still sterile as were the hoop earrings.

"Not quite sailing around Cape Horn, but close enough, right?"

Mary nor her friend understood the reference.

"Doesn't matter," Sanch said. "It's my mark of adventure. My initiation." He slurred the word initiation.

"It's whatever you want it to be," Mary said.

"Look at my ears," Sanch said, interrupting Jake's game.

"What the hell'd you do?"

"They look good, right?" Mary said.

"You're an idiot. Those are some thick hoops. You're gonna be in pain tomorrow." He then tried to thump an earlobe. Sanch dodged it.

After a few more beers and pool games, the crowd moved to the discoteca, a dance hall up the hill, a little further than the Expatriado. Sanch got a drink to go and followed the crowd, a cacophony of stumbling and shouting and some puking patrons. They all enjoyed the magic that a group of merrymakers can produce when they are riding the same wave of happiness.

"I can't leave this place," Jake said as they waited in line to enter. "We don't even need shoes or shirt to enter a dance club. I love this place," he shouted and those nearby let out a holler in agreement. About half the men were shirtless. Jake slipped as they entered and hit the floor with a thud. Sanch and Mary laughed. Jake lay for a few seconds laughing, too. The crowd stepped over him until the Tico from the pool game stopped to help him to his feet, patted him on the back and continued on.

At the bar, they each did a shot of tequila and ordered a round of beers.

"Thought you weren't going to drink tonight," Jake said.

"So'd I." Sanch lifted the bottle. Jake tapped Sanch's with his and they drank. Sanch wiped his mouth with the back of his hand. "We should've ate those mushrooms if we knew this place was like this."

"Tomorrow," Jake said.

"You two are funny," Mary said.

In the courtyard out back, people separated into groups passing joints. Five guys at a table in the far corner played cards. Jake hit Sanch on the arm and pointed to the table. Sanch already saw it and knew what Jake was thinking.

"Let's wait a little before we play," Jake said. He went to the bathroom. Sanch and Mary went to the dance floor. Sanch hadn't stepped on a dance floor for years, not since the first time he had taken Natalie dancing and she made fun of his lack of rhythm. She did it in a joking way, but he wouldn't ever dance with her again. It caused fights when she wanted to go to a dance club and he was more content at a pool hall. But in Costa Rica, it wasn't until he was covered in sweat and had danced with three other girls that he realized how much fun he was having. His ego drifted

156

away. No one judged him and he moved to his own rhythm. He closed his eyes and danced alone. The alcohol helped, but through all the distortion, deep down, stripped to the raw essentials, it wasn't the alcohol that made the decision to dance. And it wasn't the alcohol that made the decision for him to enjoy it.

The song switched to a slower melody. He opened his eyes. Jake danced too. Something Sanch had never seen. Jake didn't dance much, but enough to keep up with the girl in front of him while he talked to her. Sanch joined them.

"She's staying at the Abrigo," Jake said. Sanch shook her hand, but didn't catch her name.

"Guess who was in the bathroom?" Jake shouted over the music. The girl drifted into the crowd, dancing with another girl.

"Who?"

"Remember Paco?"

Sanch shook his head.

"From the bus ride. With the coke."

Sanch remembered now.

"He was in the bathroom with Chico."

"No shit?" Sanch swayed as he spoke.

"He gave me a few bumps. Chico was cool about us leaving. Let's play some cards."

The card players, an overweight American and four Ticos, only wanted one of them to play. Jake sat down. Sanch bought him and Jake a beer and stood watch over Jake's shoulder. They played "dealer call it," with a twenty dollar buy-in. They played mostly Texas Hold 'Em. Occasionally someone changed it up. Jake slow-played at first, but only won one hand in the first six games and that was with a Queen high. The other guys folded, but Jake showed the card anyway to let them know he was bluffing.

The other games he usually folded before the flop. The next game Jake was dealt pocket Kings. A third King was shown on the flop. Jake checked until the river card and then went all in. The American called him on the biggest pot of the night, sixty-odd dollars, a mix of colones and dollars.

"You're a goddamn cheat," the American shouted.

"I don't need to cheat," Jake said. "I had a good hand."

"The last hand you won was on a bluff," the American said.

"No rules against bluffing."

The beaten man pulled out two dice from his pockets. "Shoot dice then?"

"Not really my thing," Jake told him.

"But you know how?"

"Sure."

"Double or nothing?"

"What do you mean?"

"The money you just won."

"Sixty bucks? Why not?"

"What the hell are you doing?" Sanch asked him. "Don't you always say take the money and run?"

"I'm feeling lucky." He pinched Sanch's nipple.

The other guy rolled the dice on the table showing a four and a one.

"Let's get the rules down before I call anything. Don't want any miscommunications," Jake said. "I've already been accused of cheating once."

"All right. We'll make it easy. Just say pass or don't pass," the American said.

"What's that mean?"

"Pass—You'll win if I hit a five before I hit seven or eleven. Don't pass—You'll win if I hit seven or eleven before I hit five again."

"Not much skill involved, huh?"

"Like that last hand you had," the American said. Jake smirked at that.

"Don't pass then."

"So you're saying I'll hit seven or eleven first?"

"Whatever. I'm going to win whatever I call."

"Pretty goddamn cocky, aren't you?"

"Just roll and let's see."

He rolled. A five and a two.

"That was easy," Jake said and held out his hand.

The Ticos laughed. The American didn't.

"You son of a bitch," he said to Jake.

Jake shrugged. "I got lucky."

"I ain't paying you shit," the American said and stood to leave the table. The two Ticos on either side of him grabbed his wrist, but didn't say anything. The American understood and took out his wallet.

"All I've got is a fifty."

"That'll work," Jake said. He handed Jake the money. He then said to Sanch, "Go get them girls and tell them I'm buying."

Sanch found the girl that Jake danced with. She grabbed her friend. Sanch also told Mary that Jake was buying a round. She brought the guy she danced with.

"What did you do, tell the whole place?" Jake said as they met him at the bar.

Jake bought six tequilas. Mary and her friend downed their tequila and went back to the dance floor. The other two girls were from Holland. They said the Netherlands at first and neither Sanch nor Jake knew where that was. Anne

Frank? Still nothing. Amsterdam? That one they knew.
That led to Jake asking a barrage of questions about drugs
and whores.

"We are not from Amsterdam. We just used that as
reference. We are from another city in Holland." She said
which one, but it fell on deaf ears. She then went on to say
how much more there was to her home country besides
Amsterdam.

"Going just to Amsterdam and saying you've been to
the Netherlands would be like us going to only Disney
World and saying we've been to the States."

The girls wanted to dance some more. Sanch and Jake
played pool. Too many games and too many beers later, the
music stopped and the lights came on. They shuffled with
the rest of the drunks to the exit. The two Dutch girls
walked a few steps in front of them, hounded by a group of
guys.

"We can fuck them tonight," Jake said.

"Looks like those guys are thinking the same thing."

"Hang back a bit. Listen to what they say."

One of the girls looked back.

"You saw that. She's making sure we are following."

They walked down the hill into town.

"We better hurry if we're going to get laid," Sanch
said.

"Calm down, man. We're drunk, but we still have to
play it cool. Can't look too eager."

The girls stopped off to talk with the guys. Jake
stopped Sanch.

"Wait and see what happens now," he said.
"Sometimes you lose."

The guys only got a hug and were on their way. The
girls kept walking towards the Abrigo by themselves.

"See," Jake said. He then shouted out to the girls and asked them if they wanted to smoke a joint before bed.

"You think we are easy American girls," the tall one said. Both girls giggled.

"No. Hoping you was easy though," Jake said. "I don't care if you're American or where is it you're from again?"

"That's not going to work," the short one said. "You boys are drunk. Why don't we hang out tomorrow?"

"You want to go surfing with us?" Jake said.

"Yes. We will try surfing with you."

Chapter 11

The Dutch girls waited outside their room on the bench for the boys the next morning. Jake walked out first and waved over at them.

"Are you ready?" one asked.

"One minute," Jake said and went back in.

"Go outside and take a look at those girls and tell me those aren't the same ones we were trying to hook up with last night," he said. "We must've been drunker than hell."

"My ears are killing me. What was I thinking?" Sanch touched his earlobes gingerly.

"Go outside and take a look," Jake said.

Sanch looked outside. The girls waved. He raised a hand and the girls may have mistaken it for a wave. One had a bit of a cockeyed look to her with knobby knees and protruding hip bones. But it was the black hair sprouting from the bikini lines, like they were smuggling wigs, that sent Sanch back inside.

"What are we going to tell them?" Jake asked.

"To shave? I don't know. You're the one that told them you were going to teach them to surf."

Jake went out.

"What'd you tell them?" Sanch asked when he walked back in.

"Said you had the shits."

"Why can't you go then?"

"I didn't give them time to ask."

A few minutes went by and Jake stuck his head out the door. "I don't see them," he said and they snuck out of the Abrigo and went to the Best Western for breakfast on a suggestion from Mary the previous night. For two dollars they were served scrambled eggs, rice and beans, a tortilla and orange juice and they had some of the hottest hot sauce either had ever tried and it would become a game to see who could handle the most. Sanch also bought a coffee for seventy-five cents. Afterward, they went to Lagarto Surf to see about the ding repair job.

Vince said he would call the boss. They looked at the boards while they waited. Jake spotted the one he had repaired and sold the day before and called Vince over.

"How'd you get this board?"

"Some guy came in. Said someone sold it to him, telling him it was a great board to learn on. He took it out to try and another guy told him that was an awful board to learn on. Some asshole took a tourist for some money. Happens everyday. So, he came here to sell it and get surf lessons."

"How much you buy it for?"

"We gave him fifty bucks."

"That was my board. Can you tell where I repaired it?" Jake asked him.

Vince looked at it again. "Here."

"Yeah, but it looks good, right?"

"It's a damn good job."

The bossman arrived a few minutes later. He was well over six feet tall with a gray beard that covered his extra chin. He owned Lagarto Surf and was also head of the Police Department there. Although technically, there wasn't a police force in Tamarindo, but he lived at that house there that had a sign that said "Police" out front. Besides petty thefts, crime was relatively low.

Mr. Bruce started in Tamarindo as a charter boat captain some thirty-five years ago. He was the unofficial mayor. He was at one time a US National Longboard Champion.

"The current Costa Rican national champ is from Tamarindo," Vince added in.

"Who?" Jake asked.

"You fellas talk surf later. Right now, let's talk business. I got some boards that need repairing."

Jake showed him the board. He told him about how he worked with a shaper for six years and how he was a professional surfer at one time.

"What about you?" Mr. Bruce asked Sanch.

"He'll be my gopher," Jake said. "I'll pay him outta my cut."

"You a sidekick or something?"

"Something," Sanch said.

"Sounds like a decent resume, fellas. Follow me." He led them to the back of the shop. Hundreds of surfboards were piled together next to the shed.

"This is what needs done," Mr. Bruce said.

"Where'd you get so many?" Jake asked.

"We buy absolutely any board, in any shape. Most of these will be used as rentals, but if someone wants to buy it everything is for sale."

"How much we talking about?"

"That depends on you. What do you charge?"

Jake picked up a board on the top of the pile and looked it over. It was an eight-footer that looked like it was built in someone's backyard. It was too wide, too thick, too heavy and had bumpy rails and no rocker. The beer brand that was painted on it was misspelled.

"This one has a few dings and it looks pretty bad here." He showed Mr. Bruce where the tail had been scuffed up.

"Tell me a price and I'll say yes or no. How much would you charge if someone came to you for a repair?"

"Forty bucks," Jake said.

"Sounds good. When do you want to start?"

"Right now."

"My kind of worker. You fix as many boards a day as you want. Whenever one is finished, show it to me or Vince. I'll pay you cash for each board. Just set the price for each one. I trust you to do right."

"No problem," Jake said.

"Whatever materials you need, take one of those four-wheelers over there." He pointed to where three four-wheelers were parked outside the privacy fence. "There's a hardware store just at the edge of town. Ask Vince, he'll tell you how to get there. Tell them to put it on my credit." Mr. Bruce left them standing there and went through the back exit into his house.

"He pretty much gave us free rein," Jake said. "Nobody would ever believe this. If we go back home and tell people all that has happened, it would all sound like a lie, like we are just making shit up."

Sanch nodded. "Maybe you'll write a book about it one day."

"Fuck that. You can. So Vince, where's the hardware store and who's the national champ?"

"Follow the road out past the Best Western. You can't miss it. And have you eaten at Pedro's yet?" Vince asked.

"Yeah?"

"His son is the best surfer in the country. He'll be back in town in a few days. You should see him surf."

"He oughta see me surf," Jake said.

Sanch sat behind Jake as they roared through town on the four-wheeler, stirring up dust, honking and hollering at passers-by on the way to the hardware store. Jake bought a few gallons of resin and a few pints of hardener, too much fiberglass and too much sandpaper, a box of surgical gloves and a handful of surgical masks, and two Snickers and two cokes that they ate and drank before they went back to town.

"How do you know what all you need?" Sanch asked.

"Motherfucker, I done told you, I know what I'm doing."

"We'll see."

"Have I been wrong about anything this whole trip?"

It took Jake a few tries to get the ratio of resin and hardener just right, but he did. While he messed with that, he had Sanch sand down the dings. They started with the boards that were easiest to repair first. While Jake applied the fiberglass to the first board Sanch sanded the next. They set them both to dry. Jake figured they would let it set for a couple of hours.

"While they're drying let's go for a surf," Jake said.

They surfed the river mouth's consistent chest-high waves—still as fun as the first day they paddled out. Then they went back to Lagarto.

The boards dried and were ready to sand. Sanch used the electric sander to get the board close to finished and then Jake hand sanded it to perfection. Three hours of total work.

"I'm gonna tell him twenty-five bucks a piece," Jake said. Vince looked at them and then went to tell Mr. Bruce.

He and Mr. Bruce came walking into the shop.

"How much I owe you?" Mr. Bruce asked.

"Sixty dollars for the two boards," Jake said.

"Vince, give it to him from the register. Leave a note in there to remind me," Mr. Bruce said and left. Vince gave Jake the money.

Before heading out that night they ate the mushrooms. "You ready?" Jake said.

"Let's do it," Sanch said. They tapped the first chocolate-covered caps together and said, "Cheers" in unison and then chewed fast and swallowed hard.

"Wait and see how this goes first?" Jake asked.

"For what?" Sanch said. "If we're going, I'm going all the way."

They finished off the bag, probably less than an eighth.

Rick the kitesurfer fronted a live band that night at Expatriado and the place was packed. No stools or chairs were unoccupied. The mushrooms began to take hold upon entering and Jake went to the pool table, his safe spot. Sanch stood, watching the patterns form on the green felt and sipped on a beer, holding each sip longer than usual.

"Beer is such a weird drink," Sanch said. "It tastes like shit, but is so fucking good at the same time."

The people who controlled the pool table were playing partners and Sanch obliged. Sanch could barely hit the cue ball, but Jake zeroed in and after four games, they had won them all. Then Jake was approached with a betting proposition for a one on one game.

"Are you fucked up?" Sanch asked him.

Jake nodded yes and swayed as if he danced to the sounds in his head.

"How can you keep playing then? And keep winning?"

Jake shrugged his shoulders and did a strange dance and shined an illegal smile.

The band played and Sanch walked over to the dance floor.

He finished his beer and needed another as the mushrooms hit full effect and alcohol took the edge off.

"Get us a tequila, too," Jake said.

Sanch squeezed next to the girl who had pierced his ears the night before. She smelled yummy.

"My ears hurt like hell," he said, leaning in and having to shout as the band began a new tune. For a minute she didn't say anything and he wondered if he said that out loud or just thought it. A bit of panic swelled in him. Before he decided to say it again, she turned and smiled. The anxiety whirled away with her kindness. She touched his ears gently and looked at her work.

"They look good," she said. "Sexy."

"You want a drink?" Sanch asked. "Tequila?"

"Sure. But let me use the restroom first." Sanch watched her walk away, her body slinking with every step. He was nearly mesmerized by her femininity.

"You know she's a whore, right?" the guy to Sanch's left said.

"What?" Sanch said.

"She's a whore."

"What're you talking about?" His breathing heavied, feeling like someone pushed on his chest. He forgot how to breathe. The room spun for a quick second and then stood still. Very still, as if someone had hit the pause button during a movie. He blinked and felt his body rush towards a kaleidoscope. He opened his eyes and the world returned.

"What did you say?" Sanch said.

"She fucks for cash. Just thought I'd let you know before you start buying her drinks. Don't want to see a fellow countryman waste his money. Name's Jim." Jim stuck out his hand.

Sanch shook the man's hand. The man's hand was limp and sweaty. "How do you know she's a whore?"

The guy looked at him strangely.

"Never mind," Sanch said.

The guy smiled. His teeth were too big for his mouth and he had crusted spit in the corners of his lips.

"I've fucked her the last two nights."

Sanch looked at the man and could easily see how humans had evolved from primates, but not necessarily for the better. Pigs seemed more fitting. Swine. A goddamn ungulate. Even that was being too nice. This man was some form of creature from the dark. Sanch was convinced if the man were to take off his shoes he wouldn't see feet but cloven hooves. In his mind's eye he saw the lumpy, lard-filled Pigman smothering the pretty, petite ear-piercing girl. He ordered the drinks anyway.

"Suit yourself," Jim said.

"Thanks for the heads up."

"Just helping ya out, buddy." The man turned back around. Sanch inhaled deeply and the anxiety eased.

She came back to the bar with another girl. The other girl had shoulder-length, curly black hair and her skin a deep bronze. Her irides, the same color as her pupils, were a sharp contrast to the blue eyes of the ear-piercing whore.

The friend's name was Andrea. She took the shot with Sanch. He ordered another to take back to Jake. He heard the band play the opening to "Sweet Home Alabama." In his excitement, he didn't say anything to the girls and hurried the drink to Jake and stood in the center of the dance floor, singing along and dancing. The dance floor was empty when he started, but his enthusiasm and energy must have transferred to the band that they in turn picked up on it and transferred their energy to the crowd because by the end of the song, the bar had a livelier atmosphere and people covered the dance floor in flailing, frantic attempts of something that resembled dancing. Sanch drowned in the sweaty sea of wassailers where ambition, despair, grief, and worry ceased to exist.

The band followed it up with The Electric Prunes' "I Had Too Much to Dream (Last Night)."

In the midst of the joyful revelry, the blonde whore stopped him for a minute. She pointed to Andrea who stood off the dance floor. She waved. Sanch waved back.

"She would like to see you again tonight."

"I'll be here," Sanch said. He moved and bobbed his head to the sound of the band tuning their instruments.

"We are going to the disco," she said. "You come. Maybe later."

"I'll meet you there."

The band played one more tune and took a break. Sanch returned to the pool table. The onset of the mushrooms had leveled. Jake was up fourteen dollars. Sanch told him about meeting the girls.

"One might be a whore."

"Where are they?"

"They went to the disco," Sanch said.

"Let's go."

Through the fake fog, flickering strobe lights and pulsating music of the discoteca, Sanch spotted Mary through a blur of spastic moving dancers solemnizing temporary insanity and he shuffled near her. Jake went to the bar.

Dancing with Mary, Sanch spotted Andrea on the dance floor. She smiled and made a motion with her head, beckoning him to her. Sanch danced his way further from Mary until he could sneak over to Andrea. They danced for a bit, but then he saw Mary look his way and overcome with guilt told Andrea to wait a second and went back to Mary. Andrea left the dance floor.

"You should probably go back over there," Mary said. "I think she likes you."

"You don't mind?" Sanch said.

Mary shoved him playfully.

"Go over there," she said.

He attempted to pull Andrea back onto the dance floor, but she refused.

"You dance with me, you dance with me only," she said. That was the first time Sanch had heard her speak more than a few words. For a second he didn't know if it was the mushrooms or if her English was that poor.

"I'll dance with you," he said.

"Do not dance with her in front of me. You like her?"

"Mary? She's just a friend."

"No. You like her."

"I like you," Sanch said and he pulled her onto the dance floor.

Sanch danced with her and sweat soaked his shirt. He took it off and flung it over his shoulder. Andrea wanted to get a drink. Sanch followed her to the bar and bought himself a beer. He offered to buy her one, but she refused and opted for a soda instead. Sanch looked around for Jake and couldn't find him. Andrea found her friend and they talked. Sanch took his beer to the courtyard where Jake and Chico were. Chico offered Sanch a bump of cocaine. Sanch waved it away. They thanked Chico for the offer and went back to the pool tables.

Andrea and her friend joined them. Sanch learned that Andrea was originally from San Jose, an area called La Carpio. She had a mother still living there. Tamarindo

171

seemed to be her only hope at escaping the slums. She had an uncle who managed to make it to California where he picked strawberries and would send money to her and her mother on a monthly basis, which she used to pay rent. She also worked at the pizza place across from the Frenchman's café for a little extra cash. She earned a dollar an hour. She took half of what she earned and sent it to her mother once a month. Her mother was old and sick and couldn't work.

Jake said to her friend, "How much for a blowjob?"

Sanch and Andrea stopped their conversation and looked at Jake.

"I don't know what you heard, but that is no way to talk to a lady," she said.

"Aren't you a…I thought. Am I wrong?"

"I don't know what you heard."

"Sorry. Someone at the last bar told me you were and I was willing to pay. I think you're hot. Can I at least buy you a beer?"

Jake left to get her a beer.

Sanch apologized to her.

"You didn't say it," she said.

"I know, but that was pretty shitty of him. He's a bit messed up tonight."

An older, mustached man came up to her and said he was ready to go. She kissed Andrea on the cheek and told her to be good and left with the man.

"Her boyfriend?" Sanch asked when she left. Andrea shook her head. Sanch had a perplexed look on his face.

"Some things we don't talk about it," Andrea said.

"Where's your friend?" Jake asked holding three beers.

"She had to go," Sanch said.

"Was she still pissed at me?"

"No," Andrea said. "It is okay."

172

They played a few more games of pool and then Andrea said she was leaving.

"You walk me home?" she asked Sanch.

"I was going to play one more game," Sanch said.

"No he wasn't. Let's go," Jake said.

They started down the hill towards town and turned on the street that lead to Largato Surf and Playa Langosta, but before going that far there was a path that went back up the hill. It was a steeper hill than what they had just walked. They could see Expatriado and the discoteca down below from the road they were on.

"I didn't know this road was here," Sanch said.

"It is," she said and smiled coyly. She then held his hand. He turned to look at Jake who walked a few steps behind them. Jake gave two thumbs up. He stuck out his tongue and pretended to lick her ass. Sanch shook his head. Andrea saw Sanch and turned her head to look back at Jake.

"What?" he said.

She turned down another path that was just big enough for a car to squeeze through. It opened up to a two-story house with a wrap-around porch. A pickup truck parked in the front.

"You live here?" Jake said.

"No," she said. They walked past the house and in the back were four huts built in the only trees left in a clearing.

"You live in a fucking tree house?" Jake said.

"It is not a tree house," she said.

"They damn sure are tree houses."

"Are you making fun of me?"

"No. These are cool. I want to live here."

It was a platform about halfway up in the middle of four trees. There was a hammock below the platform and

nothing else. A ladder led to a lift up door in the platform.
She went up first to unlock the door. Jake punched Sanch in
the arm to instruct him to look up. Andrea was wearing a
short skirt and they both looked up as they followed her up
the stairs. A smile crept across Sanch's face before he
ascended the ladder behind her. Jake followed him. Once
through the flip up door, she switched on a lamp. Her house
was a mattress on the floor covered with a mosquito net
hanging from the ceiling. The windows were two holes cut
out the side of the walls. She had a radio, an alarm clock
and a stack of plastic drawers like one would find in a
college dorm room.

"How much to live here?" Jake asked.

She said it was about three hundred a month. But she
received a discount because the owner of the huts also
owned the pizza place and she cleaned his house three
times a week. She was the only long-term resident. The
other huts were used for tourists and usually rented out by
the week for about what she paid for the month.

"Where do you go to the bathroom?" Jake asked. She
pointed out the window to a rickety outhouse between her
place and the next hut on the edge of the forest. Jake went
to the bathroom. She sat on the mattress and Sanch lay
beside her.

"Are you tired?" she asked.

"Little bit." She lay next to him, putting her head on
his shoulder. He stroked her hairline. He and Natalie used
to lie like that for hours.

"Take me to America with you," she said.

"What?"

"I'm joking. Unless you want to."

"I'm moving in with you."

"Okay," she said.

174

"I was just kidding."

"You like it here? Why?"

"Seems everyone's just having a good time, you know."

"Aren't they having a good time in America?"

"Kind of. But it's different here."

"Like what?"

"I don't know. In the States, so much is emphasized on getting a good job and making a lot of money. But then you come here, and you see people who don't have hardly anything and are happier."

"That is because you come here with money. And what little bit you have now is a lot here. But for us who live here, we must do whatever we can to survive. It is not always just having fun. Look at Jennifer."

"Who's that?"

"My friend. She pierced your ears. Sometimes we have to do things we do not like to survive."

"So she is a...you know?"

Andrea didn't answer.

"You don't do that, do you?"

"Why would you ask me such a thing?"

"Sorry."

Sanch sat quiet for a moment.

"You can still rub my hair. I like it," she said.

"Why don't you go to California with your uncle?"

"He is there illegally. When he gets legal, maybe I try. Unless I meet some nice American boy to take me." She looked up at Sanch and smiled.

Sanch didn't answer.

"I scare you."

"No."

"Good," she said.

"Let's see how Jake's doing."

"He is okay."

"Let me check on him." Sanch sat up and looked down the trap door. Jake was in the hammock.

"You all right down there?" Sanch shouted to him.

"Waiting on you. You done yet?"

"Hold on." Sanch shut the door and turned back to Andrea.

"He's ready to get going."

"You love your friend, no?"

"I don't know about love, but we look out for one another." He was sitting on his knees at the edge of her mattress, and she sat up across from him.

"But you don't love him?"

"I'm not gay, if that is what you're asking."

Andrea laughed. "You are silly Sancho. I didn't say you were gay. I asked if you loved him."

"Like a brother, maybe, but that's it."

"You are too afraid of what people think of you."

Jake knocked on the door.

"I guess we're going to have to go. I had fun with you tonight."

"You have to go too?"

"I have the key."

"Give him the key then."

"I have a…" Sanch didn't know what to say. "I just…I should probably go."

"Do you have a girlfriend back home?"

Sanch paused. "No."

"Then can I have a kiss before you go?"

He leaned in to kiss her. Their lips touched, and she stuck her tongue in his mouth, and he pictured her walking up the stairs again and at that moment, Natalie never existed. He slid his hands under her skirt. She didn't resist, and he laid her on her back. He pulled a hand out from underneath and entered her from the front. She adjusted her legs to make it easier. They kissed deeper. He pulled his other hand from underneath and cupped her breasts. They were small. Everything about her was small. He stopped massaging her breast for a moment to pull her underwear off. His cock pushed tight against his shorts.

A loud knock came from under the hatch door before it lifted. Sanch jumped up.

"Hold up. I'm just saying bye," he shouted to Jake. He saw Jake's glazed eyes and heard him laugh.

"Hurry up. Tons of bugs out here." Jake shut the door and went back down. Sanch looked at her.

"Tomorrow?" Sanch said.

"Okay," she said. "You come by my work, maybe?"

"I'll do that." He saw the disappointment in her eyes and kissed her again. "You're beautiful; you know that?" She smiled. The disappointment was gone.

He climbed down the stairs. Jake was swinging in the hammock.

"What the hell are you doing up there? You get a nut yet?"

Sanch shrugged. They walked back towards the road.

"You, at least, kiss her?"

Sanch nodded.

"Bullshit."

"We kissed." After a short pause. "Maybe more." Sanch couldn't contain a smile.

"You grab some tit?"

Sanch nodded.

"Bullshit. You stick a finger in her?"

Sanch didn't answer. "Let's go."

"Bullshit. Let me smell."

Sanch kept walking.

"You stick your dick in her?"

Jake stopped walking.

"Could you have?"

"Maybe," Sanch said and continued on ahead.

"Then why are you leaving?"

"I don't know," Sanch said.

"If you say Natalie, I'm going to punch you in the dick."

"I might've been thinking about Natalie."

"Give me the key and get your ass back up there. Finish the goddamn job."

Sanch took the key out of his pocket and Jake grabbed it.

Sanch turned and ran back to Andrea. She watched through the window. She had left the door open. Sanch saw her lying naked on the mattress and fumbled pulling his cock from his shorts. He hunched on top of her, his shorts still around his ankles. He didn't so much as have sex with Andrea, but more like fucked away the memory of Natalie. He was tired of being bounded by an adolescent obsession. He hated the way she flirted with other guys in front of him without remorse. He hated her tattoo on her lower back. He hated that he fell in love with her. He hated that he had cried for her. He fucked and fucked and Andrea moaned and groaned somewhere between pain and pleasure. To Sanch it was all the same. He opened his eyes and looked at her. Her eyes were tightly shut. In the dim light, he could see the sweat beads on her upper lip as she bit her lower lip. Natalie used to do that. It pissed him off and he thrusted harder. He closed his eyes to shake the image of Natalie and reopened them. Andrea's face morphed back into

Natalie's. When it was Natalie's, he became a beast and acted on primal instinct, not afraid to hurt her. When it was Andrea's face he slowed down, but it wouldn't stay Andrea's face for very long. It shifted back and forth between Andrea and Natalie and after he couldn't hold back any longer he finished inside her.

She kissed him on the cheek, put on a robe and walked down to the outhouse. Sanch pulled up his shorts and closed his eyes.

Like a film being projected on the inside of his eyelids, he watched shapes, patterns and images of flowers exploding and waves crashing and titties bouncing. The new images entered and left quicker than he could register the change, and he lay like that and even heard Andrea return to the bed and throughout the night he didn't know if he was asleep but he never opened his eyes to check. He lay there and continued to lay there allowing his mind to speed through the colors, sounds and words. At times, it seemed as if the entire world was made up of paisley designs. He lay there floating through the abyss allowing his mind to wander and for him to cease having any control of what went in and what left and what stayed. At that moment, the external world didn't exist. It never existed and always existed. The order in which he tried to frame the universe lost its latitude and longitude. The string he had laid through the maze to help him find his way had been cut. Everything that existed and had existed would continue to exist. The world existed in his mind, and it could only exist in his mind because that was all there was, as it was in the beginning, is now, and ever shall be, a world without end.

Chapter 12

A bedside digital alarm clock sounded. Sanch rolled over, trying to get deeper in sleep, enough not to hear the alarm. He was too hung over for work. He felt a kiss on his cheek. For a brief moment, he dreamt it was Natalie and then remembered he no longer wished it to be her.

"Good morning," a voice said.

He tried going deeper into sleep, but it was useless. Through the mosquito netting, he could see Andrea brushing her hair. He took a deep breath of the cool morning air pouring through the windows. A smile formed on his face.

"You woke up," Andrea said. She entered through the mosquito netting and gave him a kiss on the lips. "I need to go to work. Will you walk me?"

Sanch didn't answer.

"Or you can sleep longer."

"No. I'll walk you," he said.

He allowed her to hold his hand as they walked to the pizza parlor. He leaned in to give her a hug goodbye, but she locked her lips to his.

"I get off at two," she said. "You come by my place then?"

"Sure," Sanch said. "If I'm not working."

"I will stop by Lagarto Surf then to see you."

"Okay," he said. "But I might be out surfing, too."

"You are funny," she said and gave him another kiss and went inside the restaurant.

Only a few people walked in the early morning hour. He went for a swim. The Tamarindo cove was placid, cool and refreshing. He swam out and dove deep. He dove a few times like that, each time with his eyes open, the burn from the salt rejuvenating. Before returning to shore, he stopped in the waist-deep water and fell backward, dunking his head under to slick his hair back away from his eyes. He splashed a bit more on his face as he exited.

"Didja fuck her?" Jake asked, sitting on the bench outside the room at the Abrigo waxing a surfboard.

Sanch shrugged.

"Bullshit."

Sanch shrugged again.

"You got laid in a tree house while tripping on mushrooms. You came to the jungle and banged a local chick in a tree house. Do you realize how epic that is?"

Sanch smiled.

"I taught you well."

"You didn't do shit."

"Tell yourself whatever you want. Did you use a condom?"

Sanch shook his head no.

"Did you pull out?"

Sanch shook his head no again.

Jake laughed. "You are going to have a little Sanch running around this place." Jake laughed again.

"That ain't happening," Sanch said.

"It isn't up to you."

"Whatever."

"I was just about to go fix a couple boards."

"Not surfing first?"

Jake nodded to a SUV parked in the courtyard.

"Who's that?"

"Guy named Greg. And guess what?"

"What?"

"I got us a ride to Playa Negra."

"When?"

"As soon as we finish with the boards. He said just wake him when we're ready. Figured we just go in there quick and sand two down real, put the fiberglass and resin on, finish them tomorrow and collect another sixty bucks."

"Let's do it."

They did it and were back at the Abrigo before nine in the morning. Greg cooked in the community kitchen.

"Want a grilled cheese before we head out?" Greg said.

"Hell yeah I'll take one," Jake said.

"How long you been here?" Greg asked.

"We've lived here about a month now," Jake said.

Sanch counted the days on his fingers and stopped at eight and looked over at Jake.

"At least," Jake said.

Greg handed Sanch and Jake a grilled cheese sandwich made with a slice of tomato, a slice of onion and chopped garlic.

Greg told them that he had driven solo from San Diego on his way to visit a friend in Panama, stopping in Tamarindo for a couple of days before continuing on his way.

"So where is Playa Negra?" Greg asked between bites.

"Dunno. We'll stop at the surf shop up the road. A buddy of mine'll give us directions."

Jake ran into Aqua Blue to get directions while Sanch and Greg sat idling out front. Sanch sat in the back seat of the Toyota Land Cruiser.

"Just follow the road past Playa Langosta. We should see signs. It's a good forty minutes or so," Jake said jumping into the passenger side seat.

On the way out of town, Jake spotted Andrea walking along the street.

"Look there," Jake said pointing to her. "Sanch fucked her last night."

"Oh yeah?" Greg said.

"Pull over for a minute," Jake instructed. "See how she liked it?"

"Cut it out," Sanch said.

"Don't you wanna say hey? Least you can do for your baby mama." Jake laughed. He shouted out the window to her. Greg slowed the car, and she approached Sanch's window.

"Where are you going?" she asked him. "I got off work early to see you."

"We're taking a ride to Playa Negra."

"That is pretty far, no?"

"You wanna come?" Jake said. Sanch smacked him on the shoulder. Jake turned around and smiled.

"I would like to. But I have to clean the house today. You have fun. I see you tonight?"

"Probably," Sanch said. She leaned in and gave Sanch a kiss.

"Be careful," she said before they drove off.

"She your girlfriend now or what?" Jake said.

Sanch ignored him.

"What about Natalie?"

"Natalie who," Sanch said. Jake laughed.

"You're about to get trapped," Jake said. "She is probably already thinking marriage, naming your baby. All kinds of shit. Planning on moving to America with you."

"She said that last night," Sanch said. "As a joke though."

Jake laughed. "She wasn't joking, was she Greg?"

"Probably not," Greg said.

"You wanna smoke a joint?" Jake asked Greg.

Before Greg could answer Jake was lighting up.

"No offense, but that tastes like shit," Greg said after taking a toke.

"Don't smoke my weed then."

"Do me a favor," Greg said to Sanch, looking at him through the rearview mirror. "Grab that blue bag behind you." There was a blue bag and five red ones. "In the front pocket," Greg continued, "you'll find a pipe. Then open the main part and pack a bowl, would you?"

Sanch found the glass pipe and then unzipped the bag and saw two-gallon freezer bags filled to the point of bursting with high-quality cannabis. "What do you think?" Greg asked.

"Let me see," Jake said looking back.

Sanch held the bag for Jake to see.

"Holy shit," Jake said. "How much is that?"

"About a pound."

"The ones in the back are filled with the same stuff?" Sanch asked.

Greg nodded.

"That's why you are visiting the friend in Panama?" Jake asked.

Greg nodded again.

"How many's he got back there?" Jake asked. Sanch told him. "What's that? Like fifty grand," Jake said.

"Close. Thirty-five," Greg told him. He allowed Sanch to take the first toke. Sanch gladly obliged.

"How do you get it across the border?" Jake asked.

"My brother works border patrol. I had six red bags when I started. The Mexican border is the only tough one. The others are a breeze."

"You grow it?"

"You bet. Drive down here twice a year. When I come down in May after the next batch is ready, I bring twice as much. Easiest hundred grand I ever made."

"You got some balls," Jake said.

"Sometimes you just gotta go big," Greg said. "But don't you try to go big." He showed Jake a pistol he had under his driver's seat. "It won't work the same for you."

"We're cool. Just wanting a ride to surf."

"I figured that."

The road out of Tamarindo was easily navigable, still gravel but in good shape. Top speed was thirty-five miles an hour. Being only twenty miles away, Negra was still a forty-minute drive. Nothing in Costa Rica could be rushed. They passed Langosta where a few cars were parked by the construction site. They continued on that road for fifteen minutes, passing the pipe back and forth, filling the cab with smoke. Sanch looked out the window, watching pristine, untouched forest pass by him. They came around a bend. Ahead a path led to the beach, while if they continued on the road it would bend once more to the left. They chose to take a break and pulled up next to the two parked SUVs and checked the surf. It was a small beach break. Good solid waves, longer rides than the Tamarindo river mouth and better formed than Grande, but no match for Langosta. They recognized four of the Canadians from the night of the bonfire lounging on the beach.

"Look who it is," Sanch said.

"Is the one you fought here?"

"Yep," Sanch said.

"He won't do anything. They said you were the one instigating that shit anyway."

"Trust me," Greg said. "They won't do shit to you."

"I'm not worried about them," Sanch said.

The Canadians sat in the sand, drinking beer.

"If it isn't the Alabama Boys, eh?" the one Sanch had fought shouted.

"We're from Florida jackass," Sanch shouted back.

"That's the one," Sanch said quietly to Jake and Greg.

"Want me to kill him," Greg said.

"He's not that big of a prick," Sanch said.

"Jesus," Jake said. "You're starting to freak me out a bit."

"Don't be such a pussy," Greg said.

The Canadians smiled and shook hands with Jake, Sanch and Greg.

The one Sanch had fought shook Sanch's hand, "It's all good, my friend. We were drunk."

Sanch shook his hand. "You were drunk," Sanch said. "I barely had a buzz."

That got a laugh from everyone.

"I was a little drunk," Sanch said.

"Shit, you were drunker than Cooter Brown," Jake said. "What's this break called?"

"Avellanes," one said.

"Good little beach break," another said.

"We are heading to Negra," Jake told him. He was told to continue on the road and that they would come across a small town, keep going past that and then start looking for signs that said "Hotel Playa Negra." The hotel overlooked the break. The Canadians stopped to surf Avellanes on their way to another town at the end of the Peninsula called Mal Pais. There was a small surf camp there that was somewhat of a secret spot with good surf and a strange character that ran it. There were majestic waterfalls nearby that were fun to jump off.

"But Witches Rock is the best surf we've had so far," one said.

They told them about their recent trip to Witches Rock, each filling in pieces of the story. They drove there instead of taking a boat, and it was the most horrendous drive they ever had. A creek blocked the road, and they had to park about a mile from the beach and walk the rest of the way. The road wasn't really a road, but a dried-up riverbed, that hadn't completely dried. But even if it had it would still be the worst driving conditions they had ever seen. But the surf was worth the adventure. Perfect head-high barrels that seemed to never end and the view of a giant rock, seventy feet high, jutting out of the water. But none of that could compare to the fact that they were the only ones there.

"To get there just follow the signs to the Santa Rosa National Park," one said.

"Thanks for the info," Jake said.

The Canadians invited them to stick around for a surf, but Jake was too eager to get to Negra.

A herd of cattle slowed their progress just outside of the small town. A man walked behind the herd, and he looked not a day over a hundred. He waved as they passed. Men constructed a wooden ring and bleachers in the field the cattle were herded from.

"Wonder what that's for?" Sanch said.

The town consisted of one crossroad with no stop sign and two crumbling stores. A group of men sat around a barrel playing cards and waved as the truck drove past. Kids, barefoot and shirtless, ran down from the bushes chasing after the vehicle.

After the town, the road deteriorated. Water from the last storm a couple of days ago still muddied the road. The potholes looked more like craters. The road became narrower, with ancient trees lining the path giving less room for error.

"I can't drive through," Greg said. He looked flustered.

"Sure you can," Jake told him. "Just punch it."

As Greg drove through the first big puddle, his back tires spun and instead of going forward the truck skidded sideways. The tires caught before he lost complete control and he made it through. The next one felt like they dropped about three feet and mud covered the windshield and splashed through the windows. Sanch and Jake laughed and hollered like kids on a roller coaster. Greg didn't seem as amused. When they got to a level dry patch, Greg stopped the car and got out.

"I'm turning around," he said. His left knee bled from having hit it on the bottom of the steering column. Jake and Sanch still laughed.

"That was fun as hell," Sanch said. "You all right though?"

"No. I'm not."

"Come on. I'll drive," Jake told him.

"You can't get through this. It's insane."

"I can drive it," Jake said. "I've driven through worse than this."

They convinced Greg to journey forward with Jake driving and Sanch in the passenger seat egging on Jake to drive as erratically as possible while Greg hollered from the back to slow down. The truck slid sideways a few times, close enough to the trees that Sanch and Jake gave each other concerned glances.

"That was too damn close," Greg said.

"It wasn't that close," Jake said.

He then looked at Sanch and mouthed the words, "That was close."

Sanch nodded in agreement.

"You see that sign?" Sanch asked.

Jake said no.

"It's the second time I've seen it. See if it comes up again."

It did. Hand painted and nailed to a tree: "Burgers as Big as your Head."

The road forked and the sign for the burgers pointed left and the one for the hotel pointed right.

"We'll eat there after the surf," Jake said and arrived shortly after at the hotel. As they exited the car and began unstrapping the boards from the roof, they could hear the roar of the surf.

"You hear that?" Sanch said.

"Is that the surf?" Greg said.

"I think so," Jake said.

"That's pretty loud," Sanch said.

"I've never heard a wave sound like that. This might be what I came looking for," Jake said. "And I don't think your board is big enough for this."

"You can use one of mine," Greg told him.

There were more surfers on the beach than in the water. It was the first time they had seen that in Costa Rica. Only four guys were out. About fifteen watched from the shore. People rumored on shore that it was ten to twelve feet with occasionally bigger sets, and it was low tide. The waves were hollower then, seeming to suck dry on the rock bottom. A line of rocks were exposed nearly to the lineup.

"We going out?" Sanch asked.

"Damn right," Jake said.

"I'm going," Greg said.

"Being from California, this is probably just another day, huh?" Jake said.

"No. This sounds like a freight train," Greg said. The weight of the wave pounding on the rock made an unforgiving sound.

"I don't think I'm going," Sanch said.

"Pussy," Jake said.

Jake walked to the beach with his chest puffed more than usual and Greg followed closely behind. Jake asked a man leaning against a tree about the break.

"Extremely shallow. Where that wave is breaking is only waist-deep. Solid rock bottom," the guy said. He lived down south in Jacos and came to Negra just for this swell.

"You already went out?"

"Yeah, man. But it keeps getting bigger."

"You going back out?"

"Probably not today. Wave is fast. Whatever you do, don't fall."

"I don't plan on it," Jake said. He walked to the water. Sanch stayed behind.

"Is that guy putting on a helmet?" Sanch asked, pointing to a guy standing next to Jake.

"I'd wear one if I had one," the Tico said.

Jake and Greg followed behind the helmeted man.

Sanch plopped on the sand next to the Tico, holding the board across his lap.

Sanch watched the guy with the helmet make it out. Jake and Greg looked as if they barely moved. One guy in the lineup dropped in on a wave and disappeared under the breaking lip. He watched the guy get spit out of the barrel and kick out of the wave just before splattering into the rocks.

"They serve food up there?" Sanch asked the Tico. He pointed to the bar attached to the hotel.

"Of course, my friend."

Sanch went to the bar.

"Tequila," he said to the bartender. He took it with him to a table and couldn't believe Jake was still paddling out, slightly ahead of Greg. The waves, although sounding murderous, looked beautiful. He sipped the tequila, holding the burning poison on his tongue, before letting it warm his throat.

Jake and Greg made it to the lineup. On the first set to come through, Jake paddled. It was easily ten feet, maybe bigger. Jake went, never looking like he wouldn't. He stood and just as quickly as he stood the wave covered him up. Sanch held his breath. Without Jake on it to give it perspective, the wave looked less menacing, slower and smaller. Sanch watched, waiting, waiting. The wave rumbled on. Jake shot out with both hands in the air as if he had ridden inside the tube like that. Sanch mimicked him, throwing both hands in the air.

"I've never seen a wave like that," Sanch said to the couple at the table beside him. It was an American guy and girl.

"That guy is good," the girl said.

"That's Jake, my friend. He used to be a pro."

"Have you went out yet?" the guy asked.

Sanch looked at the girl. She was looking at Sanch. "Not yet," Sanch said. "About to. You?"

"No way," the guy said.

Sanch drank the rest of the tequila. "See you guys later," he said and stood. He walked to the shore slowly.

On the walk to the water, he puffed his chest and walked like Jake oftentimes did in a new environment. He turned to look at the others who were watching from the sand and then looked back out at the lineup. His feet touched the cool water. He waded up to his knees. The rock bottom was flat and slimy.

He lay on the board and began paddling. He could feel the current pushing him into the rocks. He paddled harder. The further he went out, the louder the sound of the waves, as if they were warning him. But Sanch didn't listen. His biceps burned with fatigue and he was only halfway out. If he gave up now, he would be washed into the rocks. He pushed on and dug deeper. His feet felt the jagged unyielding rocks, and he heard the fins of his board scrape underneath him. He lowered his head and stroked harder, slowly gaining ground.

Ten minutes later, he reached the lineup. He sat on the shoulder, where the surfers would kick out of the wave at the end of their ride and caught his breath. He watched a few unridden waves go by, waiting for his strength to return before joining the group. He looked back at the shore. It was a long way off. If he tried paddling back in he would either be washed into the rocks or pounded in the impact zone. He made his way over to the guys waiting for the next set.

"Get out of here," Jake said when he saw him. "You're nuts. This is the scariest shit I've ever surfed. Greg hasn't even went yet."

Greg nodded in agreement. "I'm catching one and going in. I'm waiting on the smallest wave, too."

The man with the helmet paddled away getting some distance from the crowd.

"You're going to kill yourself," Jake said.

"This is what we came here for, isn't it?"

Jake laughed his deep belly laugh. "I wanna see this. You know if I'm scared riding these, you'll be shitting bricks."

"Maybe," Sanch said.

"When you're gonna go, you gotta go. There can't be any hesitation. Just make up your mind and do it. And when you go, hold on tight. Did you see the one I rode?"

"That's what made me wanna come out."

"All I remember of it is thinking, don't fall, don't fall, don't fall."

A set loomed on the horizon. The guy with the helmet and two others got into position. Sanch followed Jake and Greg as they got out of the way. The three waves of the set came through, and the three guys who were in position all went, one wave after another. The sound of the waves drowned out the sounds of whoops and hollers.

"You ever heard anything like that?" Jake asked.

Sanch shook his head no.

"How do I get back in?" Sanch said.

Jake laughed. "Only one way."

"This might be the dumbest thing I've ever done."

"Without a doubt," Jake said. "But it took balls just to come out here."

The next set approached.

"This is your set," Jake said. "You gotta go. No fucking around out here."

"I know," Sanch said.

"Good luck," Jake said and paddled away spreading out, getting into position.

The first wave came through and went by unridden. Greg went on the next. Sanch and Jake waited.

"Get ready," Jake shouted. "The next one is yours."

The wave came, and Sanch paddled hard as the peak rose above him. He took one glimpse back and watched it rise higher.

Jake shouted, "Go, go, go."

The wave was on him, and he had already waited too long to stand. He was too far inside. He air dropped down the face, floating briefly above the board before his feet reconnected. The drop was quick. His arms splayed above his head in an attempt to maintain balance while taking the almost two-story plunge. The board slammed on the surface below, his feet still attached to it, but the forceful impact caused him to fall backward. The water moved so fast he didn't penetrate it. Instead he glided, first on his ass and then on his back as the mountain of water broke over him. He was going to get barreled, just not while on the board.

He didn't know how he survived, but he did. The same couldn't be said for the board. During the washing machine tumble the board snapped from the leash and smashed into the rocks; what was left of it waited for him on shore. The current carried him in the direction of the rocks. The local from the tree, seeing Sanch paddle for the wave had already picked up his board and went out to help, reaching Sanch before he made it to the rocks.

Sanch climbed on the large board, and he and the other guy paddled together, his head between Sanch's legs and nearly buried in his ass. Once on shore, Sanch shook the man's hand.

"You saved my life," he said.

The Tico smiled. "Didn't have a choice."

Sanch removed the remainder of the leash from his ankle.

"That was stupid of me," he said to the man.

The man patted him on the shoulder, "Yes," he said before returning to his position under the tree.

A little kid brought up two pieces of the board.

"Keep it," Sanch said and made his way back to the bar where Greg waited. The bartender clapped for him as he sat down. Greg shook his head, but also shook Sanch's hand.

"Beers are on you."

"Sorry about your board."

"It happens."

They had two beers and a tequila by the time Jake joined them.

"Goddamn," Jake said as he walked into the bar. "Let's eat, you fucking lushes. I want a burger as big as my goddamn head."

Back in the truck, Jake said, "I can't believe that wave. That was by far the best session I've ever had. Didja see it? Didn't fall once."

"I fell once," Sanch said from the back seat.

Jake and Greg laughed. "Were you scared shitless?" Jake asked.

"Don't really remember much of it. I just held my breath. As soon as I went for it, I knew I was going over. Didn't have time to think about it. I just kept waiting to hit the bottom, but never did."

"We come back tomorrow, you gonna try again?" Jake asked.

"Not if it's that big."

They followed the signs through a winding, rutted road, heavily wooded on both sides and came upon a cleared land with cabana huts surrounding a large, open-aired thatched-roof bar. There were a few picnic tables, a few hammocks, and one guy sitting at the bar and one really big guy behind it. The name of the place was *Pablo's Picasso—home of the soon to be world famous Burgers as Big as your Head*. The picnic tables were engraved with names and dates of past travelers. Faded surfing pictures and yellowed surfing movie posters plastered the walls. One was signed by Bruce Brown.

"Are you Pablo?" Jake said as they entered.

"If I ain't, someone's fucking my wife," the man behind the bar said.

Jake laughed. "I'm gonna like this guy."

"Sorry. I ain't like that," Pablo said.

Jake laughed again.

"Whatta ya guys want?"

"We saw signs for burgers as big as your head," Jake said.

"You guys look a little scrawny for that."

"You serve fish?" Greg asked.

"Fish? We came for burgers," Jake said to him.

"I'm a vegetarian."

"You came to the wrong place then," Pablo said.

"I'll take a beer," Sanch said.

"Good choice. I bet if I ask what kind, you'll tell me a cold one, huh?"

"Preferably, but it doesn't really matter."

Pablo smiled. "I like him better than I do you," he said to Jake. He then got Sanch a beer from the fridge.

"Yeah, well ask him who was out there getting barreled all day and who got his ass handed to him."

"If you're trying to impress me, it'll take more than those baby waves."

"Baby waves? Did you see it?"

"I surfed it earlier."

"You surf?"

Pablo looked at the other man at the bar and smiled. "You two want burgers. What'll Vegetarian Boy have? A fish sandwich good?"

"That'll work," Greg said.

Pablo went in the back to make the sandwiches.

"He really surfed this morning?" Jake asked the guy down the bar.

The older man nodded. "Look at those pictures over there. That's him. He might have packed on a few pounds, but he still gets out there."

Sanch and Jake looked at the pictures. One was a picture of Pablo from a *Surfer* magazine from the early eighties, and he was riding what could have easily been double the size of what Negra was. Another picture had a caption with it, and it said, "Local North Shore surfer dropping in on a thirty-five footer."

Pablo came back out.

"That really you?" Jake asked.

"About twenty years ago. How do you want your burgers?"

"Medium well," Jake said.

"I only make them medium," Pablo said and went back into the kitchen.

Sanch and Jake played ping-pong. Greg sat in a hammock. They only knocked the ball around a few times, never really getting the volley started before Pablo came back out.

"Hey girls, food is served." They weren't quite medium, but slightly raw. The bottom piece of bread soaked through with the red juice and served like a burger purist preferred—meat and bread, a slice of tomato and a leaf of green lettuce.

"You weren't lying when you say as big as your head," Jake said.

"I don't lie. Stretch the truth on occasion, but don't lie. Two pounds of beef like my cock." He held both hands

197

over Sanch's burger, fingers spread. "See this here. It takes me two hands to jerk-off with. It's molded after me."

"You want us to picture your dick while we're eating?" Jake asked.

"You're on your own with that one," Sanch said. He bit into the burger.

Pablo said to Jake, "You can think of my dick while you eat, if you want."

"You are the older version of me. You're what I'll become if I stick around this place long enough, huh?" Jake said.

"In your dreams, sister."

Greg had finished his fish sandwich and fries while Sanch and Jake were only halfway into the burgers. Neither had touched the fries yet.

"I'm done," Jake said.

"Weren't you the one bragging about what a badass you are and now you can't even finish a burger? That's all right. I'll put you up on the wall of shame. When people ask, 'who is that guy?' I'll tell them some chump who thought he could surf and eat and couldn't do either."

Jake laughed.

Sanch forced down another bite. "Where's the wall of shame?" he asked.

"You guys'll be the first."

"I'm gonna finish mine," Sanch said.

"Go ahead," Jake said. "I'll watch."

"Tell you what," Pablo said, "you finish that whole plate, fries and all, you won't have to pay."

"Deal," Sanch said shoving a fry in his mouth as he chewed burger.

"How about you?" Pablo asked Jake.

"I'll pay."

Pablo, Jake, Greg, and the other patron watched as Sanch slowly downed every bite. At about the forty-five-minute mark, he propped his arms on the bar and rested his head in his hands as he chewed the final remains.

"That's gonna make a helluva turd tomorrow," Jake said.

"Need some water?" Pablo asked.

Sanch nodded. Pablo drew a cup from the faucet and set it down in front of Sanch.

Sanch sipped the water to help swallow the last bits.

"I'm impressed. Not many people ever finish that," Pablo said.

The sun set as they drove back to Tamarindo through the small village where the ring and bleachers were now constructed, and the town was in the midst of a fiesta. Villagers flocked around a makeshift arena and overflowed the seats. The little ones hung on the side of the stands with just enough room to perch on one leg just high enough to see over the crowd.

"Where the hell did all these people come from?" Jake said.

Greg pulled the car off the road.

"Let's go see," Sanch said.

Four men at the base of the bleachers facing the center of the ring pounded a melodic uptempo beat on the conga drums as a group of young girls in brightly ruffled dresses danced center ring. The crowd clapped along. The three Americans jostled for a better view, making their way to the edge of the ring.

The dance ended, and the girls exited.

Greg spoke Spanish to one of the bystanders. The old man put his hands to his head to make horns and scurried under the fence. The onlookers shouted as the old man raced to the center and acted like a bull before exiting.

"A rodeo," Greg said.

The drums started again in a slower tempo and when they stopped bottle rockets whistled into the air and burst. The crowd erupted in cheer. From an opened chute exited a cowboy gripped tightly on top of a ton of a beast.

The bull twirled and bucked, at times lifting all four feet off the ground. The cowboy somehow managed to hold on for what seemed much longer than the American tradition of eight seconds. He then launched off and landing solidly on his feet as if he were a gymnast, hat still firmly on his head. He waved his hat to the crowd. The crowd showered him with flowers. He exited as the bull continued bucking and instead of rodeo clowns entering to lead the animal to the holding stables, the crowd swarmed over and under the fence as if the home team of a college football game had just won the national championship. Instead of tearing down the goal posts, they harassed the bull.

"These people are insane," Jake said.

"Let's go in," Sanch said.

"You guys have fun," Greg said. Sanch ducked through the fence. Jake hesitantly followed. The bull stood on the other side of the ring, yet people were running and falling in every direction. One man snuck up slowly behind the standing bull and jumped on for a quick ride before falling to the ground and rolling underneath the fence to safety. The bull circled the ring in a slow trot. The crowd cheered louder. Sanch and Jake stayed close to the fence. The bull stopped center ring and turned his head, setting his eyes in the direction of the gringos.

"He's coming for us," Jake said. The bull continued his stare-down. The crowd grew restless. Inside the ring, men were hitting the bull in the haunch to try and evoke some emotion. After another thirty seconds or so, the bull feigned a charge which riled the crowd. Sanch jerked but settled down when he saw there was no danger. Jake didn't. He bolted out of the ring, having dropped and rolled under the fence. The drums beat again and the crowd emptied back to the outside of the ring. Sanch turned and saw Jake standing on the bottom rung of the fence peering over the top.

"When did you leave the ring?"

"As soon as that motherfucker looked our way," Jake said. He made room for Sanch to stand next to him.

Four men holding red capes entered the ring.

"That's Jesus," Sanch said.

"Damn sure is," Jake said.

The maintenance man from the Abrigo posted up in front of the bull, shook the cape and when the bull did nothing he shuffled closer. He shook the cape again and the bull charged. Jesus twirled as the bull came within inches of him. The crowd cheered. The bull then went after another man who held a cape and this continued for a few passes and with every charge the bull was closer to the holding stables until Jesus and the three caped men could surround the bull and lead him away as a docile, tired creature.

"Jesus is a maniac," Sanch said. "And you bitched out just when the bull looked at you."

"See them horns," Jake said. "I've had a chick's middle finger up my ass, and that's about as big as I want to take."

"You let a chick finger your asshole?"

"Knuckle deep, baby."

Sanch shook his head and looked away. He then looked back at Jake and shook his head again. Jake laughed.

"Don't knock it."

The next bull bucked wilder than the first and in a matter of seconds the cowboy slammed his forehead into the back of the bull's head and his lifeless body flew through the air. The crowd gasped, but when the cowboy hit the ground he was quick to his feet, and the crowd shouted with delight as he left the ring, waving his hat with one hand and holding a bloody gash with the other. The bull continued his rampage around the ring. The people weren't so quick to join in with this one though. A few brave men ran out, and the bull gave chase, allowing for a few more men to enter. As the bull wore down, more people entered, including Sanch and Jake.

Sanch and Jake made their way to Jesus. He was pleased to see them and gave them both hugs. They could also smell the liqueur on his breath.

"You're crazy," Sanch said to Jesus.

"Yes. Yes," Jesus said. Sanch didn't think he understood. "You try."

"What?"

"You try." Jesus handed the cape to Sanch.

"Yeah. You try," Jake said.

Jesus slung the cape over Sanch's shoulder. Jesus laughed. "Ole, Ole," he said.

"Just like the stove. Now he wants to laugh at us getting horned. No, thank you." Jake climbed out of the ring.

The bull came around and Jesus led Sanch by the arm as they walked alongside the bull. Jesus laid a hand on the bull and continued a tight grip on Sanch's elbow. In the best English he could put together, Jesus informed Sanch that a bull couldn't make sharp turns.

"Come on. Here, here. Touch," Jesus said. He grabbed Sanch's hand and moved it onto the bull.

The crowd cheered. Sanch looked around. He pumped a fist in the air, and the crowd roared with delight.

Jesus then smacked the bull hard and the bull bucked. Sanch ran towards the fence and the crowd laughed.

Another Tico came up behind the bull and grabbed him by the tail. The bull dragged him for a few feet before slowing. Jesus grabbed Sanch by the forearm again and replaced the cape over his shoulder.

"Hell no," Sanch said, trying to pull away.

Jesus laughed.

"I'm sorry. I don't do again." He led Sanch closer to the bull. "The tail," Jesus said. "Grab the tail."

"No," Sanch said.

"Sí, sí. It's okay."

Jesus grabbed it and instructed Sanch to follow. Sanch did. The crowd cheered.

Jesus slapped the bull again. The crowd laughed when the bull reared up, as if it had been pricked with a pin, and kicked his hind legs back causing Sanch to fall backward, unhurt. He looked up from the dusty ground and Jesus motioned frantically for him to stay down. The bull turned and headed for Sanch. Sanch backpedaled in an odd crab walk trying to get up, but Jesus motioned with his hands for Sanch to cover his head. The crowd sucked in air as the bull closed in on him. He balled up, tucked his knees into his chest and covered his head with his arms. The bull horns slammed on either side of him, digging into the ground. Sanch could feel the hot breath and warm snot blowing from the bull's nose while he remained in the fetal position as the bull snorted and pushed him around in the dirt and gravel, trying to find the correct angle to puncture the shirtless torso. Sanch stayed in a tight ball, rolling on the ground for a few long seconds before the bull got bored. Jesus ran to Sanch and helped him to his feet.

Another guy wasn't quite as lucky. A horn caught a pant leg and cart-wheeled him ten feet in the air. He landed hard, but quickly regained his footing and scurried out of the ring.

The bull turned back to face Sanch and Jesus. Jesus grabbed Sanch's wrist and held Sanch firmly, not allowing him to escape. But then the bull charged, Sanch broke free, running to the nearest railing. The crowd reached down and pulled him up. They cheered and shouted and rubbed his head as if he were a celebrity. Two people held him, one by each arm, from under his armpit. Another stretched over top of him gripping onto the waist of his shorts. The crowd's cheers turned from celebration to fear, and Sanch looked over and saw the bull heading for him. He lifted his legs just as the bull slammed into the fence below him. The bull backed away and then rammed the fence harder. Each time getting closer to Sanch's black-soled feet. The bull smashed into the fence two more times before moving on. The crowd dropped Sanch back into the ring where he was bombarded with hugs and handshakes from the men. Jesus patted Sanch on the back and gave him two thumbs up. The crowd exited the ring and the three men with capes walked to the center. Jesus had recovered the cape and offered it back to Sanch, but Sanch waved him off.

"I had enough," Sanch said.

Chapter 13

They drove back to Playa Negra the next morning. Although the dry season had officially started a few days ago, it rained during the night worsening the road conditions. Jake drove and avoided getting bogged down in the muddied potholes.

Passing through the town where the fiesta had taken place, the arena and bleachers were already dismantled and there was no sign that a rodeo had happened the night before except for the bare patch of trampled earth.

Arriving at Playa Negra, the three Americans stepped out to check the surf and within that twenty-yard walk from the parking lot to the beach, two men opened the unlocked doors and took the first thing they saw, which was the blue bag filled with a pound of pot.

The surf wasn't as big, and the buzz on the beach was gone.

"Goddamn it," Jake said. "I should have surfed more yesterday."

The sound of a car speeding away from the parking lot, kicking up gravel, made them turn to look back and notice the hatch of Greg's car open. Greg sprinted to the car.

"They got a bag," Greg shouted.

"Anything else?" Jake asked.

"Get in the car," Greg said.

"We won't catch them," Jake said.

"Get in the car," Greg said again.

From the passenger side seat, Greg reached across under the driver side seat, pulling up a handgun.

"Come on, man. I don't want…" Jake started to say but was cut off by Greg.

205

"You don't need to say or do anything but drive."

Jake sped off after the car.

They approached the section of road full of mud-filled potholes and there they saw the thieves had lost control and ran head-on into a tree. The two thieves sat on fallen branches, seeming to try to overcome the fact they had just wrecked a car in a nowhere town of Costa Rica after having stolen a pound of pot. Jake pulled up short of the mud holes. Greg exited the car with intent, gun aimed at the thieves. Sanch and Jake exited a bit less intent and stood just outside of the open doors. When the two guys saw the gun, they put their hands in the air.

"I'm sorry, man," one said.

"Americans?" Greg said. "You guys are real pieces of shit; you know that? Don't move."

Greg looked in their car, retrieved the bag and pointed the gun back on them.

"You have insurance?" Greg asked. The kid with the pockmarked face nodded his head yes. Greg turned and shot out the front driver's side tire.

Jake and Sanch leaned on the hood of the car and sat watching.

"Go tell him to come on," Jake said.

"I'm not telling him anything," Sanch said.

"I think you assholes should be taught a lesson," Greg said to the thieves.

"I think they've learned it," Jake said. Sanch looked over at Jake.

"What?" Greg said, looking back at Jake.

"Nothing," Jake said. "They've earned it. Earned a lesson."

Greg turned back to the thieves.

"There is nothing we can do now," Pock Mark said.

Greg aimed the gun at the kid.

"Hey," Sanch shouted. "Let's just go."

"We're going," Greg shouted back.

"Thank you," Pock Mark said.

Greg stepped closer to Pock Mark and placed the gun under his jaw and looking at the other, who was now crying without any reservations, and asked: "Whose idea was it to break into my car?" No answer. Greg turned the gun on the one who was crying. "Was it yours?"

Snot bubbles formed and popped as he shook his head no. Greg quickly lifted a foot to Pock Mark's face sending him backward. "So it was yours," he said. He stood over Pock Mark and aimed the gun into his face. The kid squirmed. Blood dribbled from his nose. Greg stood over him for a few seconds before turning toward the car and saying, "Let's go."

"You drive," Jake said to Sanch through clenched teeth.

Sanch shook his head no and turned around.

Jake stared out into the woods as Greg got closer.

Greg laughed.

"Relax guys. You didn't think I was really going to hurt them, did you?"

Sanch nor Jake responded or looked at him.

"I just wanted to scare them. Punk kids come to a poor foreign country and want to steal from people? Hopefully, they learned a lesson."

Greg got in the driver seat. As he drove by the thieves, Greg waved to them. One was wiping the blood from his face. The other one, wiping the snot with the back of his hand, waved back.

"Might want to pick up the speed," Jake said. "Or we are going to get stuck."

They did, not even ten feet from where the other car was.

"Unfuckingbelievable," Greg said. He pressed the gas some more, spinning the wheels. Jake looked back at Sanch. Sanch's face started to distort in an attempt not to laugh.

"You're just digging us deeper," Jake said. The front passenger side tire was nearly buried to the bumper.

A few yards off an old man watched as he leaned against the hood of a red pickup truck.

"How long as he been there?" Sanch said.

"What do we do now?" Greg said.

"Find some wood to place under the tires," Jake said.

It didn't help. The two thieves still hadn't moved from their spot.

Sanch and Jake then stood behind the truck to give it an extra push. The back tires spun fiercely, but the truck remained stuck, and Sanch and Jake were covered in thick globs of the wet, brownish-red clay. Sanch couldn't control his laughter anymore. Jake quickly followed. They still pushed, mud flew, and they laughed. Jake fell into the mud, and Sanch had to stop pushing so he could laugh harder. Watching what was going on through the rearview mirror, Greg jumped out, "I'm glad you two idiots are finding this so funny."

Greg looked over at the two thieves. "You think you could help?"

They did. Now all four pushed and mud splattered. Sanch and Jake weren't much help. They laughed more than pushed.

The old man slowly walked up to them with a thick rope, told Greg to stop spinning the tires and tied the rope to the car's frame. He then backed his truck up, attached the rope to his truck and pulled them free. Greg shook his hand and thanked him, placing two twenties in his hand. Sanch and Jake got back in the truck, covering the seats with mud.

"Wonder what the other guys are gonna do?" Sanch said. Greg didn't answer.

Jake then said, "Playa Negra is the other way."

Greg didn't answer him.

When they got back to Tamarindo, the mud had dried on Sanch and Jake's bodies and cracked when they moved. They took the boards from the roof of the car and Greg, without even a goodbye or nice to meet you, went into his room, got the rest of his belongings, packed up and left.

"Guess he had enough of us," Jake said.

A new guy at the Abrigo walked out from one of the rooms. "What happened to you guys?"

Jake told him the story.

The new guy told them his story. He was Richard from Oregon. He had just spent two weeks in Belize and then flew to Costa Rica to stay another two weeks. He would start grad school in the spring.

"We met some chicks that were doing the same thing," Jake said. "A lot of college kids over here."

"Why not? It's the only time I'll have the extra cash with student loans."

"Right on. Wanna go surfing, Dick?" Jake said.

"The name's Richard. I don't go by Dick."

"No shit. Most people wouldn't. But with a name like Richard, you become Dick. That's just the price you gotta pay. Thank your parents."

"I don't like it. Just call me Richard. I'll go surfing, but I don't have a board, and I've never surfed."

Jake let him borrow one.

209

They stood at the edge of the river mouth. Tamarindo Beach had started becoming more crowded as the dry season went on and every day there seemed to be just a few more people. The small knee to waist-high waves filled with first-time surfers. Richard asked why they weren't surfing that break. Jake pointed across the river. The waves easily double the size of Tamarindo's break. Only four guys were out. The sun was directly overhead. Richard swiped a streak of pink lotion on his nose and cheeks and kept his tee shirt on.

"That's what Sanch looked like the first couple of days here," Jake said.

Sanch touched his brown shoulders, "Yeah, I've gotten used to the sun now."

"Skin cancer is a serious concern," Richard said.

"I hear ya, Dick," Jake said and then jumped in the river and started paddling across.

"What about crocodiles?" Richard asked.

"It's cool," Sanch said. "We've been surfing this almost every day. There isn't any in here. It's the ocean anyway."

"What's that have to do with anything?"

"Alligators live in freshwater."

"I said crocs. You never heard of salt water crocodiles?"

"Get outta here," Sanch said. "Alligators don't live in salt water."

"Crocodiles do. You haven't been to the restaurant down the road from where we're staying. People feed their scraps to the crocs. It's on this river."

Sanch looked out at Jake, who was now more than halfway across.

"Come on pussies," Jake shouted.

Sanch looked at Richard, shrugged his shoulders and dove in. Richard stood a couple of seconds and then did the same. When they were halfway across, Jake shouted that he saw something swimming behind them.

Richard put his head down and paddled harder. Sanch stopped to look. He dangled his feet down, sitting up on his board so he could get a better view. "You fucking with me?" he shouted to Jake.

"No."

Sanch felt something bump his leg. "Shit!"

Jake laughed. Sanch flailed around in an attempt to paddle harder, but he panicked and didn't move much. He felt it again and stopped paddling. He tried to balance himself on his belly, lifting his arms and legs out of the water. It did no good on the short board. He was nearly submerged. Jake continued laughing, and now Richard had made it to the other side, and he also found Sanch's trauma a bit humorous. Sanch felt it again and thought it strange that he hadn't been bit yet. He looked back and realized it was his leash bouncing off his leg.

"Is there really a restaurant like that?" he asked when he made it to the other side.

"Yeah. I'm not kidding. There really are crocs in that water. I don't know how often they make it the ocean, but they're in there. You guys want to check it out tonight?"

Sanch and Jake both said, "Hell no."

After the surf, they went to eat. This time at a new place, the one Sanch had noticed when they first arrived that was up the hill on the beach next to Chico's with the hand-painted sign: El Pescador. Richard had heard about it from his travel book.

"You guys never wear shoes or shirts?" Richard asked on the way there. He was wearing jeans, a long-sleeved tee shirt, and hiking boots.

"The mosquitoes carry all kinds of diseases," Richard said.

They walked along the beach towards Chico's, and when they got to the abandoned boat, they turned up the path and headed underneath the wooden archway. The only part of the restaurant that was covered was the kitchen and a pool table that sat off to the side of the picnic tables. Two older men stood at the window drinking beers and three men playing pool. No one ate. They each ordered beers instead of food and went to get in on the pool game.

Sanch then ordered a tequila and asked about food. There wasn't a menu, just the special of the day. Chicken on the grill with rice and beans. Sanch ordered it. Jake and Richard decided to wait and eat somewhere else, probably Pedro's. Sanch was given his tequila and also a shot glass filled with some kind of food. He took both back to the pool table.

"You gonna eat that?" Jake asked. "You don't even know what it is?"

"I got the bubble guts. I need something in my stomach until the chicken is ready."

One of the locals, a man of about forty, thin and strong, barefoot and shirtless, as were the others, and with cut-off jean shorts, made a motion to Sanch to eat up and then the rest of the men laughed.

"See how they're laughing. Don't be stupid, put that shit down," Jake said.

"My dad once ate monkey brains in Vietnam because it was disrespectful to turn down food offered to you," Sanch said.

"This isn't Vietnam," Jake said.

"It's ceviche," Richard said. He spoke a bit of Spanish. "A kind of seafood salad. I've had some before. It's fish or some other seafood cooked in lemon or lime juice. It's usually really good."

"My stomach's feeling weird. I think I'm just hungry."

Richard told them that. They laughed some more and then said something to Richard to translate.

"They said it'll clear you out."

"That means it's gonna fuck you up," Jake said.

"I need something to clear me out. I ain't shit since I ate that two-pound burger. I got two pounds of beef that needs to come out."

"You ain't shit yet today?" Jake asked.

Sanch shook his head no and then drank the tequila and ate the ceviche. The men cheered and gave Sanch high-fives and patted him on the back.

"How was it?" Jake asked.

"Pretty good. Bit spicy, but good."

One of the locals asked if he liked it. Sanch said yes. The man went to the bar and brought back five more, one for each of them. Sanch and Richard ate theirs, as did the three locals. Jake declined and ignored the ridicule from the men.

"We'll see who's laughing when you two are shitting all night."

The chicken came out. Sanch ate while standing up, watching Jake shoot pool. They wouldn't allow Jake to play pool as he normally did. They had their own rules. The balls were racked normally, but the one ball and the fifteen ball had to be directly behind the eight ball. The one ball was on the left and fifteen on the right, if looking at it from the breaker's point of view. The one and fifteen had to be the last two balls to be hit in before the eight, and they had specific pockets they had to go in. The one had to be sunk into the left corner pocket opposite the side that was used for breaking and the fifteen had to be sunk into the right corner pocket, again on the opposite side of the table. If the one or fifteen were sunk out of order, it was a loss, just like if the eight ball was sunk before all balls had been shot in. The new rules put Jake at a disadvantage, and he lost the first three games.

"Never thought I'd see you suck at pool," Sanch said.

Jake's only highlight came when he jumped the cue ball over another. He didn't make the shot, but the locals were thrilled. It was as if they had just seen a magic trick. He showed them how to do it.

Sanch's stomach continued to give him trouble, and he started to sweat. His stomach wrenched into a knot and doubled him over in agony. "I'm gonna have to go," he said after a while. Jake thought it was funny, "Just go take a shit and come back."

"I hope that's all it is," Sanch said.

The bathroom at the El Pescador wasn't as bad as Chico's but bad enough where he didn't want to sit. He hovered over the toilet and a foul liquid squirted out onto the back of the toilet seat. He had to go back to the hotel. This wasn't just a quick shit. This was going to be something fierce.

He went back to the pool table. "I've got to go," he said. Jake laughed.

Halfway back he had to start running and made it to the Abrigo, sweating worse than before and still clutching his stomach in pain. He sat on the toilet and released some pressure, but his stomach still ached. It was far from over.

He lay down and was so hot he couldn't fall asleep until he had taken off his shorts and gotten completely naked.

He then woke up with a pain like a gutshot from a shotgun. He noticed Jake was still out as he ran to the bathroom, sitting just in time. The pain was so intense it caused him to vomit and not having anything to vomit into and being in such pain as not to care he let it spew onto the bathroom floor. He continued firing from both ends for what seemed like an hour. When everything had emptied, he collapsed onto the sordid floor. He was too weak to move and decided he would try to sleep a little to regain strength and clean up before Jake arrived. He couldn't do it. He laid, crumbled and defeated, a broken mess, still with unearthly pains running through his abdomen, sweating and dry-heaving and occasionally a rancid liquid squirting from his anus. Helpless. The pain continued. He shivered uncontrollably, unlike nothing he had ever felt before.

He fell asleep in the squalid state, not only physically destroyed, but mentally exhausted as well from the oncoming dehydration.

He laid like that in an in-between stage of sleep and not sleep.

Jake shouted, "What the hell's that smell?" Sanch lifted his head enough to see Jake standing over him with a pillow smothered over his mouth and nose. The look in his eyes let Sanch know how bad the scene was.

"What the fuck's wrong with you?"

Sanch tried to say something, anything, but only gurgled. He had lifted his head too far and again felt his stomach contract, the bile rising from the bottom of his bowels and spewing out his mouth, an acidic stench and taste as if he had shit from the wrong end. He squirmed on the floor, the pain unbearable.

"Jesus," Jake said. He still hadn't removed the pillow from his face. "You're not all right, are you?" Sanch shook his head, a line of spittle connecting him to the slopped floor. "Are you dying?"

Sanch nodded.

"I think I'm gonna puke," Jake said. "Can you stand?" Sanch laid still, no longer able to look up.

"Goddamn it," Jake said. "I'm not doing this. I'm your friend and all but this is too much." He left Sanch in the bathroom. Sanch stayed that way.

"Goddamn it," Jake said walking back into the bathroom with a shirt wrapped around his nose and mouth. He threw a sheet over Sanch and then grabbed him underneath his armpits and dragged him into the shower and turned the water on. Jake left Sanch lying on the shower floor for a second, returning with the other bed sheets. He soaked the sheet in the running water and cleaned up the floor the best he could, rinsing it out in the shower Sanch still lay in. After Jake had the bathroom as clean as he could get it, he took the sheet outside. He came back to Sanch.

"Come on. You gotta help me out a bit," Jake said to him. He put the bar of soap in Sanch's hand and helped him work a lather. He then stood back and couldn't help but laugh as he watched Sanch try to wash himself while still lying on the floor.

"You look like you're dying," Jake said.

"I am," Sanch managed.

"Clean enough," Jake said. He turned off the water and lifted Sanch's naked, deadweight body from the shower floor. "You owe me bigtime." Sanch tried to get his footing and walk, but Jake mostly carried him. He laid him on the bed.

A loud knock woke Sanch early the next morning. He opened his eyes and watched Jake open it and walk out. He heard Richard mention the smell. He heard Jake explain everything that happened the night before. Sanch then felt his stomach bubbling again. He struggled but was able to get to the bathroom on his own. What felt like liquid razor blades shot out from where it should have been solids. Sanch struggled back to the bed, collapsed on it and fell back asleep. After a few minutes, Jake and Richard came in. They both covered their noses.

"You shit on the floor again?" Jake asked.

Sanch opened his eyes and shook his head.

"Richard wanted to see how bad you were. We could hear you outside. Can smell it, too." Richard nodded in agreement. Jake laughed. "Taylah's coming in to clean the bathroom and change our sheets. Poor girl."

"Have you drank anything?" Richard asked. "You need to, or you can get dehydrated. And I got some medicine that might stop you up. I had pretty bad diarrhea in Belize and it worked for me, but I wasn't in that bad of shape. You probably got dysentery or something."

Sanch didn't answer.

"Told you not to eat that shit last night," Jake said.

"It wasn't from that," Richard said. "Me and the other guys ate the ceviche and are just fine. This is either a virus from mosquitoes or a bacterial infection from the water you drank at Pablo's. Let me get that medicine."

"Bad time for you to get sick. Richard's renting a car today. We're gonna drive to Witches Rock."

"When?" Sanch mumbled. He clutched his stomach in pain.

"We're going to get the car right now."

Richard came back with the anti-diarrhea medicine and a bottle of Gatorade. "Take this and force yourself to drink. Even if you puke and poop it out, keep drinking. At least, you get some liquid in you. That's the most important thing. Dehydration will kill you before the infection. Just take small sips, don't chug it."

"We'll be back to check on you before we leave for Witches Rock," Jake said.

They left to get the car, and Sanch took the medicine and drank a bit of the cherry flavored Gatorade and within a matter of minutes was back on the toilet where a mucousy stream fell from his rectum. He then crawled back to bed and fell back asleep.

Jake came in with Richard and Andrea following behind. "Look who we saw walking down the street," Jake said.

Andrea covered Sanch's naked body with the sheet and kissed him on the forehead and sat on his bed, stroking his sweaty hair. "Told her you were sick and she wanted to see you. Said she'll watch over you while we're gone."

Sanch smiled. "I'm going with you."

"What?"

"I wanna go. I want to see Witches Rock."

"I will make you vegi-table soup and take care of you," Andrea said. "You can stay at my place."

"I want to go. Even if I don't surf, I want to see it."

"Then get your ass in the car."

"Are you sure?" Andrea asked. Sanch nodded. She kissed him again on the forehead. "Come see me when you get back? I've not seen you in a couple of days. You don't like me anymore?"

"I like you plenty," Sanch said. "I'll see you when we get back."

"If he gets back," Jake said. "The way he looks, not sure he'll make until tonight."

"Do not talk like that, Jake," Andrea said. She kissed Sanch on his forehead again before leaving.

Jake put his surfboard on the top of the car and then came back, threw Sanch his shorts and helped him walk to the car. Sanch lay across the back seat of the rented RAV4.

"Bring me a couple of rolls of toilet paper," Sanch said. He took a small sip of the Gatorade and closed his eyes.

They drove north out of Tamarindo hitting paved road after a few miles, unlike when they headed south to Langosta and Negra where it was dirt road the entire drive. Richard had a map of how to get to Santa Rosa National Park. They followed State Road 166. They passed many smaller villages than Tamarindo, laughing when they passed one named Filadelfia. Sanch could only muster up a sheepish smile as he lay with his head bouncing against the window. After about two hours of driving they made it to a real city, Liberia, which was on the Pan-American Highway, the sixteen thousand or so miles that connected Alaska to Ushuaia. There they stopped for breakfast at the first place that looked like it served food. They were the only ones in the diner. Sanch could feel his bowels bubbling. While Richard and Jake ordered the full meal of eggs, rice and beans, toast, orange juice and coffee, Sanch put his head down. The lady who took their order asked if he was ill and Richard told her. She suggested Sanch try to eat some toast and said she would bring him some orange juice. Before the food or drinks came out, Sanch headed to the bathroom. Jake and Richard laughed as he came back.

"You're a fucking warrior," Jake said with a mouth full of eggs. "I would've stayed in bed and let Andrea take care of me."

Sanch couldn't laugh. He headed back to the bathroom without even taking his first bite or drink. He came back out, and Richard and Jake were nearly finished. Sanch took three bites and called it quits. He forced down half the cup of orange juice.

"You still puking?" Jake asked.

Sanch shook his head. "Just the squirts now. It won't stop."

They got back in the car and drove another twenty miles or so going through a town called Potrerillos and entering the park through the Santa Rosa station. From there they followed a dirt road which two weeks ago was a riverbed. The ranger warned them that some parts were impassable and didn't advise they try to make it to the beach.

"Maybe we should turn back," Richard said.

"Keep this thing moving," Sanch said. "If I die, I'm dying at Witches Rock."

"You heard the man. Dying surfer's last request," Jake said.

The first five miles started rather nicely. Then the ruts began getting deeper, and the truck bottomed out on a few.

"I think we should walk the rest of the way," Richard said.

"You bought the insurance, right?" Jake asked.

"I did. But that doesn't mean we can destroy the car."

"That's exactly what it means," Jake said.

"Keep moving," Sanch shouted from the back.

Jake laughed.

"What happens if we get stuck out here?"

"Don't you wanna surf Witches Rock?"

"I think it is way more important for you two than for me."

"Take my shitty ass to Witches Rock," Sanch said.

Jake and Richard looked back at him. Sanch lay across the back seat with his eyes closed and clutching his stomach in pain.

"You heard the man," Jake said.

"You drive it then," Richard asked.

"Bet your ass I will," Jake said.

Sanch managed a snort that could have been mistaken for a chuckle.

Jake continued the drive as if they were still on paved road. Richard couldn't help but yell for him to slow down. Jake barreled through, coming to his first stop at a crossing of flowing water, five feet wide.

"This is what the Canadians were talking about? Doesn't look too bad. How deep you think that is?" Before anyone answered, he had the pedal down and rushed towards it. The impact was sudden, and water splashed over the car and through the windows. The engine sputtered. Sanch fell off the back seat onto the floorboard.

"Just stop it," Richard said. "We can't make it through."

But Jake kept it going and made it through with water starting to seep under their feet. He then stopped the car to regain his composure.

"You guys are insane," Richard said. "Get out."

"What're you talking about?" Jake asked.

"Get out. I'm driving. You're going to get us stuck out here."

"Come on. I knew it was gonna be fine."

"Get out."

Jake did. He looked at Sanch. Sanch pulled himself off the floor and onto the back seat.

Richard sat in the driver seat, but before they could continue, Sanch stepped out and let loose in the woods.

Jake laughed. "Make sure you wipe good. I don't want that smell lingering in here."

Sanch flashed him his middle finger. He shuffled his way over when he finished and lay down again in the back seat.

"You gonna make it?" Jake asked.

"I don't know," Sanch said.

Richard drove with extreme caution for about twenty minutes, stopping when he overlooked a four-foot-deep dry ditch.

"Looks like a small creek started to form here during the last storm," Richard said.

"I can make it," Jake said.

Without looking up, Sanch said, "Yep. We can make it."

Richard let Jake drive.

Jake slammed the bumper into the rock bottom with such force Richard's knee broke the glove compartment door, and Sanch tumbled back onto the floor. Going up, Jake, being inexperienced himself but driving with confidence enough to fool Richard, attempted it on an angle which wasn't the best way to do it. The meter on the dashboard that swivels in liquid to warn when the truck is at a dangerous angle showed them that they were at a dangerous angle. Richard brought that to his attention.

"It's all right," Jake said. "Those things aren't accurate."

To make it back up, he pressed the pedal to the floor while in first gear, revving the engine until the RPM needle reached red.

"See. I know what I'm doing," he said.

Jake looked back at Sanch and Sanch flashed him a smirk.

The drive remained more than bumpy for the next mile or so until Jake stopped at a full rushing river, fifteen or twenty feet across.

"Shit. This is what the Canadians were talking about," Jake said. "Good news is that it means we're only about a mile from the beach. We try this one, too?"

"I can't walk a mile," Sanch said.

"Here we go then," Jake said.

Richard buckled up, held on tight and closed his eyes. Sanch sat up and gripped onto the oh-shit bar overhead.

As soon as the front end hit the water the car stalled. It was much deeper than they had expected. Jake started the car again and tried to go in reverse to no avail. He then tried to go forward again. It moved about two feet before the truck stalled once more and water flooded through doors.

Jake laughed.

"How is this funny?" Richard said.

"It's kind of funny," Sanch said.

Richard tried opening the door, but the water held it shut. He climbed out the window and waded back to the road.

The water flooded to Jake's knees as he continued his attempt to restart the car, pumping the gas pedal under water. Because of the steep angle in which they had gone down, the back seat remained dry. Somehow the car came alive. Jake suggested that he and Richard get in front and push while Sanch try to drive it in reverse.

That didn't work, and the engine died.

"What are we going to do now?" Richard said. "It's probably a ten-mile walk back to the ranger station."

"It's probably only a mile to the beach," Sanch said. "I know what I'm doing."

"I'm going with Sanch," Jake said and untied the boards from the roof.

"You can't be serious," Richard said.

Sanch found a tree to hold on to and squirt out a little foulness.

"Let's just go surf real quick and then I'll walk with you," Jake said.

"Bye," Richard said and started walking back.

Sanch sat on the ground and laid his head in the dirt. Jake waited to see if Richard was going to continue walking. He did.

"Wanna go see Witches Rock?" he said to Sanch.

"How are we gonna cross the river?"

"I'll figure something out."

"I'll be here."

Jake walked along the river and came back shortly after.

"There is a fallen tree that crosses the river," Jake said. Jake picked up his board and began walking. Sanch grabbed his toilet paper and a bottle of Gatorade and a surfboard and followed along.

"What are you going to do with a surfboard?"

"If I die, put me on it and push me out to sea."

They pushed through the brier bushes and spider webs to the fallen tree. With both their legs scraped, they walked across the wobbly makeshift bridge on their way to find the famed Roca Bruja as it was known to the locals. Once back on the road, they turned to look at the car stuck in the river, the muddy water swirling by it.

"We fucked that car up," Jake said.

On the walk, Jake pulled ahead when Sanch stopped for a squat.

"I'm not waiting on your shitty ass," Jake said.

Sanch grunted as his insides shot out. Then managed to say, "Don't be a dick."

Jake laughed. "Hurry up."

Sanch couldn't hurry up. Instead, he had to sit and rest a minute. He was short of breath, and his limbs were shaky and weak.

"I'm not feeling good," he said.

"I know. You're being a hell of a trooper."

The forty-minute walk was the same the entire way. Dirt road surrounded by trees. The most untouched, unspoiled piece of nature either had ever walked through. They passed a small station with boarded windows about ten minutes from the beach. A sign in front said it was some sort of research center.

The dirt road opened up to a pristine beach scene. Hundreds of birds scattered as they walked out. There were no footprints on the entire beach.

"Look at that thing," Jake said pointing to the giant rock jutting out of the surf.

"How did it get like that?" Sanch said.

"No clue, but I'm about to surf the hell out of it."

Jake sprinted towards the water.

Sanch looked for a shaded piece of sand under a bush and dropped the board and sat out of the heat, the black sand unbearably brutal in the afternoon sun.

He lay in the sand and watched Jake catch a wave. It wasn't big and adrenaline-filled like Negra or as shifty and fast as Grande. It was a playful wave, meant to be ridden for as long as his legs could stand. It wasn't meant to prove anything, to one's self or to anyone else. It seemed to exist for the sole purpose of providing pleasure to those who sought it out.

Sanch fell asleep after a bile-filled bowel movement.

The haunting darkness returned, but he was an adult now. The fear he had as a child was gone. He looked over at his father and his brother and the other men.

"You coming this time," his father said. His father held out his hand for Sanch to follow.

"I can't," Sanch said. "I don't know what we are fighting for."

"I know," his father said.

"I don't know either," his brother told him.

"Don't you think I'm afraid, too? Hell, we're all afraid," his dad said. "But we do as we are told."

"It's not about being afraid," Sanch said. "I just don't know what we are fighting for."

"We don't either," his father said. "But we said we would no matter what. So we've gotta go."

They were gone and Sanch turned to the frightening, floating blackness, the one that he couldn't face as a child. Instead, he began to laugh at it. As he laughed, the dark void transformed into an unknown face and then into his father's face floating above the waves. His father laughed at him, but he laughed too. It wasn't a laugh of humor. It was a mix of inanity and confusion. It then turned into his brother's face, and then into Natalie's, into Jake's and finally into himself. And he sat there laughing at himself and at the absurdity of it all.

"Wake up," Jake shouted.

Sanch opened his eyes. The sun was setting into the ocean.

"You were laughing in your sleep."

Sanch gurgled something.

"Why does it stink around here?"

"Sand's hot."

"What?"

His throat was parched, and he swallowed the best he could. "Sand was too hot to go anywhere else."

"That's disgusting. Let's go. Hope Dick found some help."

Sanch rose to his feet and steadied himself with the help of a nearby tree. Jake walked up the path. The sun set fast into the Pacific Ocean, creating a wonderful hue of purples. Sanch turned and looked at Witches Rock, glad that he had not died, although he had begun preparing himself just in case.

Four tents had been set up at the research center when they returned to it. Richard swung in a hammock and stood up as he saw them walking up. Others sat in camping chairs around a fire.

"Hey, Dick. How's the truck?" Jake said as he approached the camp.

Everyone turned and watched as Sanch struggled to the camp.

One girl asked if he was all right.

"I think he's dying," Jake said.

Sanch made it to the hammock and plopped down, closing his eyes.

"Has he gone to a doctor?" someone asked.

"Drink some water," Richard said to Sanch and handed him a bottle of water.

Sanch poured a little into his mouth.

"Where's the truck?" Jake asked.

"Luckily, I saw these wonderful people coming up the road before I walked all the way back. They were able to pull me out. They thought we were crazy for even attempting the crossing. It's somehow good to go. Started right up."

Jake went and talked to the campers. Sanch stayed in the hammock until Jake told him they were leaving.

"The four chicks are following us back to Tamarindo. They need to get some things. The dudes are staying here. The girls are staying the night, probably going to get a room at the Abrigo and party with us tonight," Jake said.

"Great. I'm dying."

Jake laughed. "If you don't die tonight, we'll find you a doctor in the morning."

They walked back to the cars in the dark with only one flashlight between them. Jake held it and led the way. Sanch brought up the rear, about fifteen yards behind the rest of them, barely able to make out the bouncing light up ahead.

Driving back, Jake could feel something wasn't right with the car. There was a strange thumping noise coming from underneath it. He stopped to check it out and the girl who drove behind him said it looked like the car was driving sideways. Richard got out taking a look as well. Sanch stayed in the back seat, not quite sleeping, but not fully awake.

"We broke the axle," Jake said, laughing as he got back in the car. Richard didn't find it funny. "Relax. You have insurance."

After a few more minutes of driving, Jake said, "Can you believe we broke the axle?" Sanch found it a little funny but wasn't well enough to laugh.

"I think I'm getting worse," Sanch said.

"Just keep drinking water," Richard said. "No matter what—just keep drinking it."

Sanch took a few big gulps.

Back on paved road, but still a couple of hours from Tamarindo, Sanch sat up from the back seat. "Pull over," he said.

"Why?" Jake asked.

"Just pull over."

"Gotta shit again?" Jake asked.

"Yes, goddamn it. Pull over already."

Jake pulled over, and Sanch didn't have time to run down the ditch away from the car. Instead, he held onto the door handle of the back seat and squatted. Jake laughed as did Richard this time. Sanch hadn't thought about the girls following them until they pulled up alongside the truck, having seen Sanch in the headlights.

"Keep going," Sanch shouted while he squirted hot liquid from his butthole. "Tell them to keep going," he shouted to Jake.

Jake couldn't stop laughing.

"Is he okay?" the one in the passenger seat asked. "What's wrong with him?"

Jake could only nod. Richard was in the passenger seat with his shirt pulled up to cover his nose and laughed too.

"Just go," Sanch yelled to the girls.

"Oh my God," he heard one girl say. "I think he's taking a shit."

Jake slapped the steering wheel and stomped his feet, not knowing what else to do because laughing hysterically was not enough.

The girls drove off.

Finally, Jake slowed his laughing and said, "Great way to pick up girls there, Shitty."

"Fuck you. I'm dying. I think I just shit out my intestines."

Jake laughed some more. "Hurry up. You're stinking up the car."

"I'm shitting slime. I've never shit slime before."

"You're getting dehydrated," Richard said. "You have to keep drinking, even if it comes right out. Tomorrow, you have to eat, even if you throw it up. Force it down."

Sanch reached in to get the remainder of the toilet paper to clean up before climbing into the back seat to sleep the rest of the way.

Chapter 14

"You gonna sleep all day?" Jake said.

Sanch barely lifted his eyelids.

"I've already went for a surf, fixed a couple of boards and got another fifty bucks, and ate some food."

Sanch still didn't say anything.

"Damn, you look bad. You need a doctor for real, don't you?"

Sanch nodded. His cheeks had hollowed, and his eyes were sunken.

"Richard hadn't taken the car back, yet. Let me see if I can borrow it. Tried to get him to drive back to Negra, but he's scared to drive it. We fucked it up bad yesterday."

Sanch closed his eyes again.

Jake left and came back shortly after.

"Talked to the Australian chick. She said there's a doctor up the road. An herbal doctor, that's all they've got around here. Said after the Best Western and before the hardware store there're a few apartments there. I never noticed them, but she said a doctor lives there. Let's go."

"I don't want to get up," Sanch said.

"You're just going to lay here and die then?"

Sanch nodded and tried lifting his head and then rested it back on the pillow. "I think that is best."

"Fucking A, man." Jake bent down and scooped him off the bed. Richard was outside and opened the back door and helped get Sanch in there.

They shut the door, and Richard said, "He looks really bad."

"I know," Jake said. "I'm starting to get a bit worried."

The apartments weren't much of apartments. They looked slightly cleaner than the Abrigo but built in the same fashion. It was a one-story complex with only five apartments. A lady out front hung laundry on a line. Jake pulled in fast and jumped out, frightening the lady.

"Doctor. A doctor live here?" Jake yelled. She looked at him blankly. He led her to the car and showed her Sanch in the back seat. Sanch was asleep. She understood and took Jake to the last apartment. An elderly man opened the door. He looked about ninety. Shirtless, shoeless, torn jeans.

"You a doctor?" Jake asked.

The man nodded.

"It's not for me. My friend in the car is really sick."

The man nodded again. "Bring him in."

Jake laid Sanch on a small cot and Sanch drifted in and out of consciousness.

"He's been shitting for three days now. Can't eat or keep any liquid down."

The old man nodded and then turned and went to the kitchen and out a back door. He returned to the kitchen with an armful of weeds and took some things out of a refrigerator and chopped, squeezed, crushed and grinded all that he had, finally placing everything into a pot. Fifteen minutes later he brought out a gallon jug of steaming liquid.

"Drink all."

"What is it?"

"Lemon. Hierbas."

"Herbs?"

"Sí. Cilantro. Jengibre. Granada."

Jake cut him off. "What if he's not any better?"

"He will get better."

"What if he doesn't?"

"He will die."

"Are you serious?" Jake asked.

The old man smiled. "No. Maybe."

Jake and the doctor forced the medicinal dirt-colored concoction down Sanch's throat. The doctor then handed Jake a mason jar full.

"When he wakes up. Drink more."

At the Abrigo, Sanch drank half of the liquid in the mason jar. His stomach bubbled. He farted, but didn't shit. He then lay down and fell asleep.

He was awoken by laughter. Outside, Jake entertained Richard, Mary, and Andrea with the story of driving back from Witches Rock. "He waved to them screaming keep going, keep going," Jake was saying.

"I'm glad you are finding humor in my pain," Sanch said as he stood in the door frame, squinting into the brightness.

"Look who's up?" Mary said. "How're you feeling? The whole town's worried about you." Andrea went and gave him a hug and kissed him on the cheek.

"How you feel, Shitty?" Jake asked.

"A bit hungry," he said.

"You look hungry," Jake said. "You look like you have AIDs."

Mary shook her head. "It's not that bad," she said. "He just lost a little weight."

"You look beautiful," Andrea said.

Jake said, "You slept like twenty something hours. I thought you were in a coma. It was pretty crazy."

"I feel all right now. Let's eat." He looked at everyone looking back at him. He was confused that they were all there.

"Are you sure that you are okay?" Mary asked.

Sanch shook his head no.

Jake laughed. "Are you tripping?"

"I had a pretty strange dream."

"What was it?" Jake asked.

"I don't know. It just wouldn't end. There was a large castle or something. I knew there was a castle but I never actually got to it. Never even saw it. I was supposed to go there. And I just kept walking. It was so goddamned boring, walking a never-ending road, and then I thought it was because I was dead. And if I ever found the castle it would be heaven. I knew there was no castle, but I wouldn't stop looking for it. I was to walk the road forever. Sometimes it was through a forest and other times it was the beach. I would see people on it. I saw Rob and my brother, but it was like we didn't know each other. I'd ask them about the castle, and they would just point in a direction, but the next group of people would point me in another direction."

Later, not having the strength for an evening surf, he sat on the beach with Andrea watching Jake surf the small waves of Tamarindo Beach.

Richard went to bed early because he had to return the car to the rental place in Liberia in the morning. Andrea went to work. Sanch went to El Pescador with Jake.

"Want a beer?" Jake asked.

"Better not."

"Check it out," Jake said. Jake pointed to the pool table where the guys playing jumped every ball. "They created a new game with what I taught them."

"I got next," Jake said.

"Sí, Sí," the old-timer said. "Only like this." And he jumped the cue ball.

"Every shot?"

"Sí, sí."

The game took a little longer than usual.

"I think it's time we leave the Abrigo," Sanch said. "I'd kind of like to not be reminded of me lying in a pile of shit every time I go there."

Jake laughed. "I know I'll never forget cleaning your nasty ass."

"I appreciate it. Really, I do. You might've saved my life."

"You'd do the same for me."

Jake played his turn but didn't hit any balls in.

"I've been ready to get back to camping, too. But I don't wanna go back to Chico's. I don't trust that guy," Jake said.

"Let's look tomorrow for a new place."

"You really aren't going to drink tonight?"

"I think I'm going to go to bed early."

"Stay out just a bit longer," Jake said.

"Nah, I'm still not feeling great."

Sanch walked by Andrea's work, and she saw him, waved and motioned for him to wait a second. He did. She came out with a slice of pizza wrapped in a napkin for him.

"I'm not hungry," he said.

"Save it for later," she said.

"I'm going to bed early."

"I was hoping to stop by when I got off work," she said.

"You can," Sanch said.

He gave her a hug, and she kissed him on the lips. On the way back he took a few bites of the pizza, but wasn't hungry and tossed it to a stray dog.

He was woken up by a soft knock.

"Jake is not here?" Andrea asked when Sanch opened the door.

Sanch shook his head. She came in kissing him hard and pushed him on the bed and took her shirt off.

After sex, Andrea lay with her head on his chest.

"You are not as nice as you were the first night," she said.

"Why do you say that?"

"You are more quiet. You don't like me anymore?"

"I do."

"Just for sex?"

"Of course not."

"Do you have a girlfriend back home?"

Sanch looked at her. "What makes you think that?"

"You are thinking about her now."

"I'm not."

She looked up at him.

"She's not my girlfriend anymore."

"You still love her?"

"I don't," he said. "I don't know if I ever really loved her."

"You can love me instead."

Sanch chuckled.

"You think I'm joking?"

"No."

They fell asleep like that. Shortly after, Jake stormed through the door, waking them.

"I went to the casino tonight..." he started to say but stopped when he turned on the light and saw Andrea lying naked in bed.

She rolled over, pulling the covers over her. Sanch rubbed his eyes.

"What?" Sanch said.

236

"Nothing. I just, I wasn't expecting this," he said. "But I guess you're all better, huh?"

"I make him all better," Andrea said.

Jake gave Sanch an approving smile.

"What were you saying?" Sanch asked.

"Oh yeah," Jake continued as he sat on the bed with Sanch and Andrea.

"On your own bed," Sanch said.

Jake laughed. "Damn, trying to squeeze in there. I'm horny as hell." Jake sat on his own bed. "I ain't had sex in I don't know how long and here you are just sexing away. I remember when I used to be the one to get the girls. Remember when you first got laid," Jake said.

"Whatever," Sanch said. "What were you saying?"

Jake laughed. "You remember how we were having a party, and everyone was dancing? We had taken all the furniture out of the house."

Sanch nodded. "What you were saying about the casino?"

"That's how we used to party," Jake said to Andrea.

"This true?" she asked Sanch.

"So far," Sanch said. "So, about the casino?"

"You were dancing with that chick. What was her name? The little red-headed one."

"I don't remember."

"Yeah you do. But anyway, I told her how you had never been laid before, not even a blowjob. And she said she would do it. Remember that?"

Sanch nodded. He looked at Andrea. She smiled at Sanch.

Jake laughed. "He didn't know what the hell he was doing. I had to go in there and push on his ass. I was

237

standing behind him pushing on his naked ass teaching him how to be a man."

"Is this true?" she asked.

"Not exactly," Sanch said.

"Well, he doesn't need your help anymore," she said.

"You're welcome," Jake said to Andrea.

"So what were you saying about a casino?"

"I went to the casino. Like this." Jake held up his arms. "They let you in with no shoes, no shirt. And free drinks. Dollar Blackjack. Didn't see a poker room, but that's my new hangout for sure."

"How'd you do? Win anything?"

"No. But only lost five bucks and I played for hours and drank like a fish."

"I better go," Andrea said. She gave Sanch a long kiss. Jake looked at her exposed breasts. She stood naked and pulled on her jeans.

"God damn," Jake said. "Can I watch you guys next time?"

"You are bad," Andrea said.

The next night they went to the casino, a small, dark place with six gamblers on the slot machines. There was also a craps table, four roulette wheels, and a handful of Blackjack and Caribbean Stud poker tables. The purple carpet, purple velvet walls, tuxedo-clad dealers and sexy waitresses added an element of sophistication, but Sanch and Jake easily countered that.

They sat down at the Blackjack table, exchanging twenty dollars for chips. The cocktail waitress greeted them with a warm smile. They both ordered a rum and coke. On their third drink, Sanch was down ten and Jake was up twenty.

"Anywhere to play poker?" Jake asked.

"Yes," the dealer said. She called over who they assumed was the pit boss. "These gentlemen would like to play poker," she said to the big man.

The big man informed them that there was only one poker table and that there was a wait for it. He insisted they continue playing Blackjack until a spot opened.

"Call us when it opens," Jake said. "We'll be outside."

Outside, nursing their drinks, a sleepy-eyed, angelic faced girl approached them. She held a cigarette and asked for a light. Neither Sanch nor Jake carried a lighter. She sat between them on the bench and pulled a lighter from her purse. She wore a black leather skirt that barely covered her ass, and when she sat and crossed her legs, Sanch and Jake both leaned a bit forward trying to catch a glimpse of what was under the dress. She smiled while she blew out the cloud of smoke. A skintight tank top that stopped just below her young breasts showcased a flat brown belly.

"I'm Jake," he said offering her a hand.

"Estefania," she said. Her red lips sucked on the cigarette.

"You going in the casino?" Jake asked.

She shook her head. Whether it meant no or was a lack of understanding was not clear.

"Where are you going then?"

She shrugged her shoulders and shook her head again.

Sanch felt a bulge rise in his shorts as he watched her rub her thigh with her free hand. She stood up and walked around a bit, not too far, just enough to give the two boys a preview of what she was offering and in case they needed further encouragement she bent over to adjust a shoe strap. Jake smacked Sanch on the arm and pointed as if Sanch wasn't already looking.

While lost in their state of wonder, a hand clamped down on their shoulders.

"Like what you see?" Johhny's familiar voice asked. "Told you I got girls, too. She's nice, right?"

"For sure," Jake said. Sanch nodded. She stood over by a wall, propping one leg up.

"You can have her tonight. The both of you, if you want."

"How much?" Jake asked.

"Fifty dollars each."

"For an hour?" Jake asked.

"Or three."

"One hundred dollars for three hours?"

"I don't need three hours," Jake said. "I need about twenty minutes."

"It's by the hour."

Johnny looked at Sanch. "You like that?"

"I do, but I've never paid for sex."

"This motherfucker is getting laid for free."

"Who?" Johnny asked. His face got a little less friendly.

"Andrea," Jake said. "You know her?"

"Everyone knows her," Johnny said.

"What's that mean?" Sanch asked.

Jake laughed.

"She ask you to take her back to the States, yet?"

"Hell yeah, she did," Jake said.

Johnny nodded knowingly.

"So what?" Sanch said.

"Nothing. It's cool, man. Just that she's been here, in Tamarindo, for a while, you know? She wants out."

"What're you saying?" Sanch said. "She's known for that shit?"

Jake found it amusing.

"Don't stress it, bro. Pura Vida. So you guys decide, yet?" Johnny pointed to the girl leaning on the wall.

"I have," Jake said.

"Unfortunately, it'll be the same price whether you go solo or with Lover Boy. She's one hundred dollars."

"Come on," Jake said to Sanch. "Nobody'll ever know you did this. Just chalk it up under experience when you're done."

"She's good," Johnny said. "Young. Hasn't been doing it long."

"How young is she?" Sanch asked.

"Not too young," Johnny told him. "In her prime."

"Eighteen?" Sanch asked.

"Close."

"Sixteen?" Jake asked.

"Almost."

"Get the fuck outta here," Jake said.

"Doesn't matter," Johnny nodded.

"I don't believe you," Jake said. "She's smoking hot."

At that time, the pit boss stuck his head out of the door to tell them their seats had opened.

"What're you going to do?" Johnny said.

"I've got a poker game to play," Jake said.

"After then."

"Maybe."

"You?" he asked Sanch.

Sanch shook his head. "I'm good. But what's Andrea's deal?"

"Don't sweat it, my friend. She's cool. If you like her what is the problem? If you guys change your mind, find me later. Do you want one older?"

"Probably," Jake said.

The upstairs poker room was furnished with a table and nicotine-stained walls. Aesthetics weren't a concern. Four men played through thick cigar smoke. Two recognizable faces: one was a local that Jake had played before at the discoteca and the other was the German storekeeper. They nodded their acknowledgments. A white-haired, rosy-cheeked man, loud and flamboyant, wore an unbuttoned Hawaiian shirt to showcase his equally white-haired chest. He chewed on a cigar stub. He sat next to a quiet, reserved man with a double chin wearing a black suit and black fedora, looking as if he was ready for a funeral or a murder.

Buy-in was forty dollars. Sanch didn't have enough to cover the forty dollar buy-in, but after getting the consensus of the other men, was allowed to stand and watch while Jake played.

The game rolled on as did the drinks and Jake had won a few good hands. Only the German proprietor seemed to be any competition. The other man from the discoteca was failing in desperate attempts to call Jake's bluffs, which Jake varied with great regularity. The local didn't take it kindly getting beat for a second time to an arrogant tourist, as he called him before he stormed off, busted of all his cash for the night. The more the white-haired man drank, the louder and more talkative he became and the more money he threw around, occasionally winning a lucky hand. His name was Billy Byson, and he and Double Chin were traveling together from Virginia. They were there to spend money and drink.

"What do you guys do?" Jake asked.

"Government work," he said.

"What kind?"

"Doesn't matter."

242

"Come on. I am curious," Jake said.

"We take important people around. Show them a good time."

"You here for work now?"

"You like to ask questions?"

"Yeah."

"There's a man downstairs. He was playing before you came up. He's a Congressman. And I got some things that I'd like him to consider." He then offered Jake a cigar. "Cohibas," he said. "Lanceros." Jake took one.

"You want one too?" he asked Sanch. Sanch accepted.

"What things?" Jake asked after he lit the cigar. He then looked down at the two cards he'd been dealt.

"Now you're getting personal."

Another hour went by, and Jake's chips continued to pile up. The German had already called it a night, having walked away with a good bit of American government work money. It was just Jake and the two other men. The game had slowed, but not the drinking. Then a third man came in and whispered in Bill's ear and then left.

"I think you took enough of our money, but if you want to keep the party going," he motioned to his nose, "why don't you come along with us."

He shoved the rest of his chips at the dealer. "For you, hombre."

"Let me cash out and I'll be right there," Jake said.

"We aren't waiting." Bill then wrote on a napkin the hotel and room number.

"Baxter, here," he patted Double Chin on the back, "will let you in."

Jake exchanged his chips. Six hundred and forty-eight dollars.

"And just like that, we've got another month of living. You better start earning some money soon," Jake said.

The hotel was at the American lady's place that Sanch and Jake had first inquired about prices. It wasn't a hotel room though, but a three-bedroom suite. Baxter stood guard outside. He knocked loudly before letting them enter. Music blared, cold air blew from a window unit, and empty and half-empty liquor bottles covered the counter and sink. The living room, on the other hand, looked welcoming and unused.

Bill came from one of the rooms. He wore boxer shorts and a blue suit jacket, but no shirt underneath.

"Ha. You guys made it." He hugged them both. Sweat from his forehead smeared on Sanch's cheek. "Party is in there," he said pointing to the room he had just come from. "That room's off limits," he pointed to a closed door in the middle. "And that one you can use, but it's occupied at the moment," he said pointing to another closed door. He practically screamed so to be heard over the music. "Have a seat, boys."

Sanch and Jake sat on the faded floral print couch. He opened the door of the party room and shouted, "We need some drinks in here." He pulled up a chair and sat uncomfortably close to Sanch and Jake, placing a hand on each of their knees. "What do you boys like to drink? scotch? You like scotch?"

"I'm good," Jake said, moving back and releasing his knee from Bill's grip. Sanch tried to as well, but Bill's hand stayed firm, and he even gave it a bit of a squeeze.

"You like scotch, right?" he said to Sanch, squeezing his knee and staring at him a bit too long.

"I'll drink scotch," Sanch said.

"I'll take a beer," Jake said.

"I like you," Bill said still staring at Sanch.

"Thanks," Sanch said. "You seem rather swell yourself."

"We need some goddamn drinks in here," Bill shouted. Then looking at Sanch again said, "Goddamn whores."

From the party room walked Andrea's friend Jennifer with nothing on but thong underwear. She acted like she didn't recognize Sanch or Jake as she went into the kitchen.

"You like her? Wait'll you see who comes out of that room." He pointed to the room that he had said was occupied.

"A scotch and beer," Bill shouted to Jennifer. He then began rapid fire questions to Jake and Sanch about their trip. Jake did the talking, but Bill never took his eyes from Sanch. Jennifer came over, her gaze lingering at Sanch and Jake as she handed them the drinks and walked back into the room. "We've already had our fill of her. But if you want, be my guest. I'm waiting on the new piece of ass the bossman's got in there now. Wait till you see her, boys." Jennifer looked back at Sanch and Jake before she entered the room. "In the meantime, how about some fun?"

"I like fun," Jake said.

Bill untied a baggie he had pulled from his jacket pocket. "This stuff will make you fuck like kings."

He poured some cocaine onto a small mirror on the table and cut out some lines and handed Jake the rolled up dollar bill. Jake did the largest line and then handed Sanch the straw. Sanch waived it away.

"I'm good," Sanch said. He took a sip of the scotch.

"What? You're good?" Bill said. "Motherfucker, you better get in there and get you a goddamn line."

Sanch took the dollar bill from Jake and did the smallest line.

"Come with me," Bill said to Jake. "You wait here," he said to Sanch.

Jake followed him into the room that Jennifer was in. Sanch sat on the couch sipping his scotch. He walked to the kitchen and poured the rest into the sink and opened the front door. Baxter was standing outside smoking a cigarette. He placed his hand on Sanch's chest.

"Where's Bill?" Baxter asked.

"In there," Sanch pointed to the room.

"Can't leave until I get the go-ahead from Bill. Just have a seat on the couch for a minute."

"I can go wherever I damn well please," Sanch said.

"Is that so?" Baxter showed him a gun under his jacket.

"I'll wait." Sanch walked back to the couch.

The other door of the occupied room opened and out walked Johnny's girl from the casino. She was naked, and he diverted his eyes from her newly haired snatch. She smiled as she walked by to the kitchen. He couldn't keep his eyes diverted too long, and they went back down to her bare buttocks and her legs. She watched him watch her drink a glass of water and then returned back to the room. Sanch got a glimpse of another girl in there as she opened the door, walked in and then shut it again. From where he sat, the other girl looked like Andrea.

He then tried to open the door. It was locked. He then knocked. After no answer, he pounded on it. After still no answer, he began shouting, "Open the fucking door."

Baxter opened the front door and poked his head out. "Is there a problem?"

Sanch went to the door where Jake was and opened it. Jake was standing over a dresser with his face bent over a pile of cocaine, and Bill was sitting on the bed with Jennifer in his lap and his hands clasped on each breast.

"I'm leaving," Sanch said. At that moment, he was knocked in the back of the head and fell to the floor.

Bill threw Jennifer to the ground. Baxter rocked Jake with a right hook.

Sanch slowly stood.

"This asshole is out here screaming and banging on doors," Baxter said to Bill.

Bill helped Jake to his feet. "Escort them out," Bill said.

Sanch and Jake walked back to the Abrigo.

"What just happened?" Jake asked.

"The young chick from the casino walked out of one of the rooms and then I thought I saw Andrea. I tried to go in there, and they wouldn't let me."

"Andrea's a whore? No shit?" Jake laughed.

"Why is that funny?"

"Are you kidding me? That's hilarious."

"It might not have even been her," Sanch said.

"Right. But if it was, who cares? You're getting it for free."

"Feel the back of my head," Sanch said. He moved Jake's hand onto a forming knot where he had been hit. Jake laughed.

"You think it was Andrea?" he asked Sanch.

"It doesn't matter. Not like she's my girl."

"If you say so," Jake said.

Chapter Fifteen

Packing his things, Sanch said, "You getting up anytime soon?"

Jake didn't respond. Sanch walked down to the beach.

The day was already warm, and the beach swarmed with tourists who sunbathed, surfed for the first time or bought trinkets from the locals.

Sanch dove into the ocean. He bodysurfed a few waves before heading back onto shore. He dug a hole in the sand deep enough to lounge in with his head laid back and his legs propped up. He laid his head back into the sand and the sun baked the salt into his skin.

A few minutes later sand sprayed across his face and chest. He sat up coughing and spitting. Jake stood over him laughing.

"Let's surf Langosta," Jake said. Jake had a shiner on his left eye that had already turned the color of an eggplant.

"Did you see your eye?" Sanch asked.

"Fuck you. I'm going surfing." Jake turned to go back to the Abrigo while Sanch jumped back in the water to rinse off.

A little past Lagarto Surf, Sanch noticed two tents in the yard of one of the small cinder block houses they had walked by on their first day in town. He pointed it out to Jake.

"Let's see if we can camp there," Jake said.

Two young ladies lounged in hammocks.

"Hello ladies," Jake said.

They looked up and introduced themselves, Allison and Roselyn. Both were Canadian with dreadlocks and hairy armpits. Allison's dreadlocks were more like small braids, maybe freshly done. But Roselyn had five twists each about as large as a fist.

"Living out the stereotype to a T, huh?" Jake said when he saw them making hemp necklaces. A carrying sack of hemp necklaces sat on the ground next to them.

"We could say the same about you two," Roselyn said.

They commented on Jake's eye, and Jake retold the story.

"Sanch is just lucky I stepped in," he said. "I think they were ready to kill him."

"Not sure if it was exactly like that," Sanch said.

"How much you pay to camp here?" Jake asked the girls.

"A dollar-fifty. For three dollars she will include breakfast and coffee."

"We are actually about to pack up. An apartment opened up, and we are moving in there."

"So these spaces are open?" Jake asked. "Looks like we are moving here. Let's go surf first." Then to the Canadians, "Introduce us to who we have to pay when we come back through."

"Yes sir," Roselyn said. Allison giggled.

No car came by to pick up Sanch and Jake on their walk to Langosta. Their soles had calloused, and they could no longer feel the rocks on their bare feet.

The surf wasn't large, and they rode the shore break on the other side of the river mouth.

On the way back the girls had already left the campsite but had told the old lady about Sanch and Jake. They also left two hammocks for them. They went back to the Abrigo, paid their balance, said goodbye to Jesus, who responded with a "Pura Vida," and they walked back through town.

Walking by the German store, the owner asked if they were leaving.

"Just moving spots," Jake shouted to him.

"Heading out?" Gerard and Johnny asked as they walked by the Frenchman's café.

"Nope. Just going back to camping up the street," Jake said.

"What happened to you guys last night?" Johhny shouted.

"We'll talk later," Jake said.

Mary ran to them from the pizza shop. "Are you leaving?" she asked. "Heard there was trouble last night."

"Just moving down the street," Sanch said. "Have you seen Andrea today?"

Jake laughed.

"She doesn't work today. What's the matter?"

"Nothing," Sanch said. Jake continued laughing. "Don't pay attention to Jake. He's an idiot."

"What happened to your eye?"

"Sanch can tell you later."

After setting up their tents, they went to Lagarto Surf to repair a few surfboards.

"Pedro is in town," Vince told Jake. "He just won a big contest down in Jaco. What happened to your eye?"

"Go tell him I want to surf with him," Jake said.

"Your eye though?"

"Where can I find Pedro?"

"He's working down at his father's all day."

Vince slowly lifted a finger to Jake's eye and tried to touch it. Jake jerked his head back.

"What the fuck are you doing?"

"Does it hurt?" Vince asked.

"Motherfucker, I'll give you one, and you tell me if it hurts."

Two hours, three surfboards and eighty dollars later they went to Pedro's.

A long-haired Tico asked what they wanted to eat.

"Are you Pedro, the National Champ?" Jake asked.

Pedro smiled sheepishly.

"How old are you?"

"Nineteen," he responded, his English pretty good.

"And you are the best they have here? No one can beat you?"

"They haven't yet."

"Let's go surf."

"I'm working right now," he said. "I have fish to clean."

His father walked out and said something to him in Spanish.

"He said I have a couple of hours if I want to go."

Jake and Sanch went back to the camp to get their boards.

When they returned to Pedro's the locals from the Frenchman's café were there, as was Drew, Gerard, Johnny, Mary, Vince and Beth, Alex from Aqua Blue, and the Italians from Tamarindo Adventure.

"All these people showed up to watch me surf," Jake said to Sanch quietly as he waited for Pedro to come out.

There wasn't much daylight left, so they agreed to surf Tamarindo Beach. Sanch sat next to Mary among the rest of the group as Jake and Pedro paddled out. Drew and Gerard paddled out with them. Andrea took a seat in the sand next to Sanch. Sanch looked at her, and she leaned in and gave him a kiss on the lips. Sanch pulled away and looked at her. She looked out at the ocean. After less than a minute of silence, Sanch said, "Where were you last night?"

"At Mary's. We had dinner. Why do you ask?"

"Really?" Sanch looked at Mary. The crowd cheered. Pedro was on his first wave.

"Yes," Mary said. She looked at him in a perplexed way. "You don't believe her?"

"No. I mean, yeah, I believe her. It's just that I," he paused. "I thought I saw her where I was at."

"Where was that?" Andrea asked.

"The casino. Well, after the casino. We met some guys there and went back to their place for a bit."

"I know," Andrea said. "I spoke to Jennifer. She said you were there. She also said you got into a fight."

"It wasn't a fight."

"There goes Jake," Mary said. Sanch looked up.

"We got our asses beat, but it wasn't a fight."

Jake kicked out of the wave and paddled back out.

"Are you hurt?"

"No. Jake's eye is pretty jacked up."

"What happened?"

"Jennifer would probably know better than me. I was drunk."

They stared out at the ocean as Gerard and Drew both caught a wave.

"Who was the other girl?" Sanch asked.

"Her sister," Andrea said.

"How old is she?"

"It doesn't matter."

"Is she really fifteen?"

"I think so," Andrea said. "She is very pretty, yes?"

"She is," Sanch said. He looked over at Johnny, who was sitting on his haunches smoking a joint with the Italians.

"It is none of your business," she then said. "This isn't America you know. You can't come over here and judge people. It's a much different way of surviving here. You guys come over with your own money and can go home anytime you want. It is easy for you."

Sanch looked at her as she spoke. She stared at the ocean. Mary walked over to sit with Johnny.

Pedro caught the next wave and pulled underneath the curl, getting completely covered up. Jake caught the next wave and did the same. This continued like a game of HORSE until dark. Pedro and Jake walked together from the water.

"Let's surf again," Pedro said. "Pura Vida."

"Pura Vida," Jake said to him, and Pedro walked off, and Jake sat next to Sanch in the sand.

The crowd dissolved just as quickly as they had arrived. Mary walked over and said everyone was going to the Frenchman's café.

"I'll walk with you," Andrea said to Mary. She kissed Sanch on the cheek and left. Jake sat next to Sanch.

"Did you see that?" Jake asked. "Went wave for wave with the champ."

Sanch nodded.

"Was I better than him?"

"I don't know."

"Who had more style?"

"I don't know."

"I could still be a professional, you know?"

"Probably."

"Don't need to though," Jake said. "Everyone knows I'm just as good as or better than the Costa Rican national champ. I don't need competition to prove anything."

There was a celebratory air at the Mambo Bar that night, more so than other nights. The crowd around the pool table talked to Pedro in between his turn at the table. Jake squeezed in next to Drew and Gerard. Sanch ordered a beer and looked over where Mary, Andrea and Jennifer sat together. Mary and Andrea waved. Sanch lifted his chin in acknowledgment. He then joined them at the table. Mary gave him a hug; Andrea kissed him on the cheek and Jennifer hugged him, but he avoided eye contact with her.

Jake and another guy joined them.

"Sanch, this is Lorenzo. He owns Tamarindo Adventures," Jake said.

Sanch shook his hand. Lorenzo kissed each of the girls on the cheek.

"We just opened up about two months ago," Lorenzo said. "We are looking for ways to be different than Aqua Blue or Lagarto Surf. Aqua Blue does the boat trips to Witches Rock. Lagarto Surf does almost everything. The one thing neither has is a surf team."

"Let's start a surf team," Jake said.

"Yes, yes. That is what we are doing. There is a contest to be held in Tamarindo in a little over a month. We pay your entry fee, and you wear our jersey. You win this we will pay for you to enter other ones around Costa Rica. You help to spread our name."

"I've done it before. Nothing new to me."

Lorenzo shook his hand. "We will keep in touch."

Sanch went to the bathroom. When he returned, Jennifer had left. Jake and Pedro partnered up for a game of pool. Johnny asked if Sanch wanted to play a game of foosball. Sanch did and every couple minutes would glance over at Andrea.

"You guys about fucked up last," Johnny said.

"Yeah, I know," Sanch said.

"You are getting too comfortable here. I like you guys, but there are some things you don't understand."

A few minutes later, Andrea came up behind him and pulled him away. "We are going to the Expatriado. You want to come with us?"

"I'm going to finish this game and then maybe."

"Okay." She kissed him on the lips. "Hope I see you later."

Sanch waved to Mary, and the girls walked out. Sanch turned around to finish the game, but Johnny had left.

They didn't make it to Expatriado. The night continued on in a blur until the Mambo Bar shut down. Sanch took too many shots of guaro that had been passed around in a two-liter soda bottle. He sat with his head in his arms on the picnic table, trying not to fall asleep.

"Come on, dude," Jake said.

Sanch stumbled to his feet.

"Told you not to drink that shit."

On the walk to the camp, Sanch said, "So you're getting sponsored, huh?"

He then stopped at a tree and steadied himself.

"You going to puke?"

Sanch nodded and a stream of clear liquid projected from his mouth.

Jake laughed. Sanch gave him the finger. He hurled again and then wiped his mouth on the back of his hand.

"I thought I had missed my chance at being a professional surfer, that I was too old now. But I'm getting another chance. I'll win, too."

"Why'd you ever quit in the first place?" Sanch said.

"You know why, asshole."

"You blame your kid, but you could've kept surfing."

"You're fucking drunk. Don't start that shit."

"Your kid never stopped you from anything else."

"You're going to piss me off."

"I'm just drunk. Don't listen to me."

"No shit. I'd hate to kick your ass when you're drunk."

"I don't think you could," Sanch said.

"You're crazy. I'd murder you."

They walked a bit more in silence.

"I just want to know why you quit surfing. Did you get scared?"

"I swear to God, man. I'm about to slap the shit out of you."

Sanch laughed.

"You think I won't?"

"I'm just wondering if you were too scared to really go for it and not make it."

"I'm better than you will ever be. You look like a goddamn kook out there."

Sanch laughed. "The difference is I don't give a shit what I look like. I'm just having fun."

"Then shut the fuck up and sleep it off."

Sanch stopped walking. "Or what?"

Jake stopped and stared at him.

"You don't think I'll hit you, do you?"

"I don't, Sissy." Sanch laughed when he called him that. Jake didn't. Instead, he threw a punch that landed squarely on Sanch's jaw and sent Sanch stumbling back and he fell onto his butt.

Sanch stood and steadied himself, rubbing the side of his face.

"I told you to shut up," Jake said. Jake saw him smiling. "Don't fucking do that," he said.

"I didn't think you had it in you," Sanch said. "I should kick your ass for hitting me."

Jake stared at him. Sanch walked past him back to camp. Jake followed a few feet behind him.

The next morning Sanch came out from his tent. Jake lounged in a hammock smoking from a shell.

"How long you been up?" Sanch asked.

"Couple hours. Couldn't sleep. Sorry about last night. I feel like an ass."

"We were drunk. It happens."

"You were drunker than me."

"I was."

There was a short pause.

"I got sponsored."

"I know," Sanch said and sat in the other hammock. "You still pissed?"

"I'm good. You want to hit this?" He passed the shell to Sanch. "Maybe you were right though."

Sanch blew out a cloud of smoke. "I was drunk. Forget about it."

"I was afraid to go for it and fail. When my daughter was born, I saw an easy way out. And at times, I despised her mom for not getting an abortion. I was a fucked-up kid, man."

"It's cool. We're just all trying to figure out how life works. Sometimes we fuck up."

"Some more than others."

They hitched a ride to Langosta and surfed alone for hours. By the time the first signs of a crowd showed up, they were tired and hungry.

Chapter Sixteen

Days drifted by and soon the days became weeks, spent in a routine of surf, breakfast, repair a few boards, sit in the hammock and smoke some pot during the hottest part of the day. Then maybe play some chess at the Frenchman's, maybe nap if they drank too much the previous night, or go for a walk into town to see if there was anything new to gossip about. There never was. After an evening surf, they would usually eat at Pedro's or El Pescador or the Frenchman's café and then drink at the Mambo Bar, Expatriado, or the discoteca. Andrea could sense Sanch trying to distance himself from her on some nights, but on other nights he would go back to her place. They never spoke of that night of the fight.

The routine ended when they returned to the camp after a surf, and an SUV was parked in the yard and another tent set up among theirs. They could see a naked girl inside the tent. They stopped a few feet from it, looking through the mesh window.

"Enjoying the view?" a male voice said from behind them.

"That your girl?" Jake asked without turning to see who said it.

"Yeah," he said. "Hey babe," he shouted to her, "you mind closing the window when you change?"

She turned and looked at the three men looking at her. She smiled, pulled up her bikini bottoms and then walked out still tying her bikini top.

"She does that shit. We were down on the beach in Santa Teresa, and I came out from surfing and she was just chatting away with some dude sitting next to her and she was butt-naked."

"It's natural," she said.

They were Todd and Lacy from Orange Beach, Alabama.

"No shit. We are from Pensacola," Jake said.

"Goddamn," Todd said. "What are the chances?"

They talked of favorite surf spots—Alabama Point, Terry's Cove, the Bungalows—and of favorite bars and restaurants—Flora-Bama, the Reef, Live Bait, Tacky Jack's. The four of them were inseparable for the next week. Todd and Lacy purchased hammocks from the Hammock Man on the beach, and they spent afternoons practicing the art of "hammocka-sutra," as they coined it during a stoned session of storytelling. Lacy was a phenomenal cook and instead of eating out they started cooking over open flames.

Todd and Lacy described the beauty of a waterfall they visited around Montezuma, a town near Santa Teresa at the southern end of the Nicoya Peninsula.

"We should go down there," Lacy suggested. "I'd like to visit Charlie again. He owns a surf camp down there. It's the coolest place. Such great people."

"Let's do it," Jake said.

They told the little old lady they would be back, so Todd and Lacy rolled up their belongings, but Sanch and Jake left their tents standing and only took one surf bag with a surfboard each. The drive took five hours through awful terrain and small, forgotten towns. The road then led up a steep hill into Montezuma, a village smaller than Tamarindo. It took them two minutes to drive through the town, and as they were leaving it, Todd parked the SUV on the side of the road.

"The waterfall's in there," he said. He pointed at a wooded hill. From the road, it didn't look like much of a rainforest, but once they got in it and followed a small trail through some bushes, Sanch couldn't believe how big the forest had become. They followed a small stream until the stream widened. The sounds of thousands of birds filled the air, giving them the perfect soundtrack to their hike.

"How long we got to walk for?" Jake asked.

Todd and Lacy smiled. "Not too far," Todd said. "Couple of hours."

"You serious?"

"No. It's about thirty minutes or so. It's so worth it," Lacy reassured Jake. Todd led the way up the ever increasing steepness, followed by Lacy, and then Jake and Sanch bringing up the rear.

"Look above you," Sanch said to Jake. Jake stopped. It was a mother Howler monkey with three little baby monkeys hanging onto her.

"Check it out, guys," Jake said. Todd and Lacy stopped to look as well.

"You ever heard those things scream?" Todd asked. Jake said he had and retold the story of Sanch and him running down the street when they first heard it. After they continued walking, they heard the scream once again.

The trail continued on the rise and away from the stream so that they were walking in the heavily shaded and wet forest. The trail then stopped at a cliff. Down below, the stream they had once followed was now wide enough to be called a river.

"Getting closer," Todd said. "Now we got to get down there and continue following the river trail." Down there was a good fifty feet below them.

"And how do we get down there?" Jake asked.

Todd pointed to a rope that was tied around a tree.
"Bullshit," Jake said.
"We're going," Todd said.
"Why didn't you tell us to bring shoes?" Sanch said.
"Who needs shoes?" Todd said and climbed down the rope, his feet against the cliff and his hands walking down the rope. Every few feet the rope was tied off into knots.

Lacy grabbed hold of the rope and lowered herself down. Jake looked at Sanch, shrugged his shoulders and started down. Sanch followed. Standing on the rocks by the river, Lacy bent down to stick her face in the flowing river water.

"You guys should taste this stuff. Doesn't get any fresher than this," she said. Sanch and Jake both bent down and cupped their hands to scoop the water. It was cold and crisp.

"We should bottle this shit up and sell it," Jake said.

They continued on the trail passing another group of hikers returning from the waterfall.

"Anybody else up there?" Todd asked. One of the hikers said there was a tour group swimming up there, about ten people at most.

Todd stopped. "You hear it?" There was a small rumbling through the trees. A few more steps and they could see the seventy-five-foot waterfall just beyond some branches and then they reached a clearing that gave them a view of the water cascading into a clear pool where the tour group swam.

"We going down there?" Sanch asked.

"Hell no," Todd said. "We're going up there." He pointed to the top of the waterfall.

"How did you find this?" Jake asked.

"Some people we were camping with at Charlie's brought us. You haven't seen nothing yet. Wait till we jump off it."

"Jump off that?" Sanch asked. He looked at the rocks on the bottom.

"Yeah," Todd said. "That's what we came for, isn't it?"

"Don't listen to him," Lacy said. "The one we jump from is a bit smaller."

It was, but not by much. Of the two waterfalls stacked on each other, the top one was slightly smaller.

When they reached the top of the first one, they crept to the edge and looked down at the swimmers. There was another, smaller swimming pool that they would jump into that poured over the side next to them.

"How do you get there?" Jake asked pointing to the waterfall they were going to jump from.

"The rocks," Todd said.

Jake looked at Lacy. "He isn't lying this time," she said.

"I'm not climbing that," Jake said. "I've got a surf contest in a few days. Can't be getting hurt."

"Don't be a pussy," Lacy told him as she started her climb. Todd went and Sanch followed. Jake stayed at the bottom. Once Sanch, Todd and Lacy made it to the top they shouted back down at Jake to join them, but he didn't move. Then Lacy, without a moment's hesitation ran and leaped from the top, arms flailing as she free-fell into the ice cold pool. She swam to Jake. They spoke for a minute, and he began to follow her up the rocks.

They made it to the top and Jake said, "I'm up here, but I ain't jumping."

"How you getting down then?" Todd asked, laughing. "Going down the rocks is a lot more dangerous than going up."

"Then I'll stay right here."

Todd pulled a joint that he had tucked behind his ear. "Should we have a safety meeting before jumping?" He lit it up and passed it around. The four of them sat on the rocks with their feet dangling over the edge, the thunder of the waterfall next to them and the singing sounds of the tropical birds.

After the joint, Todd said, "Just remember to swim out quick. If you swim around too long down there, it'll suck you over. Good luck surviving that fall." Todd stepped to the edge, spread his hands in the air and leaped. Sanch and Jake peered over the edge, watching him splash down.

"That's a long way down," Sanch said.

"Which one of you is going first?" Lacy said.

"I told you I ain't going," Jake said. Sanch stood quiet, peering over the edge. "Are you going?" Jake asked him. Sanch looked at him and smiled.

"You won't do it," Jake said.

Sanch didn't answer and pushed off, hollering the length of the drop. By instinct, his arms twirled to keep himself straight, if they didn't twirl, he would've fallen either too far forward on his face and belly or too far backward. And also, as if by instinct, he crossed his legs and his ankles and cupped his balls just before impact.

He entered smoothly, and he drifted down, down, down and continued submerging until he stopped, never having touched bottom. He opened his eyes and with the sun being blocked by the canopy of trees, the visibility was zero. He swam in the black coldness toward the surface but still couldn't see it. His lungs ached for air. He stroked and

263

kicked a few more times before finally breaking through, swallowing as much air as he could. The sound of the crashing water multiplied. He tossed his hands up in jubilation.

"Goddamn," he shouted. "That was great."

Watching from the rocks, Todd hollered and cheered.

Sanch made his way to the side only about ten feet from where the next waterfall began. Todd extended a hand and helped pull Sanch up. "Look how close you get to going over the edge."

"It's insane," Sanch said. They embraced and then they both looked up at Lacy and Jake looking down at them.

Lacy was clapping. Jake stood staring down with his arms crossed.

"Come on," Sanch yelled. Lacy jumped. They waited for her to swim over and all three hugged. Sanch followed Todd and Lacy back up the rocks to the launch spot.

"You gotta go," Sanch said.

"First of all, it looked like you stayed down in the water forever," Jake said. "I was starting to wonder if you were coming back up. And then you started getting pulled to the other waterfall. I thought, damn, watch that dipshit go over."

"It's fine," Sanch said. "I'm going again."

"Go for it."

Sanch did. Todd next and then Lacy again. All three climbed back up once again.

"If you are jumping, you better do it now," Todd said. "We've got to head back before it gets dark. If it gets dark, we are fucked. They don't have lighted paths out here."

"I'm not doing it," Jake said. "I'm cool."

"Come on, man. It's fun," Sanch said.

"It might be. But I surf for fun. I don't jump off waterfalls."

"We've got to go," Todd said. "Now you have to jump." Todd walked to the edge and turned around. "Dare me to do a back dive?"

"Babe, cut it out. Just jump normal."

He didn't. He jumped off in a back dive, twisting in the air and straightening out on the way down.

"He's getting cocky," Jake said. "He keeps it up and he's going to run out of luck."

Lacy jumped. They both waited for Sanch and Jake to come down. Jake looked at the rocks they had climbed to get up.

"I can't climb back down there."

"Nope," Sanch said.

"Count of three. Same time."

Sanch counted.

On take-off, Jake slipped on the wet rock, but the momentum going forward carried him far enough from the rocks. He couldn't straighten himself in the air, and he landed lopsided, making a thud as he hit. Sanch landed a few feet from him. Todd jumped in the pool. Lacy stood with her hands over her mouth. Sanch broke the surface first.

"Is he okay?" Sanch said.

"I don't see him yet," Todd said as he swam towards Sanch. "It didn't look good though."

"He's over there," Lacy shouted.

Jake swam towards her, but not at the rate he should.

"He's going to go over," Sanch said.

"It's cool," Todd told Sanch. "I was just fucking with you guys."

Lacy helped pull Jake out.

"What happened?" Sanch said.

Jake lifted his right arm and showed a bright red ribcage.

Sanch laughed.

"Does it hurt?" Sanch pushed on Jake's ribs.

"What do you think?" he said pulling back. "That was stupid. I gotta chance of going pro again, and here I am doing stupid shit like jumping off a waterfall."

Sanch laughed some more. "But wasn't it worth it?"

"No," Jake said. "Probably broke a rib. Let's go."

Sanch tapped Jake on the ribs.

"What are you doing?"

"Seeing if they are broke."

"Not going to lie," Todd said. "I didn't think you were going to make it."

"It was a bit scary," Lacy said.

"Just get us back to the car."

They drove on to the smaller village of Santa Teresa. It was dark now, but even if it had been daylight, there wouldn't be much to see except trees. Todd turned the truck down a driveway that could have easily been missed if he hadn't been there before. It wasn't until about twenty yards down the path that the headlights shined on a wooden sign reading Charlie's Surf Camp. They parked next to one other SUV and an old rusted reddish-brown pickup truck that looked from the seventies. Winged insects swarmed the lone yellow light. An electrical wire hung from around the light and connected to an RV sitting on blocks and beyond that tent cabins lined on opposite sides facing each other with about ten yards in between them. In front of each tent cabin was a picnic table. The path led all the way to the beach where a bonfire lit up the night.

266

"Charlie lives in the RV," Todd said. "You guys follow Lacy and I'll go talk to Charlie. He's cool, but a bit strange. Doesn't really let anyone new camp here unless with a personal recommendation from someone who has already camped here."

They followed Lacy to the line of tents and found two open. There were about fifteen tent cabins in total. They each slept two people and sat up on wooden slabs.

"Place is always packed," Lacy said. "Cost is only five dollars a night. That includes dinner. If you aren't in line by eight, you don't eat that night. Charlie cooks the food, but he never serves it. There's a pavilion over there where we all eat and an outdoor community kitchen. He gets everything ready, buffet style, makes him a plate and when he leaves, we all start getting our plate. Some folks have been living here for months. It's hard to leave," she said. "Kind of communal, you know. When you have been away from home for so long, it feels nice to have a family again."

"Also, underneath the pavilion," she continued, "are two refrigerators. One is beer and the other food. Everything is for sale on the honor system. Take what you need and put your money in the wooden box that was between the two fridges. Beer is a dollar. And all other food is priced on the fridge. Shower and outhouse is just past the pavilion. Shower is open-air, just a big water tank of collected rainwater."

"Hell yeah," Jake said. "Let me know when you are going to shower."

She shook her head. "You are such a perv."

Todd came back, and they joined the gathering at the bonfire. The smell of cannabis hit them before the heat of the fire. A few people stood up to hug Todd and Lacy, excited that friends had returned. Todd and Lacy introduced themselves to the newcomers who had arrived since they were last there and then Lacy turned and introduced Sanch and Jake. They were quickly offered joints and beers and swigs from the jug of guaro. The conversation went all over the place with very few transitions: from religion to music to books to life back home. Sometimes the whole group conversed and sometimes it broke off into smaller, more intimate talks. Slowly, the crowd disbursed as people headed off to bed. The few remaining talked about what they would do if they went back home.

"I'm never going home," Jake said. "Seriously."

"I think we've all said that at one time," Rory said. He was a long-haired, bearded American from Colorado.

"How long have you been here?" Jake asked.

"Three months this time. First time, about five weeks."

"Why did you leave the first time?"

"Don't know. Thought I needed to go back and have a normal life, you know."

"How long before you came back?"

"I went to school for one semester and then told my folks I couldn't do it."

"Were they pissed?" Sanch asked.

"Nah. They are cool."

"Have you spoke to them since you've been back."

"Yeah man. We talk on occasion."

"Well, I've got to head back in a month," Todd said. "Fishing season starts again." He was a deckhand on a charter boat. He worked nine months and then would spend three months in Costa Rica. He had only done it once before but was hoping to make it an annual pilgrimage.

"I've got one more semester," Lacy said. "And then I'll be an elementary school teacher."

"I have no fucking clue what I want to do," Sanch said. People chuckled.

"I'm serious. This is what I like to do. What we are doing right now. This is all I want to do. Sit on a beach, drink some beer, smoke some pot, talk to some cool people, go surfing and jump off waterfalls on occasion."

"Amen, brother," Rory said. "Who says you have to do anything different?"

"What do you do for money?" Sanch asked.

"Money is nothing but a bullshit social construction, man. It only has value because people have agreed to accept it in exchange for goods or services."

"But you need it to survive in a society," Sanch said.

"For some things. And for those things, I do whatever it takes."

"Say you're running low tonight. You don't have five dollars to give to Charlie, what do you do?"

"Fuck, man. We'll worry about it when it happens. There is always some work to do. If you need money bad enough you'll find a way to make it. There are always tourists willing to spend money. I make money sometimes just playing guide. I've made twenty dollars a head taking people to a waterfall. Isn't that right, Todd?"

"Yep. I should've charged these guys."

"They already went?"

"Took them before we got here."

"Asshole. I could've used another forty dollars."

"I'm calling it a night," one of the girls said. She gave everyone hugs and a kiss on the cheek before heading off to her tent.

"I know what I'm going to do," Jake said. "Keep fixing boards at Lagarto Surf and win surf contests. That's it. Fixing boards is making us enough money to survive in Tamarindo."

"Lagarto Surf?" Rory said. "In Tamarindo? Fuck that place. That's the most expensive place in Costa Rica, besides San Jose."

"But there is work there and tourists?"

"Fucking Lagarto Surf, man? Fucking Tamarindo? That's what's wrong with this place. People trying to turn everything into resort towns. They're already selling timeshares and shit there. That place is doomed. This whole place is doomed. It'll start down here soon, and I'm going to have to find somewhere new. I heard Nicaragua or El Salvador is the new Costa Rica. Maybe that's where I'll go. Maybe Panama. Hell, it's all turning to shit. Born just a bit too late."

"All right fellas, I'm going to bed," Lacy said, and she and Todd left the fire.

"I'm turning in, too," Sanch said.

On the walk back to his tent, he spotted Charlie sitting in an Adirondack chair under the glow of the yellow light reading a book.

"Great place you got here," Sanch said.

Charlie nodded, scratched his neck but didn't look up.

"First night here, right?" Charlie said after a few seconds.

"Yep."

"How long you staying?"

"Don't know."

"That's what I said fifteen years ago."

"Came on vacation and never left?"

"Wasn't necessarily a vacation."

"Mind if I sit?" Sanch asked.

Charlie motioned to the empty chair next to him.

"Was it hard to find a way to survive here?"

"Look kid, I'm trying to read. I get asked this pretty often. How do you make a living here? How can I move here? I don't know. It's like anything else. If you want to, do it."

"How did you do it?"

Charlie shut the book. "I came with a good chunk of change. That's the key."

"What if you don't have much money to start with?"

"Then it's harder. Isn't it like that all over the world? Hustle. That's all I can tell you."

"Is this all you do now?"

"I build these, too." He tapped the chair. "I've got a few stores that will carry them and sell them."

"Do you ever get bored?"

"No such thing as boredom, my friend. There is anxiety, and there is depression, but never boredom. Do I get depressed? Sure."

"Even over here in a place so beautiful?"

"I had a family back home, too. I had a mother. I imagine she is dead now. That hurts sometimes, knowing that I left her back home with no real explanation why I left. I had friends, too. Sometimes I wonder what my life would've been like had I not screwed up. If I would've lived a good life. But that's neither here nor there. I can't dwell on that stuff. This is where I am now, and I'm usually pretty content with my path."

"Why did you leave?"

"Ran into some trouble. It doesn't matter anymore."

"Is that the only thing that causes you to be depressed?"

"Goddamn it, kid. Are you always this inquisitive?"

"No. Just that I'm thinking of never going back home and wondering how I can make it work."

"How long have you been over here?"

"What day is it?"

"That long, huh?"

"Maybe a month."

Charlie laughed. "That's it? You're still in the honeymoon stages, kid. This place takes a while before it reveals its true self to you. Have to keep up a curtain, you know. As long as the tourists keep coming back, we are good."

Sanch nodded.

"You get what I'm saying then?"

"I think so. Some things are better not talked about, right?"

Charlie winked.

"Do those things bother you?" Sanch asked.

"What things?"

"The things best not talked about?"

"Poverty, drugs, child sex. Those things?"

Sanch nodded. "I thought those things were best not talked about?"

"Kid, all I do is rent out this property to people who want to camp, and I build chairs. Those things happen out there, and I just do what I do. It happens in the States, too. It happens everywhere. Why would Costa Rica be any different?"

"I hoped it was."

"Pretty naive for your age, aren't you? Some people can live in denial of those things, and some have had their eyes opened and can never shut them again. You might be one of the cursed ones."

Sanch nodded.

"Go get some sleep, kid. You're thinking too much."

Sanch nodded again. Charlie continued reading from *Manufacturing Consent*.

"See you in the morning," Charlie said without looking up.

"Good night," Sanch said.

Charlie looked at him again and smiled. "We're all just stardust, buddy. Passing through this life waiting on the next. You'll get through this one, just like you did the last one."

"I hear ya," Sanch said. And Charlie smiled again.

"No, you don't," he said. "But you will."

Sanch walked off into the night toward his tent.

Chapter 17

Sanch was up early the next morning to a quiet camp. He took a walk down to the water and watched small sets roll in.

"Up early, Stardust," Charlie said as he stopped and stood next to him with a nine-foot longboard under his arm.

"Yeah man, just been in a funk lately."

"What's back home?"

"Nothing I want to go back to."

"Girlfriend?"

"Not anymore." Sanch smiled.

"Family?"

Sanch nodded. "Yeah, we don't get along so well."

"Family is hard, man."

"I miss my brother, too."

"You guys talk much?"

"He's dead. I talk to him. He don't talk to me though."

"What happened to him?"

"Heard what happened with a ship out near Yemen?"

"I did."

"My brother was on that ship. He survived the attack though. Surviving the attack was what killed him."

"Hate to hear that."

"Part of me says I should join the Navy in his honor, but then another part of me says I should do something different in his honor."

"Your dad Navy, too?"

"Twenty-two years. Fought in Vietnam."

"I see why you're troubled. Just got to do what's best for you. The universe is a wonderful, strange place, my brother. We are fortunate to go through it once and get it right. We are really blessed if we are given multiple opportunities."

"Don't let me hold ya up."

Charlie walked off into the water.

Sanch watched Charlie surf for a bit before Lacy walked up behind him and sat next to him.

"Hungry?" Lacy asked.

"For sure," Sanch said.

"Todd is up there getting things started now."

They walked together and poured themselves a coffee before sitting at the table.

"Eggs and tomatoes sound good?"

Sanch nodded and sipped his coffee.

Jake stumbled from his tent with his hands down his shorts. "I gotta get laid," he said.

Lacy shook her head. "Your friend is a pig."

Sanch nodded.

Todd brought over a plate of scrambled eggs with tomatoes, a rolled-up tortilla and half of a banana.

"How much do I owe in the jar?" Sanch asked.

"Don't worry about it. We covered it this morning."

After breakfast, they surfed until lunch. They ate peanut butter sandwiches and then took a nap and then they sat under the pavilion and played chess and got high.

Some campers put together a game of soccer on the beach, and Sanch joined while Jake took a second nap. And then they all went for an evening surf. And like that, the day passed on.

At dinner, Jake said he had to get back to Tamarindo. "I don't know when the contest is."

"We're staying a few more days and then heading south, somewhere. Maybe Jaco," Todd said.

"You aren't giving us a ride back?" Jake asked.

"The bus comes every morning," Lacy said.

"Ten thirty," one of the other campers added. "You'll take it all the way to—I think the town is called Paquera. Then you'll take a ferry boat to Puntarenas where you can then get a bus to Tamarindo."

"How long does that take?" Jake asked.

"A good while."

"That's bullshit, dude. Give us a ride back," Jake said.

"We aren't heading that way," Todd told him.

"You didn't tell us you weren't going back."

"We just decided today that we wanted to check out somewhere else," Lacy said.

"What about us?"

Jake scooped up a pile of rice and beans onto his fork and took a bite and then stopped chewing.

"You don't think it's kind of shitty?" he asked.

"We didn't think we were in a committed relationship," Todd said, laughing. Some other campers laughed too. "We just said we were coming to Santa Teresa and asked if you wanted to come along."

"I thought you were going back to Tamarindo."

"Sorry about that," Todd said.

"We'll manage," Sanch said.

"I know we'll fucking manage," Jake said, "But we're pretty damn far from Tamarindo. That wasn't a short ways away, you know?"

"Most of us have to take a bus when we go somewhere," Rory said. "You'll be okay." Him and a couple other campers laughed.

"Fuck you guys," Jake said. And everyone laughed again, including Sanch.

Jake looked at Sanch. "Fuck you, too," Jake said.

Shortly after, Rory went to the beach to start the fire.

Charlie joined the fire on this night and brought out a couple of guitars and drums, and they spent the night singing, dancing, drinking and smoking. Lacy and a couple of other girls hula-hooped. Jake tried talking to one of the girls that was dancing alone, and he could be overheard saying he hasn't been laid since he came to Costa Rica.

"That's probably best," she said. "I haven't had sex in three months. I'm learning to love myself before I love others."

"I'm not talking love," Jake said.

"That's the problem," she said.

"I don't know what happened," Jake said sitting back by the fire. "I used to get laid all the time. Now nothing."

"I'm thinking of going with Todd and Lacy," Sanch said. "Maybe see some other parts of Costa Rica."

"No way. We are traveling together. You can't just leave me like that."

"Why don't you come, too? They don't mind if we ride with them."

"Surf contest. You forget about that?"

"I know. How about after the contest we do a bit of traveling then."

"That's fine. But why do you want to leave Tamarindo? That place is perfect."

"I just want to see other places."

"All right. After the contest, we'll go somewhere else."

The next day they said their goodbyes and went to the bus. "Good luck," Lacy shouted as the bus departed.

The bus ride was long and uneventful. They transferred buses at a small, dusty one-restaurant village. They met some other travelers from the Santa Barbara, California, area and shared a beer with the couple while waiting for the next bus. They then boarded the ferry. Jake rolled a joint and signaled to the California couple to follow them to the back of the boat where the wind would carry the smell away from the rest of the passengers. It was nighttime by the time the boat docked at Puntarenas.

"You guys have a place to stay?" Jake asked as they were exiting the boat.

"Yeah man. Good luck on finding one."

Sanch and Jake walked down a few alleyways out of the port area. A man approached them saying "Taxi, taxi."

"No taxi," Jake said. "Hotel."

"Sí, sí. Hotel. Follow me." They followed the man into a run-down building. Three men sat in the corner of the lobby, watching them with half-opened red eyes.

"Where the hell are we?" Sanch whispered to Jake.

Jake laughed. "No clue. Don't look like Costa Rica anymore. That's for sure."

The man spoke to the fat lady at the counter in Spanish. Then he turned back to Sanch and Jake. "She says forty dollars."

"Each?" Jake asked.

The man shook his head. "For both."

"Give it to him," Jake said. Sanch handed the lady forty dollars. While Sanch waited for the key, Jake asked the man about food.

"All around," the man said. "But be careful. Not a good part of town by the docks. People see you lost, they try to rob you." He nodded to the guys sitting on the floor.

"Thanks," Jake said. The man stood his ground.

"Anything else?" Jake asked.

"Yes, my tip. I showed you where to get hotel."

Jake gave him a few colones.

"Have a good night," the man said and left.

The fat lady led Sanch and Jake up four flights of

stairs. The stairwell smelled of urine and flying insects buzzed at the flickering lights.

"Anyone else staying here?" Jake asked the lady. She ignored him. She looked annoyed that she had to show them to the room. The room she took them to had no number on the door. "Remember fourth floor, third door on the right," Jake said to Sanch.

"Baño," the lady said pointing down the hall to the last door.

She unlocked the door to their room and gave Sanch the key and left them there.

They opened the door and stood in the hall for a few minutes laughing. Two twin beds squeezed in with no space at the head or foot of the bed.

"I can't even fit on a twin bed without my feet hanging off," Sanch said.

The surfboards barely fit in as well, wedged between the beds and then leaned against the wall. Sanch and Jake crawled over the boards to get to the beds. The room couldn't have been any bigger than six by ten with a seven-foot-high ceiling.

"Look at this," Sanch said. Jake looked over at Sanch, who had his feet on the wall. He couldn't stretch out fully.

"Sucks for you," Jake said. He was stretched out fine. Sanch tried to look out the one window in the room at the foot of his bed. It didn't open, and it was too grimy to see out.

"Wonder if they, at least, wash the sheets?" Sanch asked.

"Shut up. It's just for one night."

"I don't even want to go looking for food."

"Me neither," Jake said. "I just want to go to sleep and get out of here as early as we can."

"I didn't even know there were cities in Costa Rica except for San Jose."

"Guess it ain't all tropics. Go to sleep."

They lay in the beds for about thirty minutes before Jake said, "I can't sleep. I'm hungry as hell."

"Me too," Sanch said.

"Think you can make until morning?"

"No."

They went back down the urine smelling stairwell and into the warm night. There were hundreds of people, not all looked like tourists, wandering the streets that were lined with mid-rise buildings. They passed storefronts displaying Nike and Reebok shoes, TV sets, VCRs and CD players, watches, purses and hats. They passed people sleeping in doorways and thirteen-year-old prostitutes. They passed couples on vacation and kids running the streets because there was nothing better to do and nowhere else to go. They passed old men drinking beer and catcalling the girls walking by. They passed old men playing cards at bars and punk rock kids standing on the corners.

They walked a few more blocks, not being able to decide where to eat.

They stopped at a pizza joint and ordered a pizza with too much garlic.

"I can't eat another bite," Sanch said. "I hate to toss this though."

"Let's give it to a homeless guy then."

They offered it to the first guy they saw that looked homeless. The man thanked them. He seemed shocked they would offer him food. He opened the box and cringed his nose at the smell. He took a bite and spat it out, tossing the rest in the gutter next to him.

"Ain't that some bullshit," Jake said.

The earliest bus left at nine-thirty and then it to another six hours until they got back to Tamarindo. Sai. slept most of the way on the bus.

"You know that was the first day we went without surfing since we've been here," Jake said.

They stopped by Tamarindo Adventure and found out the contest was in three days.

"I was looking all over for you," Lorenzo said. "Everyone said you left."

They continued walking towards the camp.

"Look at that. I'm gone a few days, and people notice. They welcome me back. This is where I belong. I don't think I've ever felt I belonged anywhere as much as I do here," Jake said.

Before they made it to the campsite, Andrea caught up with them.

"Wondering when you were coming back," she said. "You didn't even tell me you were leaving."

She hugged him and gave him a kiss.

"It was a sudden decision. We woke up and decided to go check out somewhere new."

"Well, I'm glad you came back for me."

Sanch didn't say anything. She walked with them to the camp and that night she stayed with him in his tent.

The next morning she left early. Jake swung in the hammock.

"You motherfucker," he said. "I had to jerk off listening to you guys."

Sanch shrugged his shoulders.

"I told you she's your girl now," Jake said.

"I don't know what I'm going to do. It's nice having a naked body next to me, but I don't want a girlfriend."

"Well, you've got one."

The night before the contest, the town filled with excitement as people from all over the country arrived, either to surf it or to watch it. And word had spread about the new contender: Jake from Tamarindo Adventures. The day of the contest Jake woke up to Lorenzo presenting him with a striped red, white and green jersey with the lettering Tamarindo Adventures printed across the front and back.

"Hadn't put one of these on in a while," Jake said pulling it down over his shoulders.

He paraded to the beach with a string of followers, Sanch bringing up the rear.

Sanch couldn't believe the crowd. It seemed as if the town's population had doubled. Since the contest was held at Tamarindo Beach and not one of the better nearby breaks, the waves were small and mushy, which were perfect for Jake. It was what most closely resembled the breaks around Pensacola. Jake and Pedro both won their heats with ease. However, the quarterfinals weren't what people hoped for as the defending Costa Rican champ was pitted against the newcomer from America. Everyone had expected that match-up to be left for the finals, but it seemed as if the contest would be decided early.

"I win this heat," Jake said, "I got the contest. Could you imagine that? Haven't surfed competitively for seven years and then come back like I ain't missed a beat. Even if I don't win, I still did pretty damn good, huh?"

"You got this," Sanch said.

The waves were smaller than at the beginning of the contest, and there was talk of calling it for the day and finishing tomorrow with better waves. Pedro favored that idea, but in the end, the heat was held, and Pedro could not catch a wave. Jake caught everything he paddled for.

Pedro blamed the results on the wave conditions.

Others complained as well, saying the results didn't really prove who was better. Jake said it did.

Lorenzo was just as excited as Jake. Tamarindo Adventures was named a dozen times, and his new surf team was a force in the local surf circuit.

The winning amount was two hundred dollars and a tiny trophy.

"You did us proud," Lorenzo said to Jake as they were walking to the Frenchman's café to celebrate. "The next contest isn't for another month. Down in Jaco."

"We will rent you a place down there for the contest. Also, we don't want you working at Lagarto anymore."

"What will I do for money then?"

"We will give you a job with us."

"Doing what?"

"Whatever we need. Repairing boards, giving surf lessons. Do you know how to sail a boat?"

"Of course."

"We are buying a sailboat and will offer sailing trips to Witches Rock and Ollie's Point like they do at Aqua Blue."

"Sanch can be your first mate."

"Deal," Jake said, and they shook hands.

"We'll talk tomorrow. Anything you want from Tamarindo Adventures, just ask. You want to go kayaking; you got it. Want to ride some four-wheelers or dirt bikes, just ask. You are part of the team now."

When Lorenzo left, Jake said, "You hear that? How much easier could this get? I don't know how it always happens to me, but shit just falls in my lap. It's good to be me."

"I guess it ain't too bad knowing you either," Sanch said.

"Damn right. Who else could you've come here with

283

and run this town like we are doing?"

"It's been fun."

"And only getting better. We're getting a boat."

"You don't know how to sail though."

"How hard could it be? Have you ever seen me not learn how to do something? It just takes me a few tries, and I'll figure it out."

Andrea, Mary and Johnny joined them at the table for beers, which the Frenchman provided on the house. A celebration was taking place. Even Pedro came by and congratulated him.

"No hard feelings?" Jake asked him.

"Not at all, my friend. Pura Vida. I'll get you the next time. The waves were shit. You got lucky. I'm still the champ, and you know that."

"For now," Jake said. Pedro laughed.

The party went on for a good couple hours before moving to the Mambo Bar and finally ended with dancing at the discoteca. Sanch called it a night a bit early to walk with Andrea to her place.

Chapter 18

Sanch and Andrea were awoken by a revving motorbike just below her window. Sanch looked out at Jake on the dirt bike turning donuts. When Jake saw Sanch looking down, he stopped.

"Get up," he yelled. "We've got toys."

Sanch looked at Andrea's alarm clock. It was six-forty in the morning. The sun wasn't even completely awake yet.

"What does he want?" Andrea asked.

Sanch shrugged and went downstairs. Jake told him that after Sanch and Andrea left last night he was able to convince Lorenzo to let him take the bikes for a couple of days. Mary had never seen the waterfall in Montezuma, so they planned a road trip.

"But we gotta leave now," Jake said. "Remember how long it took to get there. Meet me at the shop." He sprayed dirt in his wake.

Sanch went back up to tell Andrea, and she wanted to go as well, saying there would be no problem getting a couple of days off.

Jake was on the phone when Sanch and Andrea arrived at Tamarindo Adventure. Lorenzo wasn't around.

"Long distance calls, too," Jake said. "Talking to my old man."

"Are we supposed to be here?" Andrea asked. Sanch shrugged. When Jake got off the phone, Sanch asked.

"We came back last night, and he gave me the keys to the bikes. Said I can pick them up in the morning."

"What about the phone?"

"I tried it, and it worked."

"Good enough for me," Sanch said. He picked up the

phone and had an operator connect him to home. His dad answered.

"Hey pops," Sanch said. There were a couple of seconds of silence. "Dad, it's me."

"I know who it is. Do you know how worried your mom is? We've been calling Jake's parents worried to death. You guys forget how to use the phone?"

"Phones are hard to come by over here."

"We, at least, expected a call for Thanksgiving. Your grandparents were upset."

"When was Thanksgiving?"

"Are you kidding me? It's nearly Christmas."

"No shit?" He looked at Jake. "You know we forgot about Thanksgiving?"

"My dad told me," Jake said. "Ain't that some bullshit?"

"Brian, you there?"

"I'm here," Sanch said. Jake and Andrea went outside to let Sanch finish talking.

"When you plan on coming home? Fantasy time about up, isn't it?"

"Probably not anytime soon. Going to see how this plays out for a while, you know? Things are going good."

"So that's it then. No Navy? Just like that, you've made your decision?"

"I made my decision a while ago. You just refuse to listen."

"My dad, me, your brother. All that means nothing to you? You are too good for that, huh? Your brother gave the ultimate sacrifice for your freedom, and you can't repay him with even four years of service? Not even two? Nothing? You're just going to be selfish? A man of leisure, huh? Is that how I raised you? It's time you become a goddamn man, son."

"And what's it mean to be a man, dad? Never question authority? Never question anything? Just do as I'm told? Is that being a man?"

"You ungrateful little shit. You got a responsibility, boy. To God, your country and your family."

"Is that right?"

"When are you dropping this Neverland bullshit? You think life is all just good times and rock and roll, huh?"

"Maybe."

"Maybe? So what is it you're going to do?"

"I don't know. But I'm closer to it here than I've ever been."

"Closer to what?"

"I don't know. But it's the first time I've been happy in a long time."

"Are you on drugs?"

Sanch laughed. "Not at the moment."

"Goddamn it. Can you be serious for a minute?"

"Sorry."

"What about your mother? Doesn't she deserve to be happy? She has a son in the ground and a son who doesn't give a shit about anything. Doesn't she get to be happy?"

"How is Mom? Is she around? Let me talk to her."

"She's sleeping."

"She's always sleeping," Sanch mumbled.

"What? Don't you dare. That woman has been through so much."

"Tell her I love her, will you? You guys should plan a trip. She would like it here."

"No shit she would like it there. But we aren't all as privileged as you, now are we? Some of us have responsibilities."

"Like what—having a house that you can barely afford? A car you can barely afford? Work all life just to pay off debt? Is that what you mean by responsibility?"

"You are so goddamn smart, aren't you? You have all the answers. It's all just a big goddamn joke, isn't it?"

"What if it is? And we spend our whole life fighting it instead of laughing about it?"

"Maybe Granddaddy is right about you."

"What did he say?"

"Nothing."

"Tell me what he said."

"You want to know what he said? He said, sometimes no matter how hard we try, we can't save every soul. Some souls are just lost. Maybe you're just a lost soul. And all we can do is pray for you. That's what he said."

Sanch laughed.

"And you laugh about it?"

"It's funny. I think that about you guys sometimes."

"Boy, I hope you find your way soon."

"I do too. Look, I've got to get going. But tell momma I love her, okay?"

"Yeah."

"And you take care, too."

But his dad had already hung up the phone.

Sanch walked out to Jake and Andrea.

"Have a good talk with the old man?" Jake asked.

Sanch looked at him.

"That bad?"

Sanch smiled. Jake laughed. Andrea gave him a hug.

"I've never ridden a dirt bike before," Sanch said.

Jake gave him a quick tutorial.

"Shouldn't we have shoes and pants on instead of shorts and flip-flops?"

288

"Probably, but we don't have any. Just roll it off the kickstand and start it up like this." Jake showed him.

Sanch did it.

"Now just give it some gas like I told you and it'll go. When you hear it start revving up, the handle by your left hand is the clutch. Pull that and shift with your right foot. Pretty easy. You'll get the hang of it," Jake said.

Sanch gave it gas. And after a few timid tries, he began to loosen up, picking up speed. He stopped when he came back around.

"Let's get the road on the show," Jake said. The girls hopped on, Andrea behind Sanch and Mary behind Jake. They had no idea how to get to where they were going. They took nothing with them. No change of clothes, no tents, and no sleeping bags.

After about thirty minutes on the road, Jake picked up the pace. Sanch hesitated at first, but pushed on, keeping up.

"Slow down please," Andrea said as she gripped him tighter. Sanch looked at Jake speeding further away and for a few seconds increased the speed to catch up, but as Andrea gripped tighter and buried her head into his back, he eased off.

For about twenty minutes Jake was out of sight, and Sanch and Andrea continued on the same road at a steady pace, having no clue if they were headed in the right direction. But neither did Jake. He just acted like he did.

Jake and Mary pulled over at a small stand on the side of the road that served chicken on a stick and a small bowl of rice and beans. While having a snack and drinking a soda, Jake asked, "Why did you guys slow down? Get scared?"

Sanch shook his head no, but Andrea said yes.

"I know. This guy is driving like a maniac," Mary said. "I told him to slow down."

"I've been riding motorcycles my whole life, haven't I, Sanch?"

They continued riding until just about dusk. Jake pulled off the road when he spotted a small pool hall. For hours, they had seen nothing but trees on the long, winding dirt road and then it appeared. Out front there were several varieties of vehicles: dirt bikes like Sanch and Jake rode, trucks, vans, bicycles, and cars that looked pieced together from twenty different makes and models.

"Are we going the right way?" Sanch asked. "I don't remember it taking this long. And I don't remember driving by this."

"We were driving a lot faster in the truck than on these things. Hell, half the time we ain't going but twenty miles an hour."

They walked into the aluminum shed-like bar. Four pool tables were crammed tightly into the room. Men, ranging from eight to eighty, sat shoulder to shoulder on the benches around the walls. Andrea and Mary were the only women in there.

"Will you look at this? Out in the middle of nowhere," Jake said.

"Ever been here?" Sanch asked Andrea as they entered.

Andrea shook her head. "I have not seen much of Costa Rica except Tamarindo and San Jose."

"See if we can get a game," Jake said and placed coins on one of the tables. The players looked at him. The look wasn't friendly as if they didn't know what to make of these outsiders, seeing as how that wasn't a normal stop on tourist routes. Andrea spoke to one of the men playing and explained they were just passing through.

"They selling beers in here?" Sanch asked. Andrea asked for him. The man shook his head. He pointed to a cooler, offering one to Sanch. And while Jake played using the Costa Rican rules he had learned at El Pescador, Sanch drank one of the man's beers. They only stuck around for three games before Jake said, "We should probably get going if we wanna make it there tonight."

Sanch offered the man money for the beer and the man refused. Sanch thanked him with "Pura Vida."

They continued on. Up ahead the road took a sharp left and then another sharp right before going up a hill at about a thirty-five-degree slope, if not steeper in some areas. Sanch stopped at the bottom. The dim headlights of the bikes were the only lights on the road.

"I don't know about this," Sanch said. "I can't even see the top of the hill."

"Just hit the gas and go," Jake said. "Like this."

He shouted down when he made it to the top, "Come on. It ain't bad."

Sanch could just make out a silhouette of Jake and Mary at the top of the hill as they stood in front of the glow of the bike's headlight.

"Ready?" Sanch asked Andrea.

She squeezed him tighter.

He gave it gas, but being afraid to give it too much and flip backward, he didn't give it enough and could feel the bike becoming unstable. He twisted the throttle, and the back tire fishtailed from under him and not able to correct the bike in time, he laid the bike on its side. Andrea fell off unhurt, a small scrape on her hand from the gravel and what baseball players called a strawberry about the size of a quarter on her elbow. The bike pinned Sanch's right leg to the ground, and he shouted up to Jake that he was unable to move it. Andrea couldn't lift the bike for him. Jake rode down, leaving Mary up the hill in the dark.

"What happened?" Jake said. He lifted the bike.

A bit of blood trickled down Sanch's knee.

Jake helped him up, laughing. Sanch limped around, walking off a nonphysical pain. "Take Andrea up with you," Sanch said. "I don't think I can make it with her on the back."

"This is pretty rough riding," Jake said. "Not going to lie. It ain't easy for me either. Hell, I about busted my ass on one of those turns back there. Can you make it up? If not, I can walk back down and ride your bike up."

"I got it," Sanch said.

Jake and Andrea rode up.

Sanch looked up the hill and then twisted the gas and again the back wheel spun out, but without the extra weight in the back, he stabilized it and made it to the top.

"See, it wasn't that hard," Jake said. "And we definitely didn't come across this hill riding with Todd and Lacy."

Sanch nodded. Andrea climbed back on. Jake and Mary took off. Sanch sat on the bike for a minute.

"Are you okay?" Andrea asked.

"Yeah."

Jake's tail light shrunk in the distance.

"If we don't go we are going to lose him," Andrea said.

"I'm good," Sanch said, and they continued on in the dusty unknown darkness.

After about another hour of the grueling ride, they came to a fork in the road. Jake chose the right way. The other would have turned them back towards Tamarindo.

"This hill I recognize," Sanch said as they stopped at the bottom of the hill.

"That's Montezuma right up there, right?" Jake said.

"I believe so."

The hill, although higher and longer and more winding than the previous one, had a more gradual slope. They entered the town like cowboys after a long cattle drive, covered in dust and wanting a drink and a place to sleep. Sanch and Jake entered the bar at the beach while the girls waited outside, too weary to enter the excitement. The guys bought a beer each and waters for the girls. While waiting for the drinks, Jake asked the girl next to him about cheap places to sleep. She told him the cheapest place in town was on the beach. She had been sleeping under the stars for a week now.

They downed the beers and took the waters to the girls and rode to the beach access. They walked into the soft sand and settled down at a used fire pit. Sanch and Jake scouted for firewood while the girls gathered palm leaves for bedding. Sanch and Jake found a big enough log that would burn through the night, each grabbing one end and carried it to the fire pit. With kindling, they built a teepee to start the fire and continued building the fire until it was large enough for the log, and then all four huddled around the fire on the earthen bed.

Mary eventually snuggled up to Jake and Jake put his arm around her.

"Just for warmth," Mary said.

"I'll take what I can get," Jake said.

Sanch and Andrea kissed and snuggled tight.

"Why do you three like Costa Rica so much?" Andrea asked while they lay looking at the stars.

"Surf," Jake said. "And cheap."

"I think the fact that the country hasn't had an army since the forties creates such a peaceful environment. It's as if that peacefulness transfers to the citizens. I've never met greater people," Mary said.

"What about you, Sanch?"

"I don't know. Maybe, it's all that together. There is a certain amount of freedom here that I've never experienced before."

Chapter 19

"Where's the girls?" Jake asked.

Sanch slowly opened his eyes, looking around.

"Is that them out there?" He pointed to two girls in the water.

The sun had just broken the horizon, and the thirty or so people that had slept on the beach started to wake.

"Look how many people slept on the beach. How can you ever want to leave this place?" Jake said.

"Want to join the girls?"

The girls' clothes were piled just before the water, underwear included.

"You have any clothes on?" Jake yelled. The girls giggled. Sanch and Jake looked at each other and quickly disrobed, running naked into the clear morning water and swimming out to meet them.

"You stay away from me," Mary said to Jake.

"What? You cuddled up with me last night and today I don't get any loving?"

"You aren't getting anywhere near me when you are naked though."

"That's bullshit. I haven't been laid since we got here."

"That is not my problem."

"Look at those two," Jake said pointing at Sanch and Andrea. Sanch stuck out his middle finger at Jake but continued kissing Andrea. "Don't you want that?" Jake asked Mary.

"Possibly, but not necessarily with you. Not yet at least. I will say you are starting to grow on me though."

Andrea pushed off Sanch and swam closer to Mary. Sanch swam towards her again.

"You need to calm down," Andrea said. "Too many people around right now."

Jake laughed. "I'm just going to rub one out right here."

"Shit, I might have to, too," Sanch said.

"You boys have fun," Mary said. And she swam to shore.

"Come on, Andrea. Help me out just a bit," Sanch said.

"You are funny," she said and swam with Mary.

"Damn it. I'm going in, too."

"You go on ahead. I'll be another minute," Jake said.

Sanch, Mary and Andrea put on clothes over their wet bodies.

"He's really jerking off out there, isn't he?" Mary asked.

"Probably," Sanch said.

The three sat around the coals waiting on Jake to finish his swim. Sanch added a few more small sticks trying to get a fire built again, but Jake arrived before he was able to get it started.

"Feel better?" Mary asked.

"A blowjob would be better though."

"I'm sure it would," Mary said.

They grabbed a pastry and coffee at a small café across from the beach before walking the long path to the falls and when it came time to jump Sanch was the only one who wanted to.

"I did it and nearly broke my neck," Jake said. "I don't need to be warned twice."

Andrea tried to persuade Sanch not to do it either.

"I've got to," he said. "I can't be this close to a waterfall and not jump off."

"But you have done it before."

"I'm going to do it again, too."

"You are a big kid," she said.

"I'm going to join you," said Mary. "That somehow made sense."

Sanch smiled, gave Andrea a kiss on the cheek and he and Mary made their ascent. They waved from the top and then holding hands, they jumped. After resurfacing, they swam together towards the impact zone, trying to get as close as possible to the falling water. Sanch held his hands up in celebration.

"You feel better now?" Andrea asked. She and Jake sat on the edge with their feet dangling in the cold water.

They made it to Charlie's by midday. The sound of the motorbikes interrupted a game of soccer on the beach, and the campers rushed to see who the newcomers were. Although Sanch and Jake had only spent a couple of days there the first time, the second time around, they were greeted like old friends. And not only from Todd and Lacy, who were the most excited to see them but from the rest of the campers as well. It was as if Charlie's was a mythical dwelling in the forest only visible to a certain breed of travelers, unseen by the average tourist. If you could see it, you belonged. You were accepted into the family of adventurers. But passers-by would never know it existed.

"You know all these people?" Andrea asked after the bombardment of hugs and introductions. Sanch had already forgotten half of their names.

The soccer game commenced.

"I thought you two were leaving?" Jake asked.

"We are. Just haven't done so yet," Todd said. He pulled a joint from behind his ear.

Sanch took over Todd's spot as goalie. Jake sat off to the side with Todd and smoked a joint.

After the game, Charlie showed Sanch and Andrea to the only unoccupied tent cabin.

"You two will have to sleep in a tent," he said to Jake and handed him one. "You know how to set up a tent, right?"

"Some bullshit," Jake said. "Let me get the cabin?"

"Sorry dude," Sanch said.

Lacy made a large pot of spaghetti with garlic and oil and shared with Sanch, Jake, Andrea and Mary. When Sanch ate the last bite in his bowl, Andrea took a finger and wiped the oil from his chin.

"Goddamn that was some good spaghetti," Jake said. He, Sanch and Todd broke pieces off a nearly stale loaf of French bread and sopped up the rest of the oil and garlic chips in the bottom of the pot.

"You guys want to go into town?" Jake asked.

The girls gathered up the dishes to wash.

"Me and Andrea were going to take a nap and take a walk along the beach," Sanch said.

"Fuck that. Let's go get drunk in town."

"Does he always have to do what you say?" Lacy said.

"I'm just saying. Let's get a quick surf in before dark and then go into town. That sounds way more fun than taking a walk."

"For you maybe," Lacy said. "You don't always have to be in control, you know?"

"Todd, you want to go into town?"

"That's cool," he said.

"I wouldn't mind going into town," Mary said. "Might like to do a bit of looking around. Maybe do some shopping. Find me a good looking guy."

"I'm right here," Jake said.

"I said good looking," Mary said and winked at him.

"And me and Sanch will stay here," Andrea said.

"How do you always end up pussy-whipped? Just got over one chick and you're right back into another."

Sanch smiled at him and looked at Andrea. She didn't look his way.

"You really can be a dick sometimes," Lacy said.

"You guys argue this out, I'll be waiting by the car," Todd said.

"That's fucked up, and you know it," Jake said to Sanch. "We came on this trip together, and now you're going to ditch me for a chick."

"I'm not ditching you. Just don't want to go into town and get drunk tonight. Going to take it easy."

"Whatever. I'm going," Jake said.

Todd and Lacy got into their car, and Jake and Mary left on the motorcycle. Sanch and Andrea walked hand in hand back to the tent.

Sanch was awoken from Todd's truck coming into camp at a sliding stop and Lacy yelling for Charlie to come quick. Sanch and Andrea rushed outside.

"Jake's bike slid out from under him. He was riding too fast. He broke his leg. The bone is sticking out his knee," Lacy said.

"How is Mary?" Sanch asked.

"A little banged up, but not terribly. She's waiting with him. The bike is unrideable," Lacy said. Charlie cranked his pickup and followed Todd and Lacy. Sanch and Andrea followed on the motorcycle. When they arrived, Mary sat by herself on the road, bandages on her hands and elbows and crying next to the wrecked bike.

"Where's Jake?" Sanch asked.

"They took him."

"Who?"

"Some people. They came in a van, put these on me," she held up her bandaged hands, "and then took him."

"Where?"

"A hospital in Puntarenas, they said. I don't know where that is."

"I'll take the bike," Charlie said. "You can ride with me back to Tamarindo," he said to Mary. Then to Sanch, "You two go to the hospital."

Andrea jumped on the back, and they were off, stopping in Montezuma to fill up on gas at a hardware store that poured its gas out of gallon milk jugs. Sanch wouldn't think about how fast he was driving that day until months later. At the time, he was getting to the hospital as quickly as he could and somehow weaved around potholes and passed cars when they hit paved road, and it was as if he was guided by another force.

They made it to the ferry crossing, the last ferry of the day, rolled the bike on and were across the water. Andrea asked for directions, and they rode into town, weaving through the traffic, at one point swerved around a stopped bus and squeezed beside the oncoming car and the stopped bus with just inches to spare on either side.

They followed signs to the hospital, parking the motorcycle near the front entrance.

The receptionist called down a doctor. The doctor told Andrea that the American—that was how they referred to Jake—was asleep. They had to knock him out to set the bone in place, but the break was bad and needed surgery. They would have to wait for the swelling to go down first, about three days. Sanch wasn't allowed to see him until after the surgery.

"I've gotta see him," Sanch said, but the doctor refused.

Sanch and Andrea crossed the street and split a ham sandwich on a baguette and a soda while deciding what to do.

"Do we get a hotel here?" Andrea asked.

"I gotta get the bike back. And there's nothing we can do here. We should just get back to Tamarindo. Charlie can give us a ride back with his truck."

"Doctors are good here," Andrea said. "He'll be okay. The doctors train in America and other places. They know what they're doing."

They finished the sandwich and got back on the bike for the long drive back to Tamarindo. The sun was setting, and the bugs were out. On the Pan-American Highway he got the bike up to sixty miles an hour but with no helmet, the bugs slammed into his face, and he had to keep his eyes half-shut, and his head tilted downwards so the bugs hit his forehead instead of puncturing an eyeball. Andrea buried her head into his back.

They made it into town in the early morning hours as a few revelers were just getting to their hotels from a night of drinking. They slept at Andrea's and were awake by sunup. Andrea went to work to talk to her boss, and Sanch drove the bike back to Tamarindo Adventures to tell them what happened. Charlie beat him to it. He and Lorenzo sat drinking a coffee.

"I shouldn't have ever let you guys take these," Lorenzo said when he saw Sanch. "I let him mess everything up."

"If it wasn't bikes," Charlie said, "it would have been something else."

"So how is he?" Lorenzo asked.

"Don't know. They wouldn't let me see him. I should probably call his folks."

Sanch called, and Fat Boy already knew. The doctors had called him and explained the situation. Fat Boy had then contacted the embassy to get his son home. He didn't want Jake operated on in a Third World country. He had been reassured the doctors were top-notch, but he wanted his son home.

"Go get him," Jake's dad said to Sanch.

"The doctors won't let me see him."

"I don't care what they said. Go get my son."

"I'll see what I can do."

"So what's the plan?" Charlie asked when Sanch got off the phone.

"They don't want him to be operated on here."

"Why not? They have perfectly capable surgeons. What do they suggest?"

"His dad wants me to go get him and bring him home."

"I'll give you a ride," Charlie said.

Sanch turned and looked down the road at Tamarindo. He didn't want it to end. Just yesterday they were planning on living the rest of their lives in Costa Rica, and now it was over. It was like it was all just a dream and when he opened his eyes the fantasy would be broken, and he would be right back to living a life he didn't want and working at a job he hated.

"Sanch. What do you want to do?" Charlie asked.

"Let me get one more surf in before we go," Sanch said.

They took the truck to Langosta for a session. It was still early enough that they had the break to themselves. After about three waves each Sanch said, "Let's go get Jake. I can't be out here while he's in the hospital. Surfing just isn't the same without him."

Sanch packed up the tents and Charlie helped him load up his and Jake's boards.

"Can we stop by Andrea's work before we head out?" Sanch asked.

She ran out when she saw them.

"Look, I've got to go get Jake. I don't know how to get him back to the States without me going with him. I don't know what else to do. I can't put him on a plane alone."

"I understand, Sancho. Let me ride with you to the hospital," Andrea said.

She rode between Sanch and Charlie.

"Can we stop by my place first?"

She ran upstairs and came back with a wad of money and handed it to Sanch.

"I've been saving up to go to America, but maybe you could use it to get a ticket back," she said.

Sanch counted it. Four hundred and eighty dollars.

"You saved this from working at the pizza place?"

She didn't answer him.

Andrea broke the silence which they had been riding in for the first hour.

"You are coming back?" she asked.

Sanch paused for a moment and looked at her.

"I can't take your money," he said.

"You aren't coming back, are you?"

"I really want to, but I can't take this." He put the roll of money in her lap. "You've worked for it."

A tear rolled down her cheek. Sanch tried to wipe it, but she moved her head away.

She placed her head on his shoulder and put her small hand into his hand. They rode that way until the hospital. Sanch had even fallen asleep with his head resting against hers and although she was uncomfortable that way she didn't move so as not to wake him.

At the hospital, Charlie waited in the truck parked out front, while Sanch and Andrea went to check on Jake. The same doctor greeted them. He said, "You here for the American, no?"

"You speak English now?" Sanch said. "How is he?"

The doctor made his hands into fists and raised them to eyes and wrung them back and forth imitating someone crying.

"He cries a lot," the doctor said. "Big baby."

"I'm here to take him home," Sanch said.

"I know." The doctor had already been informed by the embassy. He had argued that it wasn't advisable. But Jake's dad insisted, and the doctor had no choice. He said that Jake's leg was so bad that if it didn't get the constant attention they were giving him it would almost certainly develop into gangrene. Letting Jake out was against his better judgment, but he couldn't convince his dad. "Taking him home is a really stupid idea. If we did surgery, he would be okay. But without surgery, there is not much we can do for him. His leg is really bad. He could lose it."

Andrea wasn't allowed to go upstairs with Sanch, and she went back to wait with Charlie. The hospital was the worst Sanch had seen. The ceiling tiles were water-stained, and rust-colored streaks ran down dingy white walls. People walked the halls not dressed in scrubs, but in plain clothes. Doctors wore long white lab coats. The elevator creaked and groaned up to the sixth floor and at some point between the fourth and fifth floor it seemed to have gotten stuck for a few seconds, but the doctor didn't seem to be concerned. Sanch followed the doctor down the hallway.

"He's in the fourth room to the left," the doctor said and turned, leaving Sanch alone.

Sanch slowly walked the silenced cream-colored hall. The antiseptic smell made him half-expect to see cadavers in the beds, but all the beds were empty. Jake's room didn't have a door and as he entered he saw Jake propped up in the bed staring out the window.

"Hey buddy," Sanch said.

"Goddamn," Jake said and then cried. Sanch had never seen Jake cry and didn't know what to do. He inched closer to Jake's bed and put a hand on his shoulder. It shook with each sob.

"I didn't think you were coming for me."

"Come on, man. You knew I'd be here. They wouldn't let me in for a couple days. I was here the day it happened."

"I'm probably gonna lose my leg," Jake said.

"Looks like they're taking care of you. Got the room to yourself."

"They isolated me. Didn't you notice there isn't anyone else on this floor?"

"I did notice that. What happened?"

"I wouldn't stop screaming," Jake said. "I didn't know what was going on. No one spoke English. And they wouldn't let me use the phone, and I wanted to leave. They had me on the second floor, and I tried to break out the window."

Sanch laughed.

"I'm not kidding." Jake laughed, too. "I was going to jump out the window and escape."

"You would've probably broke your other leg."

"I don't care. It was horrible. They come in here and laugh at me. Look, they even stole my earrings. They took my wallet. They fucking robbed me of everything. I'm not bullshitting. Look at my ears."

Sanch looked. Jake's earrings were gone.

"They came in and started taking my clothes off, and I tried to fight them, and I started screaming for help, and then they stuck me with a needle. When I woke up, I was strapped to a fucking bed. Like in a straightjacket and all I had was this robe. I look down at my knee, and it's as big as a goddamn basketball with a hole in it where gelatin blobs of blood keep oozing out. Here look at it."

Jake pulled the sheet back and showed his knee which was still as big as a basketball but with a bandage around it and brownish blood seeping through the gauze. The flesh around his knee, from his thigh just above the knee going all the way up to his hip and down his calf to his ankle were colors he had never seen flesh turn—a yellowish, brownish, purplish color.

"That looks really bad, Jake. You should probably let them operate. The doctor said you could get gangrene if it gets infected. Everyone has said the doctors here are really good. The buildings look bad, but the doctors know what they are doing."

"I'm probably going to lose my leg." Jake started crying again.

A male nurse came in at that time.

"This motherfucker, watch what he does to me," Jake said.

"Hi," the nurse said to Sanch. "Let's go," he then said to Jake. The nurse laughed.

"See that shit? All they do is laugh. They think this is funny."

The nurse helped Jake into a wooden wheelchair, a fossil from the nineteen thirties. It had leather straps dangling behind on the floor. If Jake put on an aluminum helmet it would look like he was about to be fried in an electric chair. Sanch followed them into the elevator and down a few floors into another tiny room with scuffed linoleum flooring and a wooden bench. The only other things in the room were a sink and a cabinet with the doors dangling on the hinges.

The nurse put on plastic gloves and took out a wad of gauze pads from the cabinet. He undid the bandage and exposed a grotesque, bloated knee. The nurse cleared away the dried blood and a hole big enough to stick a thumb into in the center of the inflated leg. Jake winced at every move and tears rolled down his face.

"That's where the bone came out of," Jake said. "Watch what he's about to do now. I hate this so bad."

"This is when he cries," the nurse said. He then clasped Jake's knee in both hands and squeezed, the muscles forming on his forearm. A dark red almost purple jello-like substance came from the hole. Jake screamed and cried out and flailed his arms looking for something to grasp. Sanch backed away.

"See," the nurse said. "He cries. Always crying."

"You'd fucking cry, too," Jake said. The nurse squeezed again. More blobbed, coagulated blood came out.

"What is that?" Sanch asked.

"Blood clots," the nurse said. Another nurse walked in then, and the two nurses said something in Spanish.

"What? What'd she say?" Jake demanded when the second nurse left.

"Nothing," the nurse said.

"Don't tell me nothing. I heard her speak. She said something. What was it?"

The nurse smiled.

"See that?" Jake said to Sanch. "That's why I want to get the fuck home. Be in a hospital where they speak English."

The nurse cleaned the wound again, at times jabbing the alcohol soaked gauze into the wound. Jake gripped the sides of the wooden bench and gnashed his teeth and tears poured down his face. The nurse finished by wrapping it tightly with a fresh bandage.

A female nurse entered with a plastic bag filled with Jake's clothes. She helped him put on his shorts and his shirt. Both were filthy from the fall and covered in dried blood.

"Couldn't even wash my clothes?" he said. She then directed him where to get his wallet, and the male nurse told him after he gets his wallet, he must pay.

Sanch wheeled him there, and Jake signed out his stuff. A Ziploc bag held his wallet and his earrings.

"And you thought they were trying to rob you," Sanch said.

"They were. They were trying to kill me, too. I wouldn't eat. I was afraid they were going to poison me."

Sanch laughed.

"Shit's not funny."

Out in the corridor, Jake looked at the receipt he was given. It said nine hundred forty-six dollars. He looked in his wallet. It was the exact amount he had.

"Are you kidding me," Jake said.

"What?"

Jake looked around and not seeing anyone said, "Let's get out of here."

"You still have to pay, right?"

"I'm not paying. They looked in my wallet, saw how much was in there and are saying that's how much I owe them. To the penny. Let's leave right now."

"How are we going to leave without paying?" Sanch said.

"Go out that door."

It led to another hallway.

"Go that way," Jake said. Sanch wheeled him in the direction Jake said but was quickly cut off by another nurse. Sanch turned the wheelchair around nearly flipping Jake out. When the nurse left the hallway, Sanch ran down the hall stopping in front of a door that had a red salida sign over it. They went into an outdoor alleyway.

"Which ways the front?" Sanch said. "Charlie's out there with the truck."

"Go that way," Jake said. Sanch ran, pushing Jake, who yelled in pain with every bump, his leg stuck straight out nearly hitting the sides of the walls when the chair wasn't straight enough.

"You all right?" Sanch asked, slowing down.

"Keep going."

Sanch ran until they got to what they thought was the front and it ended up being the back where the ambulances arrive.

Before Sanch could turn around, a couple workers walked from inside and saw them. "Go, go, go," Jake screamed. Sanch turned and ran. He looked back and saw the workers watching them. They passed the door they had exited from, and a couple workers came out a few seconds behind them. Sanch ran the length of the hospital with Jake screaming out a stream of profanities, and they finally came out the front where Andrea sat on the tailgate.

"Where's Charlie?" Sanch asked her. She pointed to Charlie sitting across the street drinking a beer.

"Charlie!" Sanch shouted. Seeing the urgency, Charlie set his beer on the table and ran across the street with his hands extended to stop traffic. Cars zipped around him with horns blaring.

"What is happening?" Andrea said.

"What the hell did you two do?" Charlie said.

"Nothing. Just help me get him in here."

Charlie lifted Jake up by himself and placed him in the bed of the truck. Jake's stretched-out leg lay over one of the board bags. Sanch pushed the wheelchair towards the hospital entrance. It hit the curb and rolled back toward the street.

A crowd formed to see what the commotion was as a few orderlies, and the doctor came running out from the alley next to the hospital. Andrea and Sanch jumped into the truck's cab, and Charlie had the truck started and moving before the doctor could get anywhere near them. Sanch looked back and saw Jake crying and holding his leg.

"What just happened back there?" Charlie asked.

"We escaped from a hospital," Sanch said.

"What?" Andrea asked.

Sanch retold the story.

Charlie looked at Sanch, "Fucking gringos."

It was about a two-hour ride to the San Jose airport and Charlie stopped once when he looked back and saw the pain on Jake's face. He stepped out and handed Jake two pills. Jake swallowed them dry. Charlie continued driving.

After a few minutes, Sanch asked, "What did you give him?"

"Something I got in Tamarindo when I heard how bad he was. Thought he would need something for the pain."

"What was it?"

"Oxycontin. Should help him a bit. Give him two more, if he starts hurting too bad before you guys get back home." He handed Sanch the pills.

About twenty minutes from the airport, Andrea said, "You promise you are coming back for me?"

"You don't have a passport?" Sanch asked.

Andrea shook her head no.

"Otherwise, I would buy a ticket today and come with you. Would you have me?"

"Of course," Sanch said.

"Do you love me?"

Sanch smiled.

"It's okay if you don't," she said.

"I could," Sanch said.

"Jesus, man. Just tell the girl you love her," Charlie said. "What's there to be afraid of?"

"Getting hurt," Andrea said. "I understand that."

Charlie shook his head. "Yeah, I can too."

Sanch smiled and held Andrea's hand the rest of the way.

"You guys go on ahead. I'll bring Jake in," Charlie said.

"There is a plane leaving for Atlanta in forty-five minutes," the ticket agent said. "But there is only one ticket left."

"I have to go with him," Sanch said.

When she saw Jake being wheeled over, she said there was one seat in first class, and Jake could have that one.

"Once in Atlanta, when can we get to Pensacola?"

311

"That I don't know, sir. You will have to ask once in Atlanta."

The ticket agent had someone come and wheel Jake to the waiting plane. He was still dozing in and out of consciousness. Sanch, Charlie and Andrea led a baggage handler to the truck to collect the board bags.

"You two go on. I'm going to wait by the truck so I don't have to park it," Charlie said.

Sanch stuck out his hand. Charlie shook it.

"Thanks for your help," Sanch said.

"De nada," Charlie said. "When you get back over here, come see me. You're always welcome."

"Thanks."

Andrea and Sanch walked together hand in hand. At the jet bridge, Andrea cried.

"Don't do that," Sanch said.

"I'm sorry," Andrea said. "I'm just afraid you won't come back."

"I've got to save up some money and by that time you'll have a boyfriend." Sanch smiled at her.

"Then take this and come back before I find a boyfriend." She tried to hand Sanch the money again.

"I can't. When I get back though, I want some of that vegi-table soup."

Andrea laughed. Sanch hugged her, and when he pulled away, she gave him a kiss.

"Don't forget me," she said.

Sanch kissed her again and then walked to the jet. She waited, watching from the window in the terminal until the plane taxied onto the tarmac and lifted into the sky. Sanch stared out the window until Costa Rica disappeared behind the clouds.

Chapter 20

Sanch walked into Jake's room at Sacred Heart Hospital in Pensacola two days after the surgery. Jake was propped up in bed, head lulled over asleep and the bottom portion of his leg missing.

Sanch grimaced, but couldn't think of any words. The doctors amputated at mid-thigh. Gangrene, just as the doctors in Costa Rica had warned. The travel time it took to get back home had caused an infection and by the time the American doctors looked at it, there was nothing that could have been done. He needed immediate surgery. Jake's mom sat next to Jake, and she cried when she saw Sanch enter. Fat Boy stood and hugged Sanch. Sanch's daughter sat in the corner playing a Gameboy.

"You saved my boy's life. If you wouldn't have gotten him home, he may have lost more than his leg," Fat Boy said.

"I owed him one," Sanch said.

Sanch sat with Jake's parents, and when Jake opened his eyes, he cried about his leg. Sanch looked away.

"I'm sorry, buddy."

Before long the morphine put Jake back to sleep.

Sanch called Frank from the hospital phone to pick him up.

"What's up with the haircut and a tie?" Sanch said when Frank arrived.

"Got a job selling cars."

"A fucking car salesman?"

"Yeah asshole. A fucking car salesman."

"Good for you."

"What are you going to do for work?"

313

"I need a place to stay for a bit," Sanch said.

"You look rough, man."

"Can I crash with you?"

"Maybe for a few days. I don't think Heather will be happy with too much longer."

"Three days is good. Waiting on a friend to get back from Costa Rica. He's got a job for me in Orange Beach."

"How much money you need?"

"I'm good," Sanch said. He had a little over three hundred left in his pocket.

"Why don't you go to your folks' house?"

"I'm good," Sanch said. "They don't even know I'm back yet."

"Where have you been sleeping the last couple of days then?"

"Here and there."

"Besides the obvious, how was the trip?"

"Not bad. You get any surf here while we were gone?"

"Shit man. I ain't got time for surfing anymore," Frank said.

"That's too bad. Anything else new?"

"Tim is in jail."

"For what?"

"Unregistered firearm."

"See, man. That's why I've got to get out of this town. Either I'm going to wind up in jail or be a goddamn used car salesman."

"Fuck you. I make good money."

"It ain't about the money though."

"Keep telling yourself that."

Frank let Sanch use his bicycle to get around while he and Heather worked. Sanch didn't do much but ride around those three days. He rode about twelve miles each day across the Bay Bridge and the Bob Sikes Bridge and would sit out at the beach and drink a bushwacker and look out over the flat Gulf thinking about Costa Rica. It all started to feel unreal, no different than a dream. It was almost as if he had never visited. All he had was the moment he was in and everything before was a strange illusion. He was no longer living out a surfer's fantasy. He was just back to being another Pensacola beach bum drinking a bushwacker and thinking about his past instead of living in the present. And Jake, Jake was no longer the chest-thumping hero of Tamarindo who made Gerard stop dropping in on folks or the new guy who challenged Pedro or the pool player at Expatriado, he was just an amputee invalid in the hospital drifting in and out of consciousness.

On the fourth day, he left Frank's house and rode downtown to the Waterfront Rescue Mission, a homeless shelter that sat on an old piece of property where once stood a brothel during the days of Pensacola's Red Light District.

Downtown Pensacola was still years away from redevelopment and at this time, there wasn't much around but the famous Trader Jon's, a strip joint next door to it and one or two other bars and night clubs. In less than a year Trader Jon would die and then a few years after that Hurricane Ivan would come through and rearrange the landscape of the waterfront, but at the time that Sanch wandered the streets and sat in the parks there weren't many people out but a few lawyers and the homeless.

He ate lunch provided by a church group in Plaza Ferdinand.

After his third night in the shelter, he began asking around of other places he may be able to sleep. He rode over to the Army-Navy store in Brownsville where he purchased a sleeping bag since the nights dipped well below what he had been used to the last two months. One of the homeless men told him about a large twenty-seven-acre plot of overgrown land known as the Badlands down the road from the shelter that about two hundred homeless people camped at.

Once he entered the abandoned property, he saw that it was true. Some people had recliners and TVs running off car batteries with tarps spread over where they had cleared some brush and had fire pits set up nearby. Sanch rode his bike through the paths and saw people living in their cars, and he rode all the way to the waterfront. There it was cleared with a concrete dock running along the bay with giant cleats that barges could tie off on. Kids had built skateboard ramps, and there were glass shards, empty quart bottles of malt liquor, empty fifths or pints bottles, several fire pits and a couple of shit-stained diapers. The homeless camp sat next door to the only gated community on the downtown Pensacola bayfront, Port Royal.

He found a small little clearing tucked up under some bushes and he made his camp there. He had nothing to build a fire with, but his Army-issued sleeping bag kept him warm enough. That night he camped with the outcasts and the throwaways and the ghosts of ragpickers that never found their place in life's carnival tent show and most died on the fringes having given up trying to make sense or create order in a world that was not meant to have any.

The next morning his bike was gone. He counted what was left in his pocket. Two hundred eighty dollars. He rolled his sleeping bag and walked out from the property, back into visible society. He lined up with the other vagrants waiting to be fed. He devoured his peanut butter and jelly sandwich and bag of chips. He watched two homeless men bring in trout from the fishing pier. He offered to buy a six pack of beer in exchange for dinner. They cooked the fish under the bay bridge and drank beer.

That night, he walked over to the strip joint and was asked for ID as he tried to enter. He had forgotten he was still underage and was turned away. He knew Trader Jon's rarely carded and went there. When he walked in, he looked around at the memorabilia on the walls— plaques and uniforms of servicemen, squadron patches, and photos of Jon Glenn and President Herbert Walker Bush, and uniforms of former Blue Angel pilots. He remembered his brother and father talking about Trader Jon and how he never wore two of the same colored socks. When he told his father he went there for the first time to shoot pool and that he thought it was such a great place, his father had told him he should be embarrassed going there. That bar was for servicemen. But Sanch went anyway.

He went to the bar, enthralled by the museum-like atmosphere. No matter how many times he had been there before, it still felt like stepping into a life he would never live. He was taken aback when he saw Natalie tending bar.

"Oh my God," Natalie said. "What are you doing here?"

He stared at her doe-like eyes, those beautiful brown eyes that he used to get lost in but now filled him with a tinge of repulsion. Her dark brown hair that had flowed down, curling over her shoulders had been lopped off so people could see the tattoo she had put on the side of her neck. He couldn't read it.

"You forget what a razor looks like?" she asked.

He couldn't remember the last time he had shaved.

"And your hair. It's gotten so long."

"Can I get a beer?" Sanch said. He looked down at her V-neck tank top. She had new breasts, and they looked fantastic.

"That's it?" she said. "No how are you? Glad to see you? You're looking good? How have things been? Just, can I get a beer?"

"How have you been?" Sanch said.

"I'm good," she said and then got him a beer and tended to a few other people before coming back to him.

Sanch took a long pull from the beer.

"So?" Natalie said.

Sanch looked at her and shrugged his shoulders.

"When did you get back? How was the trip? Anything?"

Sanch took another drink from the beer. "It was a good trip. Jake broke his leg, and we had to come back home."

"When?"

"Been back a week or so."

"Is he okay?"

"No."

Sanch drank his beer again.

"What happened?"

"They cut his leg off."

"What?"

Sanch nodded. "Jake doesn't have a leg." He then told her the story.

"That's crazy."

Sanch nodded. "It was crazy. It all was. I sometimes wonder if it really happened."

"Did you meet anybody over there?

"What?"

"Did you hook up with anybody while over there?"

Sanch shook his head.

"I'm single again," she said. "Me and what's his face didn't work out."

"That's too bad," Sanch said.

"I got a place close to town. Stick around tonight, maybe come see me when I get off work? I'd love to hang out. Hear all about your trip."

Sanch finished his beer, and she got him another.

"Those are on me," she said and went off to the other customers.

When she wasn't looking, Sanch set the half-drank beer down and laid a ten on the bar and walked out. He had left his sleeping bag and backpack in the doorway before entering, and someone had stolen the sleeping bag.

He walked down to the water behind the Bayfront Auditorium and sat with his feet dangling over the side of the dock and stared out over the bay. He sat there for a long time, contemplating what to do. When he got cold, he walked back toward town and waved down a cab. He gave the cab driver his parents' address.

The house was dark, and he didn't want to wake them. He checked the car doors and found the passenger door open to Buck's El Camino, the one they had found him dead in. It hadn't moved since they brought it back that day. He climbed in and curled up on the bench seat and slept. He shivered most of the night. As the sun rose, he woke and was surprised he couldn't remember any of his dreams. He stepped out and saw his dad inside the house sitting at the table drinking a coffee and reading the paper. His mom, undoubtedly, still in bed.

His dad had aged. And at that moment, he knew the type of life he didn't want to live. He didn't want to be defined by a job. He didn't want work just so he could own things. He didn't want to own things. He had no use for them. He was overcome with a great sadness as he watched his father. He had a great respect for his father, but after he retired from the military it seemed as if he had given up. That he had been defined by his career and once he left the Navy, he was lost. All his father could do was live in the past. It happened to Buck, too. It happened to his mother. It happened to a lot of people. The world didn't want you to live how you wanted to live. The world wanted you to be a good consumer. Being a good consumer was good for society. It created jobs and with a job you could buy things and create more jobs. You could refuse to play the game for a while, but it seemed like eventually the world would defeat you no matter how hard you fought. Sanch hoped he could hold out for a little longer, that he could fight a few more rounds and hopefully be one of the few that wins and so he walked on.

He was too far from downtown now as his parents were victims of suburban sprawl and it took him a while just to walk out of the neighborhood.

He stopped at a convenience store and bought a hot dog that cost as much as the entire dinner of fried red snapper at Pedro's, and he took one bite of the rubbery, salty, chemically processed meat tube and tossed the rest in the garbage. He went back into the store and used the phone to call Frank.

"Sanch," Frank said. "I've been looking for you."

"Can you come get me and let me shower and what not and I'll be gone before Heather gets home from work."

"Have you not heard about Jake?"

"What do you mean?"

"Jesus, man. Jake's dead."

Sanch felt a sudden wave of vertigo.

"What do you mean?"

"Apparently the infection spread into his bloodstream. I don't know exactly. Full body septic shock or some shit like that."

Sanch stood quietly with the phone to his ear. A shiver ran down him. He felt sick.

"Sanch, where are you? I'll come get you."

Sanch told him and then he sat on the curb in front of the gas station and waited for Frank. He remembered the feeling of emptiness that he felt when he was first told about his brother. He remembered trying to comprehend how long forever was and how it created a lump in his throat and a heaviness in his chest and how he remained in a constant state just on the verge of tears for weeks it seemed, but no tears would fall after that first day.

Frank jumped from the car, and they hugged. Frank had tears, but Sanch didn't.

"I've got to get to work, but I spoke with Heather. She said you can stay here for a few more nights," Frank told him.

"I appreciate the offer," Sanch told Frank when he dropped him off at the house. "But I'm going to keep moving. I can't stay here."

"Where are you going?"

"I don't know. I'll figure something out."

"Take care, buddy. Just lock up when you go."

"I'll call you sometime."

Sanch showered, trimmed his beard, found a hair band of Heather's and pulled his hair back in a ponytail. He called a cab and went to the Greyhound bus station where he bought a ticket for New Orleans. He slept on a chair as he waited. When he boarded the bus, he looked around at the tired faces and had a flash memory of the first bus ride in Costa Rica with Jake.

He didn't know when, if ever, he would get back to Tamarindo. He knew it would never be the same. He hoped progress wouldn't ruin it, but knew it would. He wondered how long it would be before Andrea met another guy. Hopefully, the next one would be able to take her back to America. She deserved it, he thought.

The bus rolled and Sanch stared out the window at the bright orange and purple western sky.

"Where you heading?" the old man next to him asked.

"New Orleans for now. Hang out there for a while, but I want to see a bit of the country and I've never been to Canada. I've heard it's nice. Eventually, I think I want to go back to Central America. Maybe El Salvador, Nicarauga or Panama. Somewhere that hasn't been spoiled yet. But I'm worried it's too late. That every where is already spoiled. I don't know what to do. I really don't have a plan."

The old man laughed. "Sounds like a damn good plan to me."

The End

Acknowledgments

Thanks to my mother for being a strong and inspirational woman. Thanks to my wife, Tara, for putting up with me. Thanks to my daughter, Zoë, for being an amazing little human. Thanks to Izo Besares and Rick Canute for being early readers and encouraging me to chase the dream. Thanks to Jonathon Waldrop for helping me to make the hard but necessary changes to the story. Thanks to Dr. Josephs for not taking it easy on me. Thanks to the entire staff at Waldorf Publishing. And thanks to Donald Sailors for our youthful adventures.

Author Bio

Nic Schuck was born in Pensacola, Florida. Graduated with a MA in English from the University of West Florida and is an adjunct in the English department at Pensacola State College. He is also the owner and a tour guide at Emerald Coast Tours, a historic tour company in Pensacola, Florida, where he lives with his wife and daughter. This is his debut novel.